D0948448

I SPY SOMETHING

WICKED

BY
SUSAN YORK MEYERS

Doodle and Peck Publishing
(405) 354-7422
www.doodleandpeck.com

Book Design by Marla F. Jones

Library of Congress Control Number: 2019932559

To all the lovers of "bumps in the night"—
never stop peeking around corners.

SUSAN YORK MEYERS

"I already tried your three previous addresses," Mr. Dockins said. "You people sure like to move."

Prickly fingers traced down my back. I didn't like this detective knowing anything about our lives, no matter who had hired him to find us. I pushed a strand of hair behind my ear, a holdover gesture from when it had been long.

He scratched his uneven beard and asked, "Are you guys moving again?"

Sitting on our faded couch, hemmed in by boxes, I could see why he'd come to that conclusion. "Actually …"

"Yes." Mom flashed her company smile and lit a cigarette. "Lately we've found this place a bit lacking." Actually, the landlord found our rent payment a bit lacking.

Mr. Dockins massaged the back of his neck. A pit stain bloomed under his arm. Did the man live in his car?

Mom's eyes narrowed.

"You said my uncle passed away?" I prompted.

He managed to peel his gaze away from a box labeled CLOTHES. Would my smiley-face t-shirt or Mom's leopard patterned underwear interest him more?"Um, seven days ago, James Duran took a tum ble down the stairs of his house. He died shortly after. In his will, he left his entire estate to his niece, Tessa Kelling."

"Me?" My voice raised an octave.

Mom edged forward in her chair. "But Tessa's only seventeen." The smoke from her cigarette hit him full in the face. "What's it worth?"

Mr. Dockins coughed and eased sideways. "His lawyer, Mr. St. George, can give you all the details and answer any questions." He pushed a business card across the table. "Here's his phone number and address."

Mom snatched it. While she read, Mr. Dockins took the opportunity to rub his eyes.

"When was Uncle Jimmy's funeral?" I asked.

"Three days ago."

"Not sorry I missed that," Mom said. "I've never liked being around dead people." Mom's phone shrilled, but she didn't take her eyes off the card. "Get that, Tessa. It's by my bed."

I hurried to Mom's bedroom and grabbed her cell. "Hello?"

"Hey, gorgeous."

Gag. "Hello, Larry."

"The lack of warmth in your voice hurts. Put your mom on the phone."

With pleasure. "Mom. It's Larry."

Mom flew into the room, a frown pinching her face. She covered the mouthpiece and ordered, "Don't you dare say anything more to that detective until I get back." Then, her voice sweetening like she'd swallowed a whole box of sugar cubes, she spoke into the phone. "Sweetie, you're not going to believe what's happening."

I shrugged and bolted for the living room.

Mr. Dockins stood by the door. "Uh, I've got to be going."

"Sure." I opened the door, not blaming him a bit for taking the chance to escape.

The detective fished a sealed envelope out of his jacket pocket. He glanced at the bedroom door. Then in a low voice, said, "Your uncle left instructions for you to read this when you're alone."

"He left instructions?"

"That's the buzz."

"Weird." I took the envelope and peeked over my shoulder. Mom let out a shrill laugh from the bedroom. Larry and some lame joke no doubt. I shoved the envelope into my jeans pocket.

Mr. Dockins paused in the breezeway. "Be careful."

I frowned. "Huh?"

His smile stayed at his mouth. "I assumed you and your mom would be taking a trip to Ama to see the lawyer. Keep safe."

"Uh, thanks." I closed the door.

Long-lost Uncle Jimmy had made a sudden reappearance in our lives. Of course, he'd died to do so. To be honest, he hadn't been all that lost, but not having seen him since five-years-old meant no personal attachment to his death other than the "how sad" variety.

"Have you been seeing him behind my back?" Mom demanded from the bedroom doorway.

"Who?"

"Your Uncle Jimmy. When did you last see him?"

I sighed. "Not since the summer we lived with him."

"Then why did he leave his house to you and not me? I'm his sister, his only sibling."

Maybe because he didn't like you? "I have no idea."

She sniffed a couple of times and reached for her cigarette. Her breath wheezed as she took a puff. "Where did that detective go?"

I shrugged. "Guess he had other things to do."

"Well, if I'd known, I could have chatted longer with Larry. I want to get his opinion of our options. I suppose we'll have to go inspect the house. It's probably downgraded to 'dump' by now."

The thought of Larry influencing anything to do with my life gave me the willies. "Probably."

She massaged her temples. "What was your uncle thinking, leaving his estate to a child? Baby, do me a favor and get me a cold rag. The news of Jimmy's death has undone me. Not that anybody cares about my feelings." She made her way to the couch, shoved aside a box, and settled down. I got the rag. She whimpered when I laid it across her eyes. "Let me rest for a little while."

No problem. She occupied my bed, so I bolted to the bathroom and dug around in the medicine cabinet for pain reliever. Anything for the headache that throbbed square in the middle of my forehead. I fished a couple of tablets out of the bottle and washed them down with water. Leaning against the sink, I pulled the envelope out of my pocket. A note received from a dead man - exciting and creepy. It read:

Dear Niece,
If you're reading this, then I'm dead. By now you know I've left everything to you, not your mother. Wish I could have witnessed the fit she threw about that. The house comes with a condition that I didn't dare put in my will. I'll have to trust that you'll do

the right thing. Take care of Andre.

My hand jerked, knocking the water off the counter and into the sink. The breaking glass sounded far away. The note fell, beating me to the floor. Close to hyperventilating, I slid down the cabinet into a sitting position.

Andre. Andre was real.

I remembered climbing the tree, then gazing with a five-year-old's terror at the faraway ground below. "Mama! Uncle Jimmy!" No one came. They were probably still out front discussing Uncle Jimmy's plans for the fishpond.

I clutched the branch. Bark gnawed into my skin, but I wrapped my arms tighter. Tears clouded my vision. "Mama?" Okay, maybe I could climb down on my own. The toe of my tennis shoe touched the branch and then slipped. I lost my grip, screamed and closed my eyes so I wouldn't see myself hit the ground.

Strong arms caught me.

"Uncle ..." Not Uncle Jimmy, but a stranger who held me like a prince carrying a princess. His dark hair fell across my face, tickling my nose. His kind brown eyes reminded me of chocolate. With a smile, he placed me on the ground.

"Tessa?" Mama called. The dark haired man put a finger to his lips. He winked. "Tessa?" Mama's voice grew closer.

"Here!" I ran toward her voice and then looked back. The man had vanished. Mama and Uncle Jimmy came into view.

"Good grief, Baby, didn't you hear me calling?" She threw her cigarette down and ground the butt beneath her high heel. No flats for Mom, even in the country.

"I'm sorry. Guess what?" I danced from one foot to the other.

"I almost fell out of the tree. A man saved me."

Mama's eyes narrowed. "What man? And what were you doing in a tree?"

I ignored the second question. "I don't know. He was a stranger. But a good stranger," I added, not wanting to get into trouble.

"What did he look like?" Uncle Jimmy asked.

I thought. "He had brown hair like Mama's sometimes. And he was tall."

"I'm a natural blonde," Mama snapped. "Do you know this man?" she demanded of my uncle.

"I think so. His name's Andre." Uncle Jimmy grinned at me. "He's my ghost."

Mama snorted. "Jimmy, don't make up things. The child will have nightmares. She's probably imagined the whole thing anyway."

Although I searched for him, I never saw Andre again. Uncle Jimmy would grin and say, "That's the way ghosts are." Mom and Uncle Jimmy had a big fight soon after that and we left. But I'd never forgotten. No matter how many times Mom told me I'd imagined Andre, I believed.

Or thought I had. Holding written proof, I wavered. What would be waiting for me in Ama, Oklahoma? Who would I find?

Mom had revived enough to call Larry back. She paced by the bathroom door and I heard, "But I need to check this out for Tessa's sake. Besides, it comes at such a perfect time." Translation: we're getting kicked out of the apartment and you haven't given me any other options.

My fingernails dug into my upper arms. You're crazy. Nope, he's real and you've always known it. "Stop fighting," I told the two sides of my brain.

I eased open the bathroom door. Mom stared out the balcony window. Tiptoeing forward, I eavesdropped from the kitchen. "…just a few things to take care of. I expect the situation to be in order when we arrive." Ama, we're going to Ama!

"Tessa!"

I jumped even though the kitchen wall kept her from seeing me, and then rounded the corner. "What?"

"We're going to Ama. If I remember right, it's about two hours from Oklahoma City."

"Now?"

She glared. "I thought you'd be eager to see your inheritance.

You know the one your uncle passed me over to give to you."

No way would I take that bait. "What about our stuff?"

"Larry's going to store it." She couldn't get him to take her, but she could get him to take the DVD player.

It took me all of twenty minutes to pack my treasured possessions. "The car needs gas," I told Mom.

"Take care of it. I'll wait here for Larry."

I grabbed my jean jacket. Definitely wanted to get out before Sweetie arrived. I paused before heading out the door. "It might be nice to own a house."

Mom rolled her eyes. "Tessa, it was out in the boonies then and it will still be now. You don't want to live in the middle of Hicksville, trust me."

"Still, it might be …"

She stepped closer, waving her cigarette for emphasis. The acrid smoke curled like a snake waiting to strike. "We'll check it out, Baby. You can grab yourself a memento or something, though heaven knows why you'd want one. Then, we're selling."

"But it's my house."

Her eyes became slits. "Get the gas, Tessa. It's a long drive to Ama." I fled.

At the gas station, I paid for the gas and grabbed a map on my way out. Mom got lost going around the block, so I didn't trust her memory to get us from the City to Ama. I slid behind the wheel of my red Bug, an original I'd paid for it with my own money. I'd managed to hang onto it even when everything else we owned wound up sold or at the pawn shop. To avoid wasting gas, I sat with the engine off, and took a closer look at the map. Ama … Ama … there! A little dot on the map. Soon I had our course routed.

I switched on the engine and it sputtered to life. What would happen if I headed out on my own? The two bags that held anything worth anything to me already occupied the backseat. How would Mom react to being ditched? I sighed. Mom still clutched the lawyer's card. I didn't even know how to get the keys, much less locate Uncle Jimmy's house.

The wind brought the rain to play and I switched on my headlights and windshield wipers. The sound of pelting rain and the swish of the wipers relaxed me. Without taking my eyes off the road, I twisted the knob on my temperamental radio. Static hissed back.

Finally, the oldies station on 92.5 FM filtered through enough for me to sing along to Eddie Rabbitt's "I Love a Rainy Night." Yeah, corny, but I liked country music because my Grandma Petey liked it. Dad may have ditched me, but Grandma Petey had stayed. Anyway, Mom couldn't stand "hillbilly" music, so this would be my last chance to listen before she joined me.

The rain stopped by the time I reached the apartment. The sight of Larry's van parked in our spot caused me to grit my teeth. Mom and Larry stood beside it, their conversation ending the moment they spotted me. She fiddled with the collar of her blouse, always a sure sign of a scheme being hatched. A horrible thought... maybe she'd invited "Sweetie" to go with us? No! No! No!

Larry grinned and blew me a kiss. I'll let you know when middle-aged, balding men without a steady job start looking good to me.

Mom hurried over and I rolled down the window. "Where are your bags?"

She waved her hand in a vacant way. "Don't worry about me. I've taken care of everything." She wriggled her way into the passenger seat.

I eyed her, then Larry, who smirked.

"Okay. Are we going to use the van to take our stuff to Larry's?"

Mom pulled hard at her collar and addressed the backseat instead of me. "Larry's going to do that for us." Something stank. Sweetie never volunteered for work.

Larry pushed in beside her, hands jammed in his jeans pockets. "Brr, it's getting cold." He put an arm around Mom. "Sorry I won't be around to keep you warm." She giggled. I didn't hurl. Fifteen minutes later, they finished their goodbyes and we set out for Ama.

"Are you sure you know how to find the place?" Mom asked.

"Positive, take I-35 to ..."

"Don't even try to explain. You know I'm not good with directions." I headed the car away from OKC. "I spy a new life," I whispered.

"What?"

"Nothing, just a game I used to play with Grandma Petey."

"Really, Tessa, I need to rest. I've had a long day." Mom settled against the seat and closed her eyes.

In the silence, the question I'd pushed to the back of my mind demanded attention. How could I so easily accept the idea of a ghost haunting Uncle Jimmy's house? Could it be because I remembered

Andre as cute?

Mom had her secrets. Well, I had one, too. And I didn't mean Andre. I wasn't visiting Ama. I was moving there.

Two hours later, I spotted the exit and left the highway. Huge trees lined both sides of the road, their fiery red, gold and orange leaves forming a canopy over a fairytale bridge. I almost expected little winged creatures to flutter out, leftover raindrops making their wings sparkle as they danced in the sun.

"Tree sprite, tree sprite," I sang softly, "come out, come out and play with me."

Ten miles down the road, I stopped at a convenience store. Mom's eyes opened. "Are we there?"

"Not yet. I've got to use the bathroom."

"I suppose you're going to make me stand outside the car?"

"Yes, please." My car remained a smoke-free zone. One of the rare fights I'd won with Mom. I ignored her grumble as she pushed herself out of the passenger seat.

"Where's your bathroom?" I asked the girl behind the counter.

"Ya gotta buy something to use the restroom," she informed me.

I made an effort not to stare at her spiky half-purple, half-brown hair. "Sure, but the bathroom has to come first."

A skeptical glare, but she didn't fuss. Did they really have that many bathroom runners here?

After making my bladder happy, I studied myself in the mirror. My peaches and cream complexion, a present from Grandma

Petey, had sold me out. Yikes! A huge zit sprouted from the end of my chin. The angry red bump showed every sign of erupting into something disgusting, but at least it didn't have a head. Yet. I slapped powder on my shiny nose, reapplied strawberry sunshine lip gloss, and continued the exam. Rumpled clothing competed with frizzy hair for worst disaster. I sniffed my underarms. At least my deodorant still worked.

Leaving the bathroom, I made for the snack aisle. Might as well indulge in the junk food. After all, I already had the zit.

The cashier eyed the package when she rang it up. "No soda or anything?"

For real? I pasted on my best wanting-to-please smile. "I'll try and do better next time." She looked unsure as to whether she was being made fun of or not. I didn't enlighten her.

Before pulling back onto the road, I glanced at the detective's directions again. Charles St. George's office had a Main Street address. Leaving a pile of cigarette butts instead of a trail of bread crumbs, we entered town. Ama's Main Street businesses occupied buildings that had started life as houses. Suzy's Cut and Curl inhabited a single-story beige brick building with a wrap-around porch.

"That salon probably has all the up-to-date styles from the 1960s," Mom quipped. Lost-Now-Found antiques resided in a white painted house. "I'm sure antique translates to junk," Mom said.

Downtown claimed two whole blocks with the post office, city hall, public library, and Police Chief's office. At least it would be easy to find things. Not that I planned on coming into town much. Instead, I'd barricade myself in Uncle Jimmy's house and never leave, except maybe to buy chocolate. The world couldn't disappoint me if I didn't come out to play. Across the street, sprawled Will Rogers Park. Did they pop fireworks on the Fourth of July and decorate the gazebo at Christmas?

"A park," Mom remarked. "Probably the local highlight. That and a museum dedicated to some historical something or another. That's why I hate small towns. There's never anything to do in them."

I spotted the law office, a red brick, one-story building with a white porch and shutters. Surely, the vacant driveway didn't mean that everyone had gone home. But the hours listed on a burgundy and green sign read open nine to five. My watch said a quarter until five. "You called and told them we're coming, right?"

Mom glanced up from her compact. "Of course, I did. Do you think I'm an idiot?"

Thank goodness for rhetorical questions.

Exiting the car, I made a last stab at smoothing the front of my slacks. Mom reapplied her lipstick, checked to make sure her cleavage still showed and sailed toward the door, stopping short of opening it. That was my job. I did the grunt work and Mom made the entrances.

Nervous, I pushed too hard and the door slammed into a side table. "Sorry," I mumbled to the startled receptionist. Mom gave me her "can't take you anywhere" face.

"May I help you?" the receptionist asked. The frost in her voice chilled me almost as much as the wind had earlier. Unlike my wind-blown mop, her short light brown hair stayed sleek and untouched by anything but her comb. Her matching beige sweater and skirt fit sleek and wrinkle free. Probably only a few years older than me, but eons more sophisticated. Even her pearls were perfect.

Mom folded her arms and stared the woman down. "I'm Jilly Kelling. I need to speak to Mr. St. George."

The receptionist closed her laptop. Her slow gaze took in my rumpled clothing and Mom's tight skirt and dismissed them. I resisted the urge to cover my zit. "Do you have an appointment?"

Oh, stupid. All Mom had done was leave a message on the lawyer's voice mail. We should have called and made sure Mr. St. George could, or would, see us. The receptionist waited, hands folded, a satisfied smile on her lips as if she already knew the answer, which of course she did.

Mom said, "I'm afraid we don't have an appointment, but …"

The sleek hairdo started shaking at the first word out of Mom's mouth. "I'm sorry, but without an appointment it's impossible to see Mr. St. George today. Perhaps you'd like to make one for tomorrow morning?" She reopened the laptop and typed. "He has a ten o'clock opening."

"But …" I heard the desperation in my voice, swallowed and tried for confidence. "He has the key to my house." My house—strange and wonderful words!

The receptionist's eyes widened as something clicked inside her brain. She suddenly appeared a lot younger, less sure of herself. She stood and motioned toward the chairs stationed in front of her desk. "Please have a seat. I'll see if Mr. St. George is available." Leaving a strong sent of musk behind, she disappeared down the hall.

Mom settled into one of the chairs. "Help should know their place. I may have to tell Mr. St. George how rude she behaved toward us." She glared at me. "You were quick to tell her it's 'your house,' weren't you? Well, keep the dream until it sells, baby."

Could she really sell it without my consent? I took a deep, mental breath and studied the room. All in beige and brown tones, it said classy but without any personality, nothing to offend a potential client. That the receptionist matched the room, probably not intentional.

From down the hall came a raised voice, and then nothing. A door opened and a slight, somewhat excited man hurried into the front office, his hand extended in greeting. He stood about the same height as his receptionist, tall for her, short for him, cute in a Stargate's Daniel Jackson sort of way.

"Let me do all the talking," Mom stage whispered.

"Mrs. Kelling, how nice to meet you. And this must be Tessa. No, no don't rise." He shook Mom's hand and then clasped both of mine in his. "I'm Charles St. George."

"That detective gave us your card," Mom said.

His grip squeezed. "Detective? Oh yes, Mr. Dockins. Err, what exactly did he tell you?"

I couldn't help it. "Mr. St. George, you're hurting me."

He released my hands, a horrified expression covering his face. "I'm so sorry. I guess I got lost in the excitement of meeting James' family. His leaving us was so sudden. I still have a hard time believing he's gone."

"That's okay." I wanted to rub my fingers but resisted.

He ran a hand through light brown hair. "I am sorry. I should have contained my emotions better. My own father passed away about six months ago. He and James were close friends. It's been hard losing them both so close together."

"Really, it's okay. I'm sorry about your father."

"Thank you."

Mom's throat clearing could have called cows.

He focused his attention on her. "Mrs. Kelling, you didn't say what information Mr. Dockins gave you."

"Simply that my brother's dead and he left my daughter his house. You look about twelve years old. Are you sure you're a lawyer?"

His shoulders relaxed as he leaned against Anna's desk. "Believe me, I get that all the time. Really, I did graduate from law school. Cross my heart." And he did. "It's the first time we've used Mr. Dockins, but it sounds like he did his job."

"Do we owe you anything?" I asked.

He frowned. "Owe me for what?"

"For hiring Mr. Dockins."

"No, the estate takes care of that."

Feeling ignorant, I mumbled, "Of course." I didn't dare meet Mom's eyes.

The receptionist spoke. "Would you like something to drink? Coffee?" She smirked my way. "Or maybe a coke?"

"No, thank you," we both replied. An uncomfortable silence descended.

"I like your glasses," I blurted out.

"Oh." Mr. St. George touched his glasses as if he'd forgotten what kind of eyewear he wore. "Thank you." He removed the glasses and handed them to me. "The frames are completely wooden." I ran a finger over the smooth, light-colored wood. "I bought them on eBay. My optometrist fitted the lenses."

"They're cool." I handed them back.

"I think so."

"I did phone," Mom broke in. "I naturally assumed you'd call back if there was a problem."

"Of course, of course." He half-glared at his receptionist. "I'm afraid Anna didn't recognize your name at first, or there wouldn't have been a dilemma." Anna's mouth uttered a quick apology that her eyes didn't second.

Mom's eyes sent out a "so there." "I suppose there are papers to sign?"

"Yes, Mrs. Kelling. May I call you Jilly?"

"Of course you can." She actually fluttered her eyelashes.

I tried to bring us back on track. "If we could sign the papers and get the key to the house, we'll get out of your way."

"Out of the way!" he cried. "You are most certainly not in the way." He crossed his arms as if settling down for a long chat. Inwardly, I sighed.

"We didn't expect you so soon," Anna said.

He dagger-eyed her, but his smile shifted back into place when he returned his gaze to us. "Anna's right. When you phoned and left the message you were coming, we didn't realize you meant today. You indicated there were things you needed to take care of before traveling to Ama."

"Is there something wrong with our taking possession of the house right away?" Mom demanded.

Mr. St. George cleared his throat. "No, of course not, but you do realize the house has been closed since your brother passed?"

"The house is locked?" I asked.

"We acted per James' written orders. The doors were locked as soon as the ambulance took him to the hospital. No one has entered since," the lawyer confirmed.

"All the utilities are still on?" Mom demanded.

"Yes."

Excitement flitted through my stomach. "So someone could live in it?"

His forehead wrinkled in a frown. "Well, technically, yes."

"Musty," Anna said. Her button nose crinkled. "It'll be musty and dusty. Really, don't you think it would be better to view it first thing in the morning?"

"Yes," her boss agreed. "Besides, you don't know the condition in which Jimmy left things. As I said, he departed rather suddenly."

"That's true." Mom had a convenient allergy to dust. She only started sneezing when someone asked her to clean it.

"My aunt's friend owns a wonderful bed & breakfast a couple of streets over," Anna said. "It's called the Red Rose and the rooms are quite cozy. You could get a good night's sleep and start fresh in the morning."

"I don't know ..." Mom began.

"It's not hard to find," Anna pressed on. "When you leave here, take a right on Elm, go two blocks and then left on Ash. You can't miss the sign. Willa cooks everything from scratch. I sometimes stop by in the mornings to have breakfast."

Good grief, did she own part of the place? Or maybe Willa gave Anna extra biscuits for every person she steered toward the B&B?

"Now that does sound wonderful," Mom agreed.

They all beamed. I wanted to scream. But at least things progressed after that. I gave proof that I was Tessa Kelling and we signed the necessary papers. Charles St. George handed Mom a cream colored check.

"What's this?" she said, snatching it.

"James set up a monthly allowance for Tessa. However, the first two checks will be made out to you until Tessa is eighteen."

"As they should be. Where can I cash this?"

Charles St. George covered his shock by adjusting his glasses. "The Ama National Bank is on Second Street."

Mom folded the check in half and tucked it into her purse. "Can we sell the house?" she asked as we stood to leave.

I stopped breathing.

Charles opened the front door and stood aside to let us pass. "It would be difficult to do before Tessa turns eighteen," he said. My breathing returned to normal. The office phone rang.

"Charles," Anna called, "it's your mother."

"Have a good night," he said before closing the door behind us.

I backed the car out of the drive. "The B&B is on Elm, right?"

"Forget that. We're heading to your uncle's. No need letting those nosy parkers in on our plans though."

My heart thudded. Andre, here I come!

Two left turns and a right left Ama's city limits behind. I shoved the folded map into the glove box. Uncle Jimmy's country road didn't appear on it. "Are you sure you know the way?" I asked.

"Baby, as I said before, it was the boonies then and still is. Nothing's changed."

I concentrated on following the winding country road. A falling mist gave the illusion that the rest of the world had deserted, leaving me stranded alone with Mom. Cheery thought.

"Boy," Mom commented, "wouldn't this be a lovely place for a serial killer to hide? The faster we check out your uncle's dump and get back to the City, the better."

The thought of leaving here washed over me like a cold soak of panic. If only Uncle Jimmy could've waited two more months to fall down those stairs. Not that I wanted him to fall. But in two months I'd be eighteen and wouldn't have to deal with Mom trying to sell the house. Despite Mom's "help," I almost missed the mailbox with DURAN neatly lettered on its side. I stopped at the driveway's edge and peered down the graveled road. Did home wait at the end?

"What are we sitting here for?" Mom wiggled in her seat. "My butt fell asleep fifteen minutes ago."

"Sorry." I inched the car forward. A rumbling in my stomach reminded me that we should have stopped for dinner before venturing into the country. My tired brain refused to even consider driving back into town, though. I'd make do with the peanut butter and crackers I'd bought at the convenience store.

A crackling sound reached my ears. Mom popped one of the cracker sandwiches into her mouth. Oh well, at least there would be running water. Soaking the evening away in a hot bath sounded wonderful.

But first I had to find Andre.

The two-story brick and stone house at the end of the drive could have stepped out of the same fairytale as my tree sprites. The bricks were red, but not too red. They went perfect with the sand stones across the bottom and along the corners. I'd plant some ivy so it could be a true ivy-covered cottage. The yard, an oasis surrounded by trees and nature allowed to stay wild, had a stone pond in the center. It stirred a memory of dragging my hand through sun-warmed water. Fish?

"I see your uncle never got rid of that pond," Mom mumbled around cracker. "He said he liked seeing it covered with wild summer strawberries. I know for a fact he never ate those strawberries. And he never kept any fish in the pond. Should have knocked it down years ago."

I'd keep the strawberries and add fish to the pond. My eyes went back to the house. A figure strolled around a van parked next to it. My heart hit my chest. Andre! But then the man stepped out of shadow. Bile replaced excitement. "What's Larry doing here?" I demanded.

Instead of answering, Mom rolled down her window. "Larry! Here we are, sweetie."

Like he couldn't see my Bug. I stopped short of Larry's van, giving him plenty of room to leave. My jaw ached from clenching. I opened my mouth wide and wiggled it from side to side until the pain went away. A deep breath and I asked again, "What's he doing here?"

Mom jumped from the car and ran toward Larry. I rubbed my temples. Her ignoring me meant she felt guilty about something, probably something rotten. She threw herself into Larry's arms as if his ship had come in after a long, dangerous voyage. I got out of the car.

Mom snorted. "Really, Tessa, uncross your arms. You look like the disapproving housemother of an all-girls school."

Larry grinned. "Yeah, unclench those butt cheeks already."

I glared at Mom. She fiddled with her collar and avoided my eyes. "What's he doing here?" My screech would have filled a cackling witch with pride.

She grabbed Larry's arm and smiled. "Guess what, baby. Larry and I are getting married."

Married? But the chance of going to hell wasn't supposed to come until after you're dead.

"Well, isn't it terrific?" Mom demanded. She gave Larry another squeeze. "Poor thing, afraid I'd move out here to Ama and he'd lose me forever. So he popped the question."

No way would Mom ever consider moving to Ama. Ya got bluffed, Larry. As much as I hated Larry, I realized the jerk might actually be doing me a favor. If Mom got married, she'd be less likely to care about what I did.

"When's the big day?" I asked. They shared a gaze.

Mom smiled at me. "Well, Baby, that's something I need to talk to you about. We're eloping tonight."

"You're leaving tonight?"

She let go of Larry and latched onto me. "I knew you'd be happy for us." She waved toward the house. "I'm sure you'll be safe here while we tie the knot. You can poke around as much as you please. Maybe even find a few souvenirs to take back to the City."

So, no invitation to the wedding. Probably for the best. I don't think I could have kept my mouth shut when asked, "Does anyone object?" "When will you be back?"

Larry grinned. "Get hitched, gotta have a honeymoon."

Mom giggled.

How come the perfect solution suddenly appeared so scary? "You'll be gone longer than overnight?" Another exchanged glance that I couldn't read.

Mom got a funny smile on her face, as if the burrito she'd had for lunch had come back to haunt her. "You don't think you'll like being here all alone?"

"I think," I said in a steady voice that didn't match my knocking knees, "it'll be fun." After all, getting to stay was what I wanted, right?

Larry shoved his hands in his pockets. "I don't know about that. There's no one out here in the boonies to hear you scream."

I expected Mom to say something to that, but instead she told Larry, "Let me get some things out of Tessa's car. I'll only be a moment."

As she walked away, Larry leaned in close enough for me to smell the onion burger he'd apparently had for lunch. "You and me are going to be family now. And I like for family to be real close and loving."

For me to step back would have let him win, so I held my ground. "You remember what happened the last time you got too close."

He retreated two steps, his hands crossed in front of his crotch. The name he hissed didn't sound at all loving.

"Larry?" Mom watched us, her purse in hand. She shifted her wary gaze from him to me.

"Just giving Tessa some last minute advice, you know, like don't open the door for mass murderers."

Again, I expected at least an "Oh, Larry" from Mom, but nothing. She hurried forward and planted a mush kiss on my cheek. "I'll see you in a few days, baby."

And they left, leaving me standing alone in the driveway of a dead man. As the van's taillights disappeared, Mom's hand still clutched the check from Charles St. George. No problem. Ever since the age of thirteen, I'd worked part time jobs, everything from babysitting to dog walking. I wouldn't starve.

Mom had a plan. And dawn couldn't have burst any brighter than the realization when it came. In Mom's mind, being alone would break me. She expected to come back to a terrified, sobbing girl who'd be compliant to anything she wanted, including selling the house.

Mom didn't know me at all.

I grabbed my purse out of the car and climbed the steps, imagining the colorful plants that would bloom in the hanging pots come spring. Actually, pansies would be beautiful right now. Maybe I'd go into town tomorrow and buy some. That would be the first project in my new house.

My house … or Andre's?

I traced the outline of the exquisite stained glass window that filled the center of the front door. Jewel-colored squares and rectangles would let the sun dance inside. A memory surfaced. I'd played in the foyer beyond this door.

No going inside until I'd tried somewhere else first. I half ran to the backyard and then stopped with a jolt. Shouldn't the tree be smaller to me at seventeen than it had been at five? It still appeared imposing. How had I gotten up the nerve to climb it? Twilight, the perfect time for meeting a ghost. "Andre?" I whispered.

Only the breeze answered.

"Andre!" The shout came from deep within my fear that he'd moved on. Had Andre never really existed? That would make Uncle

Jimmy's note a cruel joke. Rough bark scratched my forehead as I leaned against the tree.

    If I climbed it and started to fall, would Andre catch me?

As crazy as things could get with Mom, she gave me an anchor in the world, even though we pulled anchor every time the rent came due. Standing on the front porch of Jimmy's house, I knew I'd found my real home. Forget finishing high school. I had no intention of enrolling anywhere after fall break. Here's where I'd build my own nest that the world couldn't take from me. Maybe then there'd be room for school, dreams, and having a normal life.

But what if Andre had moved on after Jimmy died? Isn't that what ghosts did? Did I want a normal life or one with a ghost?

The key slid into the lock. I opened the door with caution. No idea what I would find – from rancid food to dead plants. Hopefully, no beloved dog, still patiently waiting for his master to return. Luckily, there hadn't been enough time for doggie to die of starvation. But, plenty of time for him to get hungry enough to gnaw the leg of any stranger who walked through his front door. I peered into the dim, dark paneled entryway. No mad dog, dead or alive appeared.

Well, Mom, you could have at least stayed for the tour.

"Hello?" No mystical voice answered. I pushed open the door and walked inside. Turning on the overhead light helped dispel some of the gloom.

A really ugly vase stood on a small side table. Splotches of orange, blues and yellows ran through it like someone had left it in the rain before its paint had completely dried. Ugh. Hopefully, the beautiful stained glass in the door and not the tacky vase indicated my uncle's decorating style. I didn't remember much about Uncle Jimmy's house. We'd moved so many times that, like the colors in the vase, our makeshift homes tended to run together.

To the right, six potted plants separated the entry from the living room. Green and leafy, they apparently didn't need much water. Straight ahead an open door led to the kitchen. On my left rose a wooden staircase. Sigh. I'd always dreamed of owning a two-story house. Actually, any house would do, as long as it didn't come with an eviction notice.

Might as well get the worst over. I cautiously entered the old-fashioned kitchen and sniffed. Thankfully, no smell of rotting food greeted me. I spotted the wax fruit bowl in the middle of the yellow Formica table and grinned. I knew for a fact, the red apple sported a bite out of its underside. Still grinning, I toed the edge of the linoleum floor. Sliding across the orange and white squares in stocking feet had been one of my favorite activities.

I ran a finger along the black and white checked countertop. No dust. Okay, maybe there hadn't been enough time for a dog to die or plants to whither, but enough time had passed for dust to settle. Out of curiosity, I tested the soil in the plant hanging over the porcelain sink. Someone had watered it.

Could a friend of Uncle Jimmy's be taking care of things? A friend Charles St. George didn't know about? Or maybe a ghost with a cleaning fetish? Chills tap-danced across my spine.

The screened-in back porch also served as the laundry room. A calendar hung over the washer. I laughed. Blocky numbers said 1987. It reminded me of a 1962 Norman Rockwell calendar Grandma Petey hung in her kitchen. "I like the pictures and each month my art changes," she'd explained. When I'd pointed out that a lot of people framed calendar pictures, she snorted and said, "Too much trouble."

The kitchen led to the sparse dining room, which then led into the living room. Two built-in book shelves flanked the stone fireplace. A big bay window overhung the front of the house, its wooden seat matching the wood in the shelves. The furniture seemed old, but comfortable. The easy chair in front of the fireplace appeared cushy enough for snuggling down with a good mystery.

Back in the entryway, I peered behind the door under the stairs. A tiny half bath complete with a cute pedestal sink nestled in the nook.

I took a deep breath and faced the stairs.

Jimmy had been fifty-three when he died. Fifteen years older than Mom, not the twenty she claimed. Did Uncle Jimmy cry out in terror when he fell? Did he try to grab the railing? I tested it with a yank. Seemed sturdy. I held on tight as I ascended. Halfway up the stairs, I paused on the small landing to study another stained glass window. Round, about the size of a porthole, it featured a sailing ship in the middle.

A door led off the landing. I opened it and found narrow, un-carpeted stairs that ascended up into the gloom. Definitely could wait to see the attic. On second thought, wouldn't the attic be the perfect place for a ghost?

"Andre?"

No answer.

I closed the door and climbed the rest of the stairs. Another stained glass window flashed its colors from the end of the hall. I stud-ied an image of a trellis with climbing red roses. One section of glass had been broken and then badly repaired. Globbed-on paint made the rose uneven and heavy. How much would it cost to get fixed? More than my baby sitting money I bet.

My heart jumped at the sight of the small marble fireplace in the bedroom on the left. I remembered it! A clean, white chenille bed-spread covered the twin bed. Faded rosebud-patterned sheets peeked out from under the spread. Mom had slept on the bed, and I'd had a pallet on the floor. Uncle Jimmy worried I'd roll into a fire, so the fire-place had remained cold.

An old-fashioned bathroom, complete with a claw-foot bath-tub, stood across from the bedroom. Yes, I could soak in that tub. The linen closet even held clean towels.

The next room proved to be Uncle Jimmy's. I blinked in disbe-lief at the mess. No one with a cleaning fetish or even a strong urge to dust had ever slept here. I tugged the door shut, not yet ready to deal with the emotional reality of a dead uncle, even an estranged one. My eyes fell on the locked door. I'd never seen the room beyond. It had ticked off Mom that Jimmy wouldn't let me use it as a bedroom. But the door had stayed locked.

The knob turned under my hand. Shaking off the feeling of being a naughty child, I pushed it open. The door creaked and I found a room identical in size to the one down the hall. No furniture. Instead, a drop cloth littered with tubes of paint covered one end of the carpet. A gorgeous mural of an enclosed garden covered the far wall. Ivy clung to its gray stone walls and a cobblestone walkway connected blooming bushes. An old-fashioned picnic table, perfect for afternoon tea, filled the middle of the scene. Jimmy obviously hadn't wanted a five-year-old disturbing his work. Or a sister putting out her cigarettes in turpentine. I traced the detail on the trunk of a half-finished elm tree and a lump formed in my throat.

Jimmy would never finish it.

Only one room left and I still hadn't found Andre. The door at the end of the hall stood open. My mouth gaped. Shelves lined every inch of the walls, holding more books than I'd ever seen outside of a library.

But only one book caught my attention. The floating one. And then a drop-dead gorgeous guy held it. He faced me, a look of interest in his eyes.

I wish I could say that I held my ground and demanded to know how he'd pulled off the trick. I'd like to say that, but instead I fainted. When I next opened my eyes, I lay stretched out on the guest-room bed. A voice from somewhere near my feet cautioned, "Don't be alarmed, but I'm going to materialize again."

A slight shimmer and there he stood at the end of the bed, his hands clasped in front of him. Dark hair fell in silky waves to his shoulders, giving him the kind of tousled appearance that's sexy, unmade, and rugged, all at the same time. He wore gray flannel slacks and a light blue V-necked sweater over a white shirt. Brown splotches of paint on the pants kept the outfit from being too perfect.

"I'm Andre," he said.

"I know you," I said.

"Would it scare you if I came closer?" At least he seemed a polite ghost. Of course, when I'd called him drop-dead gorgeous, I hadn't meant it literally. He waited for an answer.

"I guess it would be okay," I said, sounding like the five-year-old I used to be. With fluid grace, Andre sat on the edge of the bed. No indention, the covers stayed smooth. His nearness made me push myself to a sitting position.

"Would you like some water?" he asked.

I shook my head.

"Would you like me to leave?"

Afraid he might, I reached out to grab his knee.

"Wait," he said, but too late.

My hand went through him, hitting the bedspread. "I can't touch you!"

"It takes a lot of energy for me to be both visible and solid," he explained.

"But you carried me in here." I clasped my hands to my chest in a move that would make melodramatic heroines everywhere jealous. "Didn't you?"

"It takes less energy to manipulate objects when I'm incorporeal."

I remembered the floating book in the library. "Incorporeal?"

"Can't be seen."

"I know what it means," I snapped. "I've just never met anyone who could actually do it."

"Forgive me." For what? Thinking I didn't know what incorporeal meant, or for being able to do it? My mind tried to grasp ghostly concepts.

"You're saying you were invisible when you carried me in here?"

"Yes."

Definitely grateful I hadn't come to in the middle. "But sometimes you can be both visible and solid?"

He smiled, amused. "Yes."

A tickle in my stomach alerted me something had happened. Andre held out his hand. Swallowing hard, I took it. His larger one closed around my smaller one. A sensation not of cold, but rather a lack of warmth flowed through me. Without taking his eyes off my face, he turned my palm and kissed the inside of my wrist. My heart skipped. He released my hand and again I felt that small tickle. I tried to touch him again, but my hand went right through his. Andre let me take my time adjusting.

I peeked from under my eyelashes. He had the darkest brown eyes, smooth and rich like melting chocolate. It took all the willpower I possessed not to check and see if my zit had somehow disappeared. His eyes looked kind, exactly like I remembered them from the tree incident. "You can't stay visible and solid all the time?"

Andre shook his head. "I need to rest."

Lack of food caught up with me. Or perhaps the reality of talking to a ghost began to sink into my hazy brain. Either way, a feeling of lightheadedness crept over me. I pushed it away. "Why can't I see through you?"

"Would you like to?" So slow I almost couldn't perceive it, he went transparent. Soon the dresser appeared behind him.

Breathe deep, Tessa. "Thanks for the demonstration, but I like you better the other way." I waited until he wasn't so see-through. "You saved me. I fell out of a tree and you saved me."

"I'm surprised you remember." He appeared solid. An illusion maybe, but one I liked.

"You disappeared. Even at five, I knew people couldn't do that. Uncle Jimmy told me you were his ghost. My mom called Uncle Jimmy crazy."

He laughed. "They were both right."

Definitely a ghost of few words. Realization. "You're the one who's done the cleaning."

His smile teased. "Did you think Cinderella's little mice were doing the work?" I felt the heat from my blush. He gave instant apology. "I'm sorry."

"No problem." So, I really did have a ghost with a cleaning fetish. Another realization. "You're the reason my uncle ordered everything locked."

"Yes." Andre moved on the bed as if trying to find a more comfortable position. Did the action stem from when he'd lived and could still feel discomfort? "He knew I would take care of things until you came."

"Are you the one who found Uncle Jimmy? After…"

Those delicious eyes clouded with pain. "Too late, I'm afraid."

"Was he still alive?" I whispered.

"Yes, but unconscious. I had to leave him to get Willard, uh, Dr. St. George." Andre's voice cracked. "That was hard."

"St. George is the name of Uncle Jimmy's lawyer."

"Willard St. George is Charles' uncle. He and Charles' father, Barney, were Jimmy's closest friends. That's how Charlie got your uncle as a client. To be honest, he's kind of a flat tire, at least in Jimmy's book."

"So, Dr. St. George came to the house …"

"Too late. He couldn't help, and Jimmy died. Willard told the police that he'd stopped by to make sure your uncle took his medication. Since everyone knew how stubborn Jimmy could be, no one questioned Willard's word."

"Uncle Jimmy sent me a note."

"I know. He gave it to Willard about a week before he died. Willard hired Mr. Dockins to find you." Almost like Uncle Jimmy had known.

I shook the thought out of my head. "Dr. St. George hired Mr. Dockins? Charles didn't tell me that."

"Well, after he found out, ol' Charlie threw a fit. He said it was his job as executor of Jimmy's will to find you."

"So, Dr. St. George knows all about you?"

"Yes."

Jealousy stung as if the doctor had somehow taken what should have belonged to me all these years. "Does Charles know about you?"

"No."

Good. I had more questions, but my stomach overrode them. It growled. Not a dainty gurgle, but a deep rumble that brought conversation to a halt. I winced and shrugged. "I haven't had dinner yet."

"There's food in the kitchen. Meet me downstairs and I'll heat something for you." He vanished.

A guy who cleaned and cooked? His being dead appeared the only problem. I ran down the stairs, eager not to miss a moment with him. At the kitchen door, I stopped as a can of soup poured itself into a saucepan.

"Have a seat," said a voice near the stove. I slid into the first chair at the table, my eyes never leaving the pan on the stove. The ladle rose and then dipped, and then Andre shimmered into view. He must have read my unsure gaze, because he asked, "Is this better?"

"Yes." He filled a bowl and then placed it in front of me. "Thank you."

He frowned. "I had to throw out all the perishables so it's only condensed soup." This fact appeared to cause Andre some anguish.

"I like it," I assured him.

"You haven't tasted my homemade soup yet." He moved to the sink. "James liked tea, but I haven't made it since he passed. Will water be okay?"

"Fine, but I can get it myself."

There was that grin again. "I don't mind." A great-looking guy who waited on me? I didn't argue. "Could you please put ice in it?"

"Of course." The ancient fridge didn't have an ice maker. Still, the old-fashioned aluminum tray with the metal lift handle caught me by surprise. It resembled something Grandma Petey would've sold in a garage sale years ago. My uncle sure hadn't been worried about impressing anybody. Andre took a seat, so near I could've touched his knee, if he'd been solid.

"Isn't the air supposed to grow cold whenever ghosts are around?"

"People are as different dead as they are alive. However …" The temperature in the room dropped. A numbing cold seeped into my bones.

I gasped and rubbed my arms. "Okay, okay!" The chill eased and then disappeared.

"Eat your soup. It's getting cold." I groaned, but took a slurp. I felt weird with him watching me eat, but hunger overrode awkwardness. "Are you getting tired?"

Andre shook his head. "I'm fine. I'll rest when you go to sleep. Uh, I expected your mother to be with you." The spoonful of noodles plopped back into the bowl. I managed to splash both myself and the table. Andre handed me a napkin.

My stomach twisted again, but not from hunger. "She's getting married."

He frowned. "You're not invited to the wedding?"

"It's complicated." I shrugged. "For the moment, you're stuck with me."

"I have no problem with that." From the force with which he assured me, he must have remembered Mom rather well. Andre leaned back and stretched long legs. "It must be hard to leave all your friends back in the City."

"Not really. You have to have friends to miss them." I pushed my empty bowl away. Andre immediately carried it to the sink. "Hey, I can do that."

"It's okay." I yawned, barely managing to cover my mouth. "You're tired."

"Yeah."

"Then any more questions can wait until morning, don't you think?"

"You'll still be here?"

The amused look returned to his chocolate eyes. "I never left."

You've got the rest of your life to talk to him. Do you really want to embarrass yourself by falling asleep, maybe drooling? "Where, uh, where do you stay at night?" I asked.

"I like to … haunt the library." He grinned. He must have seen the hesitation in my eyes because he made a little bow. "Don't worry, Tessa, I never enter a bedroom uninvited, visible or otherwise." This time, instead of disappearing, he walked me up the stairs. At the top, he paused and asked, "Would you like me to light a fire?"

"That'd be great."

In the bathroom, I passed on the hot bath. I'd probably fall asleep taking it. I cleaned my face, dabbed a little acne medicine on my pimple, and hurried across the hall to my room. In the fireplace, a low flame snapped and crackled. I snuggled under the chenille bedspread and gazed at the fire. Its warmth calmed my jumpy nerves.

What would practical Grandma Petey think of Andre? I'd found him again.

What did I think of him? Exhaustion warred with excitement and finally won. I slept deeply. For about two hours.

Then Larry entered my dreams.

I'm your new daddy, Tessa. And I like for family to be real close.

Awake, I gasped for breath and pushed myself to a sitting position. Sweat soaked my shirt as I frantically searched the room. No Larry, thank goodness. Fumbling for the light, I found the switch. Fringe brushed my hand. That's when my semi-awake brain remembered my change in address. I pulled the lamp's chain and peered at the shadows beyond its pale semi-circle of light.

Had Andre holed-up in the library to spend the night reading his floating book? What else did ghosts do for fun? Wide awake, I decided to find out.

I slipped my robe over my smiley-faced tee. The fire had died to embers, but even in the dim lamplight, the robe screamed ratty. But it beat wandering around in just the tee. Stopping by the bathroom, I faced the mirror. Should I put on makeup? Get a grip, Tessa! I ran a comb through my hair, then cupped my hand over my mouth and blew. Could ghosts smell bad breath? I brushed.

Back in the dark hallway, I hesitated. The memory of my uncle falling down the stairs made me hesitate to wander around with only the moonlight to guide me. Still, I felt weird about turning on a light.

Okay, silly, this is your house. Act like it. I pulled my robe tighter and flipped on the light switch. Now what?

As I stood there indecisively, or as Mom would say, "Not knowing whether you're following your butt or your head," I spied a light underneath the door of the mural room. Did my resident ghost live there? Did ghosts need light? What would a ghost put in a room? It's not like he needed a bed to sleep in or a dresser for clothes.

I knocked. The door opened as if of its own accord, but fast, not slow motion spooky. Andre appeared. "I saw the light," I stammered.

"Please come in." He stood aside and I entered. Andre held a paintbrush. He'd drawn the mural, not my uncle. Delicate strokes had added branches to the half-finished tree.

"It's beautiful."

"Thank you." Fresh paint splattered the tarp and the smell of turpentine permeated the air.

I eyed the brown on Andre's gray pants. "How can a ghost get paint on his clothes?"

"The splatters were there when I died."

"Oh." Time to take your foot out of your mouth, Tessa. "Is this a painting of a real place?"

"It's a spot I once knew." His voice held no invitation for me to ask where, so I didn't. Andre moved in front of me. "Your uncle gave this room to me. But perhaps you'd like to use it for something else?"

I shook my head. "Not a thing. I figure this house is big enough for us to share."

"What about your mother?"

"I'm working on that."

"I beg your pardon?"

"Nothing." I returned to the mural. "You were a painter in, uh, when you were alive?"

"Yes."

Even though he wasn't exactly volunteering information, I still had to ask. "And that was?"

"The 1920s."

My mind tried to process that. "How old were you when you died?"

"Nineteen."

Okay, that added up to about 120 in people years. Good grief, Tessa. He's a ghost not a dog. "It's a great painting, Andre."

He laughed. "I've had a few years to improve my technique."

"I don't have the talent to be a painter."

A brush pressed into my hand. "The bench needs some tan."

"No!" Panic welled inside me at the thought of destroying his creation.

"You can't hurt it. Follow the outline, and I'll add the details.

36

Go, on," he urged, "see what it feels like to create." When I still hesitated, his hand took mine, steady and sure. A strand of his hair brushed my cheek.

Breathe or pass out, Tessa. I gulped air.

Andre guided my hand to the bench. He let go. "Paint."

I did. With slow strokes, careful not to go outside the lines. No toddler with a crayon could've been prouder. "Finished." I stepped back and almost cried. The tan blotch stood out like a dirty bandage. "Andre, I've ruined it!"

"Not at all." He took the brush. Subtle shading and deft strokes transformed my blotch into a nuanced wooden bench.

"Someday," I gushed, "I'd love to be able to do that."

"It's important to fulfill your dreams," he told me.

He didn't offer to teach me.

No problem. I'd fulfilled one dream by finding him again. I'd fulfill my only other dream if I managed to keep Mom from taking my house. Then, I'd work on the big dream. A life no one could screw up but me.

Through the open door came the distinctive tinkling of breaking glass. We stared at each other. "You didn't by any chance forget to mention a cat?" I asked.

He shook his head and disappeared.

I raced down the stairs two at a time. At the bottom, I rounded the corner too fast and found myself riding the hall rug like a surfboard. Moonlight streamed in the open front door where a dark figure loomed. I slammed into the intruder sending him sprawling back outside—me right along behind. Did the high-pitched shriek come from him or me? He bounced down the porch steps, gained his footing, and took off.

Two strong arms wrapped around my waist kept me from going airborne. Grasping the nearest rail, I glared at the broken hole that used to be the stained glass center of my front door. "You're a ghost," I wailed. "Couldn't you have scared him or something?"

"Worse than you did?" Andre reappeared, doubled over with laughter.

My glare deepened.

He snickered. "I'd managed an unearthly 'Who's there?' when you made your entrance. Are you okay?" he asked in what seemed an afterthought.

"Fine!" I attempted to make a dignified exit and immediately regretted it. "Ouch." A trickle of blood oozed down my left knee.

"Tessa, you're hurt." Before I could say something nasty about stating the obvious, Andre lifted and carried me into the living room. Thank goodness he stayed visible for the trip. I wrapped my arms around his neck, my brain torn between giving attention to my knee pain and the serious attraction building in other areas. Oblivious to my dilemma, Andre gently laid me on the couch. "Stay here," he ordered. "I'm going to see if I can find any sign of our friend." I closed my eyes and willed my knee not to hurt and my dignity to come back.

After forever, Andre reappeared with a first aid kit. "Whoever it was, hightailed it. Of course, there are numerous places to hide on the property and he definitely got a wiggle on."

"A what?" I asked.

"He scrammed, left in a hurry."

"Oh. Couldn't you see him hiding?"

"I can be seen through, but can't see through," he retorted. "Here, let me check the damage." I bit my lip as Andre straightened my leg. "A few bruises and small scrapes. It's going to be sore in the morning." He knelt, his dark head bent over my leg. Skillful fingers applied ointment and then a bandage. I resisted the urge to reach out and wrap some dark strands around my finger, but the thought did help keep my mind off the pain. "Done," Andre announced.

I winced and stretched my leg along the couch. "I guess I should call the police." I obediently swallowed the ibuprofen and water he held out to me.

"Do you have a cell phone like Willard?" Andre asked. "Jimmy didn't own a phone." He spread the brightly colored afghan from the back of the couch over me. At least he didn't tuck it under my chin.

"What?" My head whipped left and right as if I could make a phone appear on demand. "You're kidding."

He shrugged and even in my distress, I had to admire the perfection of the movement. "Jimmy enjoyed his privacy. He liked contact with people only when he needed them. That usually meant showing up unannounced and banging on their front doors."

"He didn't have to answer the phone if he didn't want to," I shouted. "It's called Caller ID."

Andre sat cross-legged on the floor, no longer solid. His entire body went motionless, his attention focused on me. "Your uncle was a funny old bird."

"Car?" I asked.

Andre frowned. "I beg your pardon?"

"I didn't see a car. Is it in the garage?"

"No, he walked everywhere."

"But, Andre, it's at least seven miles into town."

"Jimmy liked to walk."

I sat back, closed my eyes again, and groaned. "Do you think whoever broke in will come back?"

He didn't answer. I peeked, but Andre gazed past me, his eyes studying the broken front door. "I think the intruder thought the house empty. I also think he's still running." He chuckled.

"Mom took our cell with her." I could afford a car or my own phone, not both. "Do you think I can wait until tomorrow to report it?"

"I should think so."

Silence fell. I leaned against the back of the couch. Should I report the break in? It risked letting other adults know I lived by myself. And gorgeous Andre didn't really count as company in the eyes of the law.

"Has your mother developed a better opinion of living in the country?" Andre asked. "Or 'the boonies' as she called it."

Huh? What? "How do you know my mother doesn't like the country?" I laughed. "Oh yeah, from our stay here." I struggled to sit straighter. The afghan fell from my shoulders. I gave up and snuggled back under its cozy warmth. "I wonder who Mom thought did the cooking and cleaning."

"Your uncle. Let me tell you, Jimmy took great pleasure in her compliments. He strutted around in an old apron like he'd won first prize in a cooking contest. Your mother never struck me as the type to appreciate a ghost cooking eggs for her in the mornings. So, we kept up the pretense."

"You read her right, although she'd probably have eaten the eggs before screaming her head off. Mom's practical when it comes to free food."

"Your uncle once suggested that I surprise her by appearing in the mirror and yelling, 'Boo' But I declined."

"It must have been hard on you having us here, to have to stay hidden."

His smile went straight to those delicious brown eyes. "I didn't mind."

"Mom and Uncle Jimmy never got along, even before we came to live with him."

"I know he didn't approve of her marrying your father."

It felt natural talking to Andre. Natural, maybe. But normal? A part of me wondered about my sanity, but another part told my sanity to shut up. "Yeah, the usual Grade B movie plot. Jimmy didn't like my dad and told Mom that if she married him, she'd never be welcome in his house again. She married him anyway. I saw my father for the last time at my eighth birthday party." What a blast. Daddy drunk and Mommy screaming. "Mom was Dad's second wife. The wife he brought to my party was wife number four. The whole time he kept introducing me to stepbrothers and sisters I'd never met and haven't seen since."

Andre grimaced. "Charming."

"Yeah, I used to cry every time Mom suggested throwing me another party. Which usually happened because she liked some cute single dad and wanted to trick him over to the house. Anyway, after the divorce, we parked on Jimmy's doorstep. Even he couldn't throw his homeless sister and her kid out. But that only lasted for about a month." My knee stung. I twisted sideways in another a vain attempt to get comfortable and the afghan slipped off my feet. "According to Mom, Jimmy started every morning with 'Hello' followed by 'I told you so.'"

"He did, I'm sorry to say. Your uncle was a very obstinate man." In a seamless move Andre knelt beside the couch. He tugged the afghan back into place, one hand brushing ever so slightly against the arch of my foot. Oh, wow, if his touching my foot could create tingles …"So, for you this is a little like coming home?"

Huh? What? Pay attention or continue to come across like an idiot, Tessa. I shook my head as much to clear it as to answer him. "Afraid I don't remember much about living here. Half the places Mom and I lived are blurs. I used to envy the kids at school who went home to real houses and real beds. My bed was the couch, or if we'd sold it that month, a pallet on the floor."

"I've always rather liked the bohemian lifestyle myself," he commented.

"Yeah, well, I never found anything romantic about being shaken awake at two in the morning so we could sneak out before the landlord came for the rent."

"Understandable."

"Andre, why is it the only time I remember you is when I fell out of the tree?"

"Since you were so vocal about seeing me, as any child would be, we didn't feel it best to make a habit of it."

My eyelids drooped. Even the novelty of talking to a ghost couldn't keep me awake. I declined Andre's offer to help me climb the stairs. Later, nuzzled under the covers, I listened to the thud of the hammer as he nailed a board over the broken window. I'd really liked that stained glass and I hated the thought of an ugly piece of wood taking its place. Guess what, Uncle Jimmy? I'm here only one day and I'm already trashing your beloved home.

I rolled over trying to make my aching knee comfortable. Andre had been right, it would really, really hurt in the morning. My thoughts drifted to other topics. What would happen when Mom and Larry appeared? How would I keep her from dragging me back to Oklahoma City? She still held the purse strings for another two months. Mom had a plan. What if tonight put it in motion? Had I fought with Larry downstairs?

A knot in my stomach pulled tight. Better leave me alone, Lar. Better leave me alone!

The next morning I awoke to a howling wind that shook the rafters. I tested my knee - stiff rather than bendy. Self-pity hit. How long would it take Andre to start worrying and check on me? Before or after starvation?

Both knee and mind muttered protests as I angled myself to a sitting position and examined my injury. A puffy bruise had formed around the neat bandage. The bruise immediately throbbed twice as hard. It might be wise to soak the bandage before trying to remove it. Hopefully only dried blood would come away and no fresh skin.

Part of me wanted to throw my clothes on and find Andre right away. But the other half, the one that told me I really needed a shower, won. I hopped halfway to the door before remembering my robe. Ghost or not, Andre equaled male. I fumbled my way back to the bed and grabbed it.

Balancing in the tub on one leg and one tiptoe, I let the warm water run, thankful for Uncle Jimmy's orders to keep the utilities turned on. I soaped myself off to a belted-out chorus of Crystal Gale's, "Don't it Make my Brown Eyes Blue." My eyes were already blue, but that didn't stop me from putting real feeling into the song. My knee loosened. Time to deal with the bandage. My uncle apparently hadn't believed in anything modern like ouchless bandages. I yanked, then yelped and carried on like a two-year old. It hurt! Tears mingled with the soothing water flowing down my skin.

I dried off and pulled on a pair of jeans, faded from wear, not style, and a peach colored cable knit sweater that hit almost to my knees. A keepsake of Dad's I'd saved from the bonfire my mother had made of all his other stuff. I ran my fingers through my hair to fluff it and considered makeup. Nope. I slathered Beeswax balm on my lips. If we were going to be housemates, Andre would have to get used to the real me, and that wasn't makeup and stilettos.

Speaking of … every part of me wanted to find him.

Halfway down the stairs, a delicious smell hit my nose. Mmm … cinnamon. Unfortunately, my knee warned against any pace faster than a quick hobble. "Hi," died on my lips as the dishes washed themselves.

Andre took form. "Good morning. Did you sleep well? How's your leg?"

"Yes and sore." I sat, grabbed my spoon and peered into a bowl of oatmeal. Yuck! "Um, looks good." I scanned the table for help. "Is there any sugar?"

A slight crease crossed his forehead. "Have you even tasted it yet?"

"I don't really like instant."

"Instant!"

His wounded gaze made me backpedal. "I – I never dreamed you'd make me *real* oatmeal." Was real the right term?

"I don't make instant foods. Notice I said make and not cook."

"I'm sorry." To restore peace, I took a big bite. My eyes widened.

Andre grinned. "Better than instant?"

"Delicious!"

"It's my own recipe. I use all natural chunky applesauce with a dash of cinnamon."

I took another bite, savoring the warm apple taste. "It's great."

"And good for you." Inwardly I groaned. Who'd ever heard of a ghost on a health kick? He placed the pan in hot soapy water. "I enjoyed the concert."

"What?" Oh, my shower. "Please tell me you didn't hear."

"Afraid I can't do that." I resolved to learn to hum. Andre took the chair next to me. He wore the same blue sweater.

"Can ghosts change their clothes?"

"We can alter our appearance." He studied himself. "I admit I don't keep up with changing styles. Also, it takes a lot of energy to keep the alteration going."

"Don't worry. A good-looking guy never goes out of style." I slapped my hand over my mouth. Had I really said that out loud? The grin on his face said I had. My pimple competed with the rest of me for brightest red.

He let me off the hook by pointing to a piece of paper beside my bowl. "I've made a grocery list."

Wouldn't you know it? Not a single piece of junk food on the list. "I don't like raisins," I said, trying not to sulk.

"Then don't buy them. It's your kitchen. You're in charge."

Who was he trying to kid? I searched for a last bite of oatmeal. "How'd you meet my uncle?" A morbid thought struck. "This isn't the house where you died?" Maybe Uncle Jimmy had been so worried about taking care of Andre because the ghost had lived here in life?

"I died in another place." His eyes didn't meet mine.

"Oh." Not wanting to push a painful memory, I stayed silent.

"I met Jimmy at a used bookstore."

I remembered the upstairs library. "He liked to read?"

"He had certain types of books he favored."

What a funny way to phrase it. "Andre, how did you meet? I mean …"

"I know what you mean. Your uncle could sense ghosts."

My spoon clattered to the table. "Really?"

Andre grimaced, probably wondering if I made a habit of dropping my spoon at every meal. "Jimmy sensed me. I can't tell you how much it surprised me when he spoke."

"I can imagine. No, honestly, I can't." I retrieved my spoon. "You weren't the first ghost he'd talked to?"

"Down the road about a half mile is a cemetery. Jimmy claimed he had a lot of friends there. I never could tell if he was kidding or not." He wiped the place where my spoon had fallen with a napkin.

The dearly departed were my neighbors? "Is that where Jimmy is buried?" I asked, suddenly ashamed that I didn't know.

"Yes." Andre read my discomfort correctly. "It's okay, Tessa. You didn't really know him."

"I should visit."

"When you're ready. Anyway, I was pretty much a wanderer at that point, death imitating life, if you want to be poetic about it. Jimmy invited me to his home. We got along and he asked me to stay. I did." Simple story, except that one of the participants could disappear at will.

"I don't have to stay," he added.

"What?"

"It's your house."

"I've waited twelve years to find you again. Don't you dare decide it's time to move on now!"

Andre laughed. "What about your mother? I doubt she'll like the idea of an invisible man living with her now any more than she would have twelve years ago."

"It's not her house." I didn't like the subject, so I changed it. "Can other people hear you?" I gestured between the two of us. "I mean when you're talking to me, can anyone else hear you?"

"Not unless I want them to."

"Andre, could my uncle come back as a ghost?" I didn't mind sharing the house with Andre, but Uncle Jimmy didn't sound so fun.

"I don't think so."

"Why?"

"The ghosts I know all have some kind of guilt left over from their lives." He chuckled. "I don't think Jimmy ever felt guilty about anything in life. He wouldn't start in death."

What's your guilt? I didn't ask. And if he ever resolved it, did that mean he'd fade away for good?

"I went to see Dr. St. George last night." Andre said. "After the break-in."

"You ditched me?" I'd been all alone in the house?

"You were asleep. I promise I wasn't gone long." He frowned. "But, I shouldn't have left at all. I'm sorry. But I wanted to make sure he knew you'd arrived."

I gathered my tattered dignity around me like a worn blanket. "You're not my babysitter. You can come and go whenever you please. Anyway, what did the doctor have to say?"

"He and Elma want me to bring you by later this evening."

"Elma?"

"His wife."

"She knows about you too?"

"Yes."

Maybe meeting someone else who knew about Andre would help me stop feeling like I had knocked on the door to Looneyville. "Sounds great."

"I'll let them know." From the look he gave my empty bowl, I

46

knew Andre couldn't wait until I left to clear the table.

I scooped up the list. "I need to report what happened last night. While I'm out I'll do the shopping, so I won't starve." Dang, that meant even more time away from him. But I had to buy food before barricading myself in the house, never to come out again. But now, knowing he had gone places with my uncle, I asked, "Would you like to come?"

"No thank you. But, I agree, you probably need to get a wiggle on."

"Beg your pardon?"

"Get going. Get that break-in reported."

"Uh, right." I paused in the doorway and watched him carry the dishes over to the sink. Dead or not, I'd have to get the boy some other interests besides cooking and cleaning.

A pile of junk mail lay on the entry table beside that awful vase. Not only does he cook and clean, but fetches the mail too. I set aside a clothing catalog, to browse through later, maybe during a hot bath. Everything else went in the trash.

The board replacing the front door window fit perfectly. Another of Andre's talents revealed. The break-in felt fuzzy and unreal. Did I really have to report it? The nagging feeling the intruder might have been Larry bothered me. Had the guy been tall or heavy enough? Had I seen a beer gut?

Outside, the wind had died, making the fall day crisp. "Sweater weather" Grandma Petey called it – my favorite. Driving past the abandoned stone pond, I imagined it covered in wild strawberries in the summer.

No one will let a seventeen year old girl live out in the country on her own. Mom will win. Shut up! I told my brain. Today, this was my road and Ama my town. Not a place where we'd crashed because the gas money ran out. I owned a house. I belonged. Someone even waited for me at home. That thought almost made me head back home. I already missed those chocolate brown eyes.

Downtown, baled hay, scattered pumpkins, and scarecrows decorated storefronts. All down Main Street, festive fall garlands wrapped Victorian style street lights. At the end of the street, sat "Ma and Pop's", the perfect name for a small town grocery. Had Uncle Jimmy shopped there?

I exited the car, one fist holding the list so it wouldn't blow away if the wind decided to come roaring again. Get the groceries, report the break-in and get back to Andre!

"Tessa? Tessa Kelling? I'm so relieved to see you." Charles St. George charged down the sidewalk looking as earnest as a flop-eared puppy. He grabbed the hand not holding the list. "I stopped by the Red Rose this morning to check on you and your mother, but Willa said you'd never showed."

I felt like an idiot as he clutched my hand in both of his, but didn't know how to yank it back without being rude. "I'm sorry, Mr. St. George."

"Call me Charles."

Never been called Chuck in your life, have you? "I'm sorry, Charles, but we decided to drive to my uncle's house … my house."

He squeezed my hand. "I guess I should have realized you'd be anxious to see it. I was *trying* to be helpful."

My need to please surfaced and I passed the blame. "Mom made a last minute decision." I'm not sure how that explained things, but Charles brightened.

His head swiveled back and forth like someone watching a tennis match. "Where is your mother?"

"She didn't come into town." He pulled me along the sidewalk. My knee protested the sudden movement. "Ouch!"

Charles stopped. "You're limping. Are you hurt?"

I didn't want to talk about the break-in while standing on the busy sidewalk. "Strange house equals bumped knee." His face said that if we'd taken his advice, I'd have been tucked in at the B&B and not wandering around a strange house at night. But he said nothing, and instead walked a bit slower down the sidewalk, me in tow. We headed in the opposite direction of the grocery.

"Uh, Mr., err, Charles, where are we going?"

"We need to get you some breakfast."

Another guy intent on taking care of me. At least this one still breathed. However, I usually took care of myself. "Thanks, but I've already eaten."

He frowned. "But there you couldn't have found anything fresh at your uncle's."

"I ate some oatmeal."

He screwed up his face like a little boy told to eat his broccoli. "I hate that instant stuff."

"Me too."

Charles grinned. "So you'll come to the café with me? My treat."

He looked so hopeful I gave in. "Sure."

The café, a freestanding white-bricked building stood two doors down from where I'd parked. We slid into the bench seats of a red vinyl booth covered with a red and white-checkered tablecloth. Both had tears in them, but were clean. The waitress, dressed in a red sweatshirt with "Eat at the Café" printed on it, knew Charles by name. "The usual?"

"Yes, ma'am." He grinned at me. "I'm afraid I'm the typical bachelor. I don't do any of my own cooking."

The waitress, whose nametag said Donna, winked. "Your being single is your own fault. There are plenty of us who'd like to change that." He ducked his head as if embarrassed and she laughed. She gave me an appraising glance. "Of course, maybe he likes 'em young?"

"Huh?" It took me a moment to realize what she meant.

Charles sputtered. "For Pete's sake, Donna, she and her mother are clients."

"Really? And what will your client be having?"

I glanced at the menu and thumbed an imaginary nose at Andre. "I'll take a glazed donut, please."

"That's all?"

"And some orange juice," I added. With a shrug, she left to place our orders.

"Sorry about that." Charles reached across and took both my hands in his, something that wasn't going to sell Donna on the completely true client story if she happened to glance our way.

I pulled my hands away and placed them in my lap. "It's okay."

He stared at his empty hands then folded them on top of the table. "I feel terrible about you and your mother going alone into that dusty, shut-up house last night. I hope there weren't any other shocks or surprises."

No surprises other than the attack. Since the age of five I'd known I'd find Andre again. "Actually, it wasn't that bad."

He leaned forward. "So, besides your knee, you had a good evening?"

"Someone tried to break in." It came out of my mouth before my brain could shout "Whoa!"

"What?" His eyes bulged and he straightened. "That's awful. Did they take anything?" Then a horrified, "Did they attack you?"

"Sort of." I explained about the rug and how I'd scared the would-be burglar when I'd sailed through the door after him.

"What did the Police Chief say?"

"We haven't reported it yet."

"Why not? Oh!" He hit his forehead. "No phone. One of your uncle's little peculiarities. Haven't you got a cell?"

"No." I didn't explain that Mom had taken off with it.

"Maybe you and your mother should move into the Red Rose until you decide what you want to do with the house."

"We think whoever broke in thought the house still empty. He had no idea anyone lived there until I slid into him."

Charles put on a funeral face. "I'm sorry your stay in our town is being spoiled by such an outrage."

Good grief. Did he always talk like an eighty year old?

Donna brought our food with a wink at me and a flirty grin for Charles. I munched on my donut while Charles consumed a bran muffin, orange juice and fruit. For a young guy, he ate like my grandmother. Afterward he insisted on accompanying me to the Police Chief's office.

Could be a bad, bad move. Mom would kill me if I got Larry arrested.

Police Chief Mason, a stocky, red-haired woman in her early fifties, agreed my visitor hadn't expected to find the house occupied. While I sat trying to wipe the sugary donut glaze off my sweater, she expounded on her theory. "Probably a kid up to mischief. And I hate to say it, but we probably won't catch him. Still, I'll send someone to check around." She frowned at the phone in her hand. "Still no answer."

"She doesn't always take her phone with her," I said. *Doing great Mom. Whatever your plan, did it include evading the police?*

Chief Mason stopped trying to reach Mom on her cell. "You say she's on her honeymoon?"

I ignored Charles' surprised gaze. "They didn't see any need to postpone the wedding. After all, she couldn't do anything for my uncle."

"Well, when she gets back, tell her I said she needs to answer her phone."

"I will," I assured her.

"I'll be taking care of Tessa until her mom gets back," Charles said. Oh really?

"Yes, you do that," Chief Mason said. She addressed me. "Like I said, either I or a deputy will be out later today to poke around. Also, I'll keep my ears open for anyone who's bragging about almost getting caught." She chuckled. "Or, limping."

"Thank you."

Back on the sidewalk, Charles fussed. I clasped my hands

behind my back in case he felt the need to comfort me again. "I could follow you home and check things out. I don't like that you're living in the country alone." He cleared his throat. "Tessa, why didn't you mention to me your mother had left on her honeymoon?"

I widened my eyes and put on my ready-to-please smile. "Charles, I didn't think it wise to tell people I'm all by myself."

"Yes, yes, I guess I understand." His eyes moved passed me. "Well, if you change your mind, please let me know." Charles gave my arm an absentminded pat and left at a gait just short of jogging.

I scanned the area. In front of Suzy's Cut 'n Curl, I saw one of the few people in town I recognized, Anna Gleason. Why would Charles run away when he saw her? Maybe Charles did have a reputation for "liking 'em young," as the waitress had teased. People were walking around my imitation of a statue, so I made my legs move.

Since I'd been old enough to skip to the corner store, I'd bought the groceries. Inside Ma and Pop's I grabbed a blue basket from behind the front door and started down the nearest aisle, Andre's list in hand. Since he seemed more than willing to do the cooking, I'd decided to let him. To thank him, I'd purchase any food he wanted. On *my* list a temperamental cook beat opening a jar of peanut butter or popping frozen dinners into the microwave, which we probably didn't own anyway. Fresh veggies, tomatoes that I loved and cauliflower that I didn't, headed his list. Guess I'd try a healthier lifestyle. It wouldn't hurt to lose a few pounds. Not that I could ever emulate the models in Vogue.

A funny feeling tickled my neck. I peeked from under my eyelashes. The attention of my fellow shoppers focused on me. A young mother with a fussy toddler smiled and ducked her head when caught staring. An elderly woman adjusted her glasses and gawked harder. The familiar flush covered my neck. Why the interest? Ama wasn't so small that the sight of an unfamiliar face should stop business.

Then, in the process of hunting for tuna, I spied Anna Gleason standing inside the front door, her head close to the cashier's. At my stare, she gave me a smirk and a wave. Feeling overexposed, I half-heartedly waved back, but she'd already left. The cashier, a friendly looking redhead, stared at me with her mouth open. She realized it, blushed redder than even I could, and quickly got busy at her register.

I barely knew Anna, so what was her problem? Had my talking to Charles set her off? Was she stalking him or something?

I decided I'd had enough shopping and hurried to the front of the store. The cashier, whose tag said Chloe, grinned. "Hello. Welcome to Ma and Pop's. Did you find everything you needed?"

"Yes." After all, I couldn't blame the store for the things I couldn't find for lack of trying.

As she totaled my purchases, Chloe peered at me from under what would have been pale eyelashes if they hadn't been dunked in green mascara. I longed to demand that she tell me exactly what Anna Gleason had said, but the words stuck in my cowardly throat. "Twenty dollars and twenty-three cents," Chloe announced. Her grin said expensive dental work. "Is it true?"

I paused, the money still in my hand. "Huh?"

"I hope it's okay to ask."

"Um, is what true?"

"That you live in the house that's supposed to be haunted?"

Would Andre be pleased to know of his fame? "My uncle was James Duran," I said.

She finally took the money. "Really?" Her dark green eyes bulged and her left hand played with a dangly earring. "Is it really haunted? Have you seen the ghost?"

Yes, I've seen him and he's gorgeous. "I've heard a few things," I hedged.

"Like bumps in the night?" She clutched my money to her chest.

"Sort of." Although, most of the bumps had come from the would-be burglar and me.

"Awesome!" I shrugged."You're not afraid?"

"Not really."

"You must be so brave. I don't think I could last more than a few minutes in that house! Haunted equals pretty creepy to me," she explained in a rush.

Did everyone in this town have a slightly off side? "Well, if there is a ghost, he never hurt my uncle."

"How do you know it's a he?" she asked handing me my change.

"I guess you could say it's male energy."

She let out her breath in one big "whoosh" and ran her hands down her arms. "That gives me goose bumps." Her smile widened. "Are you a junior or senior? 'Cause if you're a senior, I can show you around school when fall break's over."

"Thanks, but I don't know when I'll be enrolling."

"Oh. Well, fall break ends this week. Hey, if y'all need anything else, well, maybe I can get you some store credit."

Huh? "No, we're fine. Where did you get the idea…?" Anna! "Chloe, what did Anna Gleason say to you about me and my mother?"

She repeated it to the grocery bag and not me. "That you guys are destitute and can't wait to live off Jimmy's life savings."

Okay, Tessa, deep breath. "I can take care of myself."

"Hey, forget I stuck my foot in, okay? I want you to consider me your first friend in Ama, okay? Anything y'all need just let me know!"

"Sure, no problem." Weird. I pushed open the glass door and then paused. "I'll take one of those," I said, pointing to a bin filled with pumpkins.

"Which one?"

"The biggest."

It took me two trips, one for the groceries and one for the pumpkin. I stuck it in the passenger's side with the seatbelt snuggled around it.

Once in the car, I pondered. Why had Anna Gleason said that stuff to Chloe? Hateful didn't even begin to cover it. I spied a real rat.

At the stoplight, I spied Mom. Maybe. No. The woman wore a similar brown tweed coat. Spiky blond hair instead of wavy. Mom tried that style a few years back, spiky, with purple tips. It was like living with the aging ghost of punk rock. I rolled down the window to yell, but the woman darted into the post office.

Had she pulled at her collar? A stranger or Mom playing games? No Larry in sight. Could he be nursing the bruises I'd given him the night before?

Forget Mom and Larry and their schemes. Forget Anna and her malicious gossip. Even forget sweet Charles and his threat to take care of me.

Andre waited.

Entering the house, I tossed my keys on the side table. The catalog, along with the junk mail, had disappeared. My ghost was obviously something of a neat freak. "Andre?"

"Behind you."

I jumped and whirled around. A sack of groceries floated behind me. "Did you shut the car door?" The question came out in a squeak.

"Yes, Ma'am. I also put the pumpkin on the front porch. Went for the jumbo size, did we?"

"Thanks and yes. I wasn't in the mood for something small." He followed me to the kitchen. "You're a celebrity."

"Me?" He materialized. Gone were the sweater and slacks, replaced by a pair of jeans, a long-sleeved polo in deep black and sneakers. He'd pulled his wavy dark hair into a ponytail, pirate style. I've always found pirates sexy. He stuffed his hands in his pockets and studied himself. "You like?"

"Very much." Oh so very much!

His edges ripped ever so slightly. Not solid. "I decided maybe a change wouldn't be bad." The ripples disappeared. Solid and visible gave the illusion of a living man.

I tried to help Andre with the groceries, but soon tired of the refrain, "That doesn't belong there."

"You're very organized," I muttered, silently substituting the word organized with anal retentive.

"You bought the groceries, so I'll put them away," he said as he snatched the sugar out of my hand. If Andre wanted to be that picky, I wouldn't feel bad about sitting and watching him work. Not a bad view. He had a cute butt. "I can't find the flour."

"Huh?" I woke from my daydream. "Sorry, I didn't get everything on the list. I'll grab the other items next time."

"Not a shopper, huh?" He sat in what I'd started to think of as his chair.

Anna's claims stuck in my throat. It would kill me if Andre also thought of me as a freeloader. "Like I said, you're famous."

Andre raised an eyebrow. "Really? What's the word?"

"Nothing definite. Apparently you're on the mysterious side."

"So, what did you tell them?"

"I might have made a reference to 'bumps in the night.'"

He looked flabbergasted. "You reduced me to bumps?"

"I deemed it the safest thing to do. Vague enough to be intriguing, yet not concrete enough to bring ghost hunters around."

He still looked like he was deciding whether to be insulted or not when something else caught his attention. Leaning forward, Andre brushed his finger across the lower part of my sweater. The combination of sight and touch made my stomach contract. "You have something on your clothes," he said.

I peeked down. "It's glaze. I ran into Uncle Jimmy's lawyer and had a donut."

Andre frowned. "And after I fed you a good breakfast."

"Don't pout. You can't expect me to go off sugar all at once. I'd probably have a heart attack or something."

"You'll probably have one if you continue to eat that way," he predicted.

"You think I'm fat, don't you?" I snapped. His wide eyes and sputter didn't fool me. "You're so worried about me eating sweets because you think I need to lose weight."

"I do not! But I do think you're projecting your own insecurities onto me."

Way too much! I slammed my hands on the table and shoved my chair hard. It teetered, but didn't fall. "Just because you don't have to worry about gaining weight anymore, doesn't mean you can judge me."

Andre stood. "I think being crackers must run in your family."

He shimmered.

"Don't you dare disappear on me!"

For a moment, we glared at each other. Then Andre turned and stomped away. He reached the wall and kept going, shimmering right through it, leaving me open mouthed furious.

Andre's assurance, no arrogance, that he knew best grated on my nerves. Still … I fingered the little fruit magnets on the refrigerator door, flicking the edge of a piece of notepaper stuck under one. Okay, a grownup girl should apologize after going psycho. My ticked-off boarder sat and sulked at the top of the landing.

"I'm sorry," I said. "Truce?"

"I don't have ulterior motives, Tessa."

"I know. Friends?"

A heart pumping moment, then he grinned. "No beefs here."

I took that as a yes and joined him on the landing. "What do we do for fun now?"

"Would you like a tour of the rest of the house?"

"Sure. Can we start with Uncle Jimmy's room?"

"Uh …"

Way to be an unfeeling clod, Tessa! "I'm sorry. Uncle Jimmy and I were strangers. But he was your friend and I guess my wanting to paw through his things must seem cold to you."

"No." His smile went all the way to those liquid chocolate eyes so I felt reassured. Andre stood and held out his hand. "Come on. Let me reintroduce you to Jimmy."

Again, the combination of sight and touch did funny things to my brain. I stood, and he let go. A shimmer told me I could no longer touch him. "How do you sit?"

"Beg your pardon?"

"I mean, when you're not solid. Why don't you sink through the couch, or partway into a chair?"

"Practice."

Drops of rain played a steady beat on the roof—slow at first but gaining pace. "It's a good day for rummaging through the past," I said. The door to the mural room stood open. I spied the clothing magazine. Ah, Andre's inspiration. We stopped outside Uncle Jimmy's room. "Have you been in here since he died?" I asked.

"No."

"How about we search through the attic instead?"

"It's okay, Tessa." Andre reached out and turned the knob. He stood aside, and I entered my late uncle's domain. And people claim teenagers are messy! How to describe Uncle Jimmy's room? Slobs 'R Us? A mournful look played across Andre's face. "He wouldn't allow me to clean in here."

No kidding. Tossed and forgotten clothing covered the worn gold brocade chair. The moldy smell that had been missing in the rest of the house lived in this room. I half wanted to close the door so it couldn't get out, but afraid that I'd die if trapped inside with the smell. Survival won out.

More than a dozen candy wrappers littered the nightstand. So, Uncle Jimmy had insisted on having his junk food. Taking a peek inside a coffee mug, I shuddered. Half full, it wore a thin layer of gray skin on top. Ugh.

And when had Jimmy last changed the dingy sheets? Andre sat on the edge of the bed, making sure the faded bedspread covered them. How much of his behavior came from old habits? Of course, even a ghost might not like the idea of sitting on grungy sheets, much less one as obsessive about cleanliness as Andre. An almost fanatical gleam entered his eyes. Probably already started thinking about giving the whole room a good scrubbing. I'd hate to see what that mop water looked like afterward.

"Okay," I said, trying to not to take a deep breath. "I guess Uncle Jimmy tended to be a slob?"

"Yes."

In the bathroom, soap scum covered the pedestal sink. Either a tossed moss green towel or mold grew on the grungy floor. Forgetting, I took a deep breath and immediately gagged.

"Sometimes not breathing can be a blessing," Andre muttered.

I giggled and then stopped to examine a three-foot-high dirty yellow vase. "I've never seen so many pennies."

"Jimmy said when the vase got full, he'd take a winter vacation to someplace warm." The jar missed being full by an inch. Wonder where he would have gone?

I came to a beat up old dresser and my heart skipped. An envelope sat propped against the dirty mirror with two names written on it —Andre's and mine. "What's this?"

Andre shook his head. "I don't know. Jimmy never said anything about leaving a note."

I joined him on the bed after making sure the bedspread also covered my spot. "This is his second note to me." I held the envelope out to Andre. "You should open it. He was your friend."

"But you're his niece."

"You're the one who knew him."

"Your name is first on the envelope."

Very aware of his peering over my shoulder, I opened and read:

To my niece, Tessa. I'm assuming you've remembered or figured out who Andre is by now. I always told you I had a ghost. Guess I wasn't as crazy as your mama tried to make me out to be. Remember, the deed to the house may now have your name on it, but it's as much Andre's house as yours. Isn't legal to leave your home to a ghost, though. I'm hoping you've got grit and know how to handle your mother.

Nice to feel wanted. I'd have to stop thinking of Andre as my boarder. As for handling my mother, that remained to be seen. I continued to read.

Andre, I hope she's halfway decent. Scare the pants off her if she gives you trouble.

I glared at the ghost, who appeared suspiciously doubled over with silent laughter. "Real charmer, my uncle."

Andre straightened, but his eyes twinkled. "He always spoke his mind."

I turned back to the letter.

I learned in life how to get mine, and if the two of you can

work together, and follow directions, you can get yours too.

"What's he talking about?" I asked.

He shrugged. "I haven't a clue."

I waved the paper in the air, "Actually, we have one right here." Thunder clapped overhead. Maybe that should've been a warning. Getting a teensy bit excited, I asked, "You knew my uncle. Do you think there's anything to this?"

Andre shook his head. "Tessa, I wouldn't put it past Jimmy to have a 'got ya' at the end of the trail."

"Still, we have nothing to lose." I pointed to the rain pouring down the windowpanes. "Hunting for treasure is a perfect rainy day activity."

We focused on the paper again and this time Andre read:

"When I am dead, I hope it may be said: 'His sins were scarlet, but his books were read'" (Hilaire Belloc).

There weren't many books in the room. "You met Jimmy in a bookstore, right?"

"He collected certain types of books."

"Do you think a clue could be hidden in any of these books?"

"Maybe."

It didn't take long to search through the westerns my uncle favored. Nothing fell out or was underlined in code. Checking the bathroom, I found both my earlier assumptions to be correct. A towel covered with mold.

"Gross! Why don't we try the library?"

"Why not?" Andre replied, but not with enthusiasm. Had he already grown tired of our game?

My first visit to the library, my eyes had been on the floating book. Today I gazed in awe at the wooden shelves that stretched from floor to ceiling, stopping only at the two windows and the door. The room even had one of those rolling ladders.

I started for a shelf. "I spy books, lots and lots of books."

"He didn't read any of those," Andre said.

I crossed to another.

"Or those." Andre moved about the room, his fingers resting lovingly on book after book.

My uncle had first encountered the ghost in a bookstore. "He bought these for you, didn't he?"

"Yes."

"How did he know what to buy?"

"We'd make a day of it. Estate sales, auctions, used bookstores ..." Andre laughed. "Sometimes Jimmy would forget and start talking to me. We'd get the entire section of the bookstore to ourselves when that happened."

A mental picture appeared of my uncle wandering a bookstore chatting away to the air. No wonder people thought him eccentric. "But he didn't usually read what he bought?"

"No."

"Then why are we in here? Okay, what books, besides the westerns in his room, did he read?" Andre didn't answer, but I got the feeling he knew. "What?"

"I need to check something out."

"Without me?"

"Give me a moment." Before I could protest, he did his convenient disappearing act.

Although blonde, I'm not dumb. I scurried back to Uncle Jimmy's room. Stopping in the doorway, I observed the top mattress leave the bed. "What have you found?"

The mattress dropped and Andre appeared, looking sheepish. "Those certain books he liked to read."

"Okay, let me see them."

"But ..."

"Hey!" I crossed the room. "We're a team, right?"

Instead of replying, he stepped back and bowed at the waist. "Be my guest."

I straightened my shoulders and studied the bed. No creepy crawlies were in evidence, so I slid my hand underneath the mattress. My fingers came in contact with an object. I hauled it out. A book covered in faux, royal blue velvet. Andre stood with his arms crossed, an interested gaze crossing his face. Another suspicious twinkle played in his eyes. The title page read *Tales of Erotica* in bold script. I held it out to Andre. "Maybe you should see if there's anything hidden in here."

He shoved his hands in his pockets. "Oh, no, I found it. You get to search it. We're a team, remember?"

"You're not funny." I flipped the spine up and fanned the pages. Nothing fell out. I shook the book.

"It could be wedged in pretty tight," Andre observed.

I glared and then flipped the book over. A blush crept up my neck and I didn't dare glance at him. Quickly I flipped through the pages. No notes. But the book gave me the desire to take a long shower with plenty of soap. I closed it and tossed it on the bed. "How many are there?"

"At least two."

I reached back under the mattress and pulled out another book, identical to the first except for its red cover. "Why did he hide them?"

"Maybe he felt naughty."

This book looked even more worn than the first. Luckily, I found what I needed pushed between the second and third pages. The red book joined the blue one on the bed. "If the next clue is as easy to solve, we should be finished by the time the rain stops." I held out the notepaper. "I found it, so you get to read it."

He unfolded and read, "All art is but imitation of nature'" (Seneca).

Before either of us could venture to guess the meaning, the doorbell rang.

Mom? What would she do if I refused to answer?

The doorbell shrilled again. I stomped down the stairs and threw open the door, ignoring my new "conscience" who insisted I peek out the side window first. If a big, bad guy stood on the other side, my conscience could earn his keep.

Not a guy, but a girl occupied the porch. Good or bad remained to be seen. Relief flowed through my chest. At least it wasn't Mom.

Anna stood calm and dry under her umbrella as if the rain didn't dare fall on her. "Hello." Her tight smile made me feel like she wanted to be anywhere but at my door.

"Hello." My tight smile mirrored the sentiment. She made me feel even younger than seventeen. Not to mention huge and gawky, even though I was at least two inches shorter. Besides, her comment to Chloe about Mom and me living off Uncle Jimmy's savings still stung.

"May I come in?" she asked.

"Sure."

"Thank you." She sailed past me, the water from her umbrella drip-dropping onto the top of my head.

I shook my hair, feeling like a wet dog. I stopped when her umbrella found its way into my hands.

"I'm sure you have a place for that."

Did I ever! Instead, I played nice and dropped it on the area rug to dry. My uninvited guest wandered into the living room. Like at the law office, her musky scent saturated the air. Maybe she used it to mark her territory? But this territory belonged to me.

"I've always loved this type of old-fashioned decorating," Anna said as she prowled the room. "It's cozy. Your uncle had good taste."

Maybe I should take her to his room, give her a present of a couple of books? Would she raise a tweezed eyebrow or hunker down for a good read?

Without waiting for an invitation, Anna eased down onto the sofa, pushing the afghan aside as if it had cooties. Her legs were encased in a pair of rust suede pants. I'd have spilt something gooey on them. Elegant clothes and I don't mix. "It must be awfully hard."

I blinked. "What do you mean?"

"To live in someone else's house. You and your mother must feel like you don't belong, especially since you're here because of Jimmy's death." She hugged herself and shivered. "I don't know how you sleep at night."

I should've thrown her out. But years of trying to please everyone doesn't get erased overnight. "Is there something I can help you with?"

"I'm here as a favor to Charles. He told me about the attempted break-in. I must say, he's worried. I know he suggested the two of you move into the Red Rose for a while, but you refused." She shook her head, as if wondering at our stupidity. "Charles is such a busy man, but he was going to come all the way out here to check on you. Naturally, I volunteered to do it instead. I thought maybe I could talk some sense into your mother. Where is she?"

You mean Charles didn't tell you? "On her honeymoon."

Anna leaned forward and clasped her hands around her knees. Manicured nails matched her pants. "You're alone?"

I smiled, though inside I screamed. "I'm not a baby."

"Still, I definitely think the B&B would be a much better place for you until your mother returns."

Good grief. She only had five years on me at the most. I resented her talking to me like I was a little kid. "What am I supposed to do, Anna? Live in the house in the daytime, leaving as soon as the sun starts to set?" Kind of like a reverse vampire.

Her mouth dropped open. "You mean you're staying in Ama?"

"Yep."

"Oh. Charles and I assumed ..." She rubbed her temples. "Would you happen to have anything for a headache? The rain is playing havoc with my sinuses."

Think hard. Where had the ibuprofen of the night before ended up? "Let me check." I tried the kitchen. A bottle of sinus medication and a glass of water stood on the counter. I had the feeling my housemate wanted to get rid of our uninvited guest as fast as I did. Returning, I found the living room empty. For one brief moment, I hoped she'd slipped out. But her umbrella still dripped on my rug. I followed a sound upstairs.

Anna stood inside the doorway to Andre's room. "I went searching for a bathroom and got lost."

"There's one under the stairs."

"Oh." She studied the mural. "It's gorgeous."

"Thank you."

"But you're not the artist."

"How do you know?"

She shrugged. "There's no way you could've painted it in the short time you've been in town."

"My uncle was a man of many talents." Notice I didn't say painting. "Here." I held out the water and tablets.

"Thanks. You know," she said between sips, "I'd really love a tour."

"Mom's a much better guide than I am."

"But she's not here."

"Right."

Anna's eyes narrowed. She handed the glass back. "You know what?"

"What?" I asked cautiously.

"I'm going to stay with you until your mother gets back." She held up a hand. "No, I insist. It'll be fun, kind of like a slumber party. I used to love slumber parties in high school. Didn't you?"

I thought I heard a book drop from the library. "Thanks, but I'll be okay." I couldn't tell if my declining her self-invitation made her happy or distressed.

"Suit yourself. Well, I'd better scoot. I'll tell Charles you're doing fine."

"You do that."

Anna stopped at the top of the steps. "I can't believe I'm standing where Jimmy died. It's kind of creepy. Don't you find it a little creepy?"

I fought a sudden, violent urge to put my hands in the small of her back and push—just to give her the full effect of Jimmy's death, you understand.

Anna shivered. "Is there a draft on these steps? It's freezing." The air had grown chilly.

"Old house," I mumbled.

"Well, I'd get that fixed." The cold numbed and we could see our breath. "This is creepy!" She took off down the steps.

In the foyer, Anna grabbed her umbrella and held it to her chest. I had the satisfaction of seeing a large, wet stain appear on her silk blouse. She giggled. "It almost makes you give credit to all those ghost stories."

"You do like spreading stories, don't you?" I asked sweetly.

She frowned. "I don't know what you're talking about."

"You told Chloe at Mom and Pops all about Mom's and my business. You know, talking about clients has to be some kind of breach in ethics. Maybe that's a question I should ask Charles?" I smiled big.

Her eyes narrowed. "Chloe is quite a little gossip. You can't trust a thing she says. You'd do best to keep that in mind."   Her eyes dropped first. Her umbrella sprayed droplets of water all over the hardwood floor as she opened it. "Well, I've done my good deed. Please let me know if you need help. That way we won't have to bother Charles."

I somehow kept from shoving her outside.

The door shut itself with a bang. "Halloween is missing one of its witches," Andre said when he appeared. I laughed. He busied himself mopping the water with paper towels. "Maybe she's trying to keep an eye on you. She seemed more than determined to keep you and this Charlie fellow apart."

I sat on the bottom stair. "It's Charles St. George. She's his receptionist."

"Hmm, a little hanky-panky going on in the office between the typing and the filing?"

"Or maybe she wants there to be. But why she thinks I'm a threat is beyond me."

"He didn't strike me as a Casanova when he came here to visit Jimmy. More the fussy sort who'd have to be hit over the head before he figured out a girl was interested in him."

"Is Willard the only St. George who knows about you, besides Elma?"

"Yes. The doc's the 'real McCoy', a great guy. He and Jimmy went way back."

"Charles is his nephew?"

"Yes. Charlie's father, Barney, and Willard were brothers. Barney passed away a few months ago."

"How did he die?"

"Heart attack."

"You might be right about Charles and Anna. Although ..."

Finished with his wiping, Andre leaned against the newel post. "What?"

"When we were talking on the sidewalk this morning, he all but ran away when Anna came into view. I don't think he wanted us to be seen together."

Andre snapped his fingers. "That's it then. He's got an eye for pretty girls and she's the jealous type." Had he called me pretty? Andre tossed the paper towels in the wastebasket underneath the entry table. "Jimmy didn't like Charles."

"Yeah, you said Jimmy thought he was a flat tire, which I took to not be good."

Andre rubbed the back of his neck. Some phantom ache? "It isn't. Jimmy never thought Charles was quite Jake."

"Jake?"

"On the up and up."

"Oh." I didn't want to talk about the lawyer anymore. "Where did my uncle get that vase? It's hideous."

Andre grinned at the watercolors-gone-wrong. "It was a present."

Oops. Had Andre given it to Jimmy? No, the ghost had better taste than that. I had a mental image of Andre handing a ghostly credit card to a cashier. "Who gave it to him?"

"I believe you did."

"Not funny."

"I'm serious." He picked up the vase and stuck his hand inside. Fishing out a yellowed card, he handed it to me. On the front, a cartoon mouse waved. On the back were the words, "Happy Birthday, Love Jilly and Tessa."

I had to admit the vase did look a lot like Mom's taste. She had a decorated sweatshirt for every occasion. "I didn't know she tried to make contact with Uncle Jimmy after we left. Did he reply?"

"I don't think so. But he never got rid of the vase."

"Forgive me if I'm not touched. Who knows, maybe if he'd said thank you we could have come back here to live. And don't say that's probably why he didn't." I tossed the card at Andre. He caught it and replaced it in the vase. "It's funny," I mused.

"What?"

"I lived here. This was my home. Yet there's no part of me here."

"It was a long time ago."

"I know." I shrugged. Not his elegant shrug, but we can't all have broad shoulders. Not that I wanted broad shoulders...okay, how crazy did you have to be to get confused in your own mind?

I must have looked pitiful, because Andre asked, "Ready for more clues?"

"Not right now. I'm more in the mood for unpacking." So there, Ms. Gleason, I'd make myself right at home. There would be plenty of time later to discover the punch line to Jimmy's joke.

"Want some company?"

"Sure."

Some of Anna's observations had hit a sore spot. She and Mom would have gotten along. They could both zero in on a person's weakness the way animals track oozing blood.

No matter how hard I'd tried pretending, this was still Uncle Jimmy's home. I didn't want to erase him from the house. For one thing, I didn't think Andre could handle that. But I could make my room really my own.

Andre perched on the edge of the bed while I opened my last suitcase. My clothes were already unpacked. I rummaged through the few keepsakes I always kept with me, no matter if we moved to a rent house in Stillwater, or the garage apartment of Mom's former best friend.

As I decided what to put where, Andre reached over my shoulder and tapped the glass of a wooden picture frame. "When was this taken?"

I struggled to breathe normally as his arm brushed mine. Thankfully, my voice came out squeak free. "About a year ago. That's my best friend, Monica, and me at the Oklahoma City Zoo." It'd been one of our last fun times together before she'd moved to Arkansas. I'd received a post card saying she'd met a really hot guy, and then nothing. Bet her hot guy wasn't as hot as the guy next to me!

"I like your hair."

What was it about guys, even dead ones, and long hair? "I wore it like that until about a year ago. I made the mistake of letting Monica's older sister cut it while she was on the phone having a

70

screaming fight with her boyfriend. Right in the middle she said 'oops' and slammed the phone down. She'd cut a huge chunk out of the side. She blamed the whole thing on him and cut my hair into a short bob. At first I freaked, but now that it's grown out a little, I kind of like it."

"So do I." But not as much as the long waves, I bet. He moved away and breathing became a lot easier.

I placed the picture on the dresser, and concentrated on un-wrapping the newspaper from around my most prized treasures, a matching vase, tray and dish. I'd found the set in a thrift store on a rummaging expedition with Monica. They'd cost me way too much and Mom's fit had been huge, but I'd kept them. A border of pink and blue flowers ran around the edges of the yellow tray and small dish. The vase, also yellow, had a flower border close to its lip. They represented all the pretty things I'd ever dreamed of owning. They'd helped me ignore the third-hand furniture and transported me away from our tiny apartment on days when Mom had been at her worst. I shuddered to think of how Andre's artistic eyes saw my treasures.

I tried to arrange them on the dresser without comment, but he wouldn't let me get away with that. "Does that boudoir set have a story? Was it your grandmother's?"

I fingered the dish. "No, I bought them. Is that what they're called? A boudoir set?"

"Yes." He joined me at the dresser. "You have a good eye." I raised an eyebrow. No, he wasn't joking. Andre flipped the vase upside down. I'd seen the writing, but never paid much attention. "This is an A. J. Wilkinson pattern, probably from the 1920s. Very nice."

"So I did okay?"

"Very okay."

I pointed. "There's a crack in the back of the vase."

"If it doesn't take away from your pleasure, then it shouldn't matter." It didn't. "The set would make an exquisite focal point in your room."

"Huh?"

Andre waved his arm like a maestro leading the symphony. "You could paint the walls yellow and use blue and pink for accent colors. I'll bet you could even find a border that's a good match to the flower design."

"Since when did you morph into Martha Stewart?"

"There are some very good decorating shows on TV." I digested this as he continued, "Would you like me to paint a mural for you?"

I envisioned a field of flowers running across the bottom of one wall. But, would he understand? "No, thank you. You can do anything you want to the rest of the house, but this room is mine."

"I'm going to make you stick to that promise." Animated, he paced the small room. I watched. His feet didn't touch the floor. "There are a lot of changes I've wanted to make in this old house. The paint in the hallway is much too dark and the kitchen hasn't had any remodeling since it was built."

"Remember," I warned him, "we're on a limited budget." Especially since Mom had taken off with the check. All I had was my savings.

He waved an impatient hand. "I know, I know, but ..."

I only half listened to Andre's plans, already knowing whatever he did would be fantastic. My room wouldn't equal the rest of the house by the time he'd finished, but it would be mine. If I had the 'grit', as Uncle Jimmy had said in his note, to handle my mother.

After a yummy dinner of grilled chicken and veggies, Andre and I set out to see Dr. St. George. "I know it's silly, but meeting friends of Jimmy's will make me feel like I knew him a little better," I commented. And maybe not so jealous.

"I'll give you directions. It's not hard to find."

I stopped in the act of opening my car door. "Aren't ghosts allowed to travel in cars?"

He shrugged. "I don't like cars."

"But you must have ridden in them when you were alive?"

"Like your uncle, I preferred to walk. I never owned one, never even got my license." If a ghost could sweat, Andre would have been soaked to the skin.

"You're really scared. I can't believe it. You can do whatever it is you do to get around, but you're afraid of riding in a car." Another thought struck me. "What in the world do you think is going to happen to you? You're already dead."

He folded his arms across his chest in the universal body language of stubbornness. "I didn't say it was a rational fear. Follow my directions and I'll meet you there."

Two things occurred in my brain at once. One, the vivid memory of Larry sneering at me and saying, "Don't try and think, Tess, just do what your mom says." The other, the clear memory of fighting with an intruder in the dark. Maybe it had only been a tramp or kid who thought the house empty, but that didn't really help with the night-time shakes. And it would be a dark drive to the doctor's house.

"I don't want to go by myself," I said.

"I could …"

"No." We glared across the hood of the car at each other. He vanished. I waited a heartbeat and then the passenger's side door opened. The seat scooted back as far as it would go. Then the door slammed shut.

I slid into the driver's seat. Before starting the car, I asked, "Could you please stay visible for the drive?"

I found myself staring into those delicious brown eyes. "Thank you."

In answer, he jutted out his chin and glared straight ahead.

My little car bounced along the driveway. Before turning onto the main road, I peeked at my passenger. Panic filled his wide eyes. I almost relented, feeling guilty about asking him to face his fears so I wouldn't have to face mine. But then the wind shook the trees, and the gloom swelled around the car.

Andre would have to get over it.

However, by the end of the trip, I'd started to wonder if a ghost could have a nervous breakdown? He clutched the strap above the door with fingers that would have turned white if they hadn't already been so pale. Funny, because he wasn't solid, so the strap did him no good. After his initial appearance, he refused to look at me, but instead continued to stare steadfastly ahead. He broke his silence only to give the address in a strained, but civil voice.

The St. Georges lived in an older neighborhood where the homes were two-story with little concrete steps leading to the side-walk. In my mind, I pictured mothers pushing baby carriages, grand-mas sitting on porch swings, and little boys and girls playing ball with Rover. As we pulled to the curb, an older man with bushy white hair and a mustache charged out the front door as if he'd been waiting for our arrival. He stood beneath the glow of the porch light, ready to welcome us into his brightly-lit home. If an apple pie cooled on a window ledge in the kitchen, I'd know I'd been transported back to Ama of the 1950's.

I parked and realized Andre no longer sat beside me. He stood next to the car, either sulking or car sick, if ghosts could get sick. "Thank you," I said as I joined him.

He glared at me. But even furious, he remained polite enough to stay visible and walk me up the short brick walkway.

"Hello, hello!" Dr. St. George beamed at us.

I grinned. "Hello."

"Hello, Willard," Andre said, happy to be out of the car. "Tessa, this is Dr. Willard St. George. Willard, this is Tessa Kelling."

"Pleased to meet you." He hastened down the steps and engulfed me in a big bear hug. "Welcome, Tessa. Welcome to our home."

"I second that," came a female voice from behind him. "Now, all of you get in here. It's chilly out." The gray haired lady wore a floral housedress, the picture perfect wife for the doctor, except she stood several inches taller and spread twice as wide. "Hello, Tessa, I'm Elma."

Reaching the door, I found myself engulfed in an even bigger hug, this one lilac scented. "It's nice to meet you. Thank you for having me over."

"A pleasure," she assured me before addressing Andre. "Stay where I can hug you." He got his bear hug. They stood head to head and Andre had to be several inches over six feet. She ushered us into a warm, comfortable living room. "Andre, how stylish." Elma said. "I don't think I've ever seen you in anything but those splattered gray pants."

"Spiffy," Dr. St. George agreed.

Andre spread his hands wide and made a little bow. "Thank you. I'm feeling rather sheik."

"I'll assume that's 1920's for 'good'. Well come and sit," Elma instructed. After perching on the navy blue couch, I observed Andre as he settled next to me. A subtle shimmer said me he'd gone insubstantial. Dr. St. George and Elma settled into flowered easy chairs across from us.

"Although you arrived in town a lot earlier than Willard and I expected, we're glad you're here," Elma said. "Can I get you anything? Tea? Coffee? Pie?"

Earlier than expected? That had also been Charles' take on my arrival. "No, thank you, I'm fine." I resisted asking what kind of pie. "You have a nice house."

"Thank you. It's over one hundred years old," Dr. St. George proudly informed me. "I've always thought this would be the perfect home for a ghost." He winked at Andre.

Okay, I didn't care for that turn in the conversation.

Luckily, Elma took it upon herself to change the subject.

"This house has been in our family for over seventy-five years. The St. George's are one of the oldest families in Ama. The town library is named after us."

Uh, she had married into the family, hadn't she?

Willard cleared his throat in obvious embarrassment. He took his turn at changing the subject. "Elma and I are so sorry about Jimmy."

"Thank you." A twinge of guilt hit. They'd been closer to my uncle than me. I smiled at Willard. "I understand you and Uncle Jimmy were good friends."

He leaned back in his chair, a broad grin covering his face. "For over forty years. He was one of my first patients when I started practicing medicine. Jimmy used to call me one of the few people he could stand. I took it as a compliment." He pointed at a small table in the corner that held a chessboard. "He's the best player I've ever played against. I'm going to miss those games."

Silence fell. I glanced at Andre who'd leaned back with his arms casually crossed in front of him, sitting in that still way of his, seemingly content to let the time pass. Of course, he'd had more experience at that than any of us.

The doctor coughed and came back into the present. "Andre and I became acquainted about ten years ago when your uncle had a particularly nasty bought of pneumonia. I was urging him to go to the hospital, and he was threatening to die on me if I succeeded. I thought he'd gone delirious when he kept telling me he had someone at home who could take care of him. But then he introduced me to Andre." Another silence, this one warm, as both he and Elma beamed at the ghost. "I took it as another great compliment to be let in on that secret. When he …" Willard shifted in his chair, "…well, I broke the speed limit getting to James the night he fell. I couldn't do anything for him, his injuries were too severe."

"If I had …" Andre began.

"Stop it," his friend ordered. "His internal injuries killed him and would have no matter what you did."

"I was here playing chess," Andre said to me.

"Are you sure," Elma said, "that you wouldn't like some tea."

The abrupt change of subject caught me off guard. I saw the doctor resting his forehead in his hands. He'd lost a good friend. "I'd love some," I said. "Please let me help."

Standing, I managed to hit my knee on the coffee table, causing it to lurch sideways and threaten to topple over. It bumped right where I'd skinned my knee during my midnight fight with the burglar. I yelped and collapsed ungracefully back down on the couch. At the same time, Dr. St. George jumped to avoid getting hit by the table and Elma moved to catch the flower arrangement that decorated its center. Andre, in a lightening switch from insubstantial to solid, caught and righted the table.

"Willard, I've always told you that table is too big for this room." Elma smiled apologetically at me. "It was his mother's, so I've never had the heart to throw it out behind his back."

"So that's what happened to my bowling ball," the doctor muttered. He peered over his glasses at me. "I'm so sorry."

"Please don't be." I eased my knee out and silently promised it that I'd never, ever move it again. "You can't protect against the truly clumsy."

"Tessa hurt her knee last night," Andre said. "We had an intruder." To me he asked, "Do you think it's bleeding again?"

"Intruder?" Elma squealed as she clutched the flowers to her chest. "Andre, you didn't mention this when we saw you earlier. What happened?"

But her husband had other concerns. "Have you been examined by a doctor?"

"Not needed," I said. "It's only a scrape."

"Do you mind if I beg to disagree? Why don't you let me make that judgment?"

I couldn't pull the leg of my jeans up far enough to let him see the scrape and had no plans to take off my pants in somebody else's house. "Really, it's fine." But he and his wife overruled me and I found myself being herded into the den.

Elma handed me a throw. "Here, put this over anything you want to cover." She smiled. "Our family is so blessed to have both a lawyer and a doctor in it."

Oh boy. Left momentarily alone, I considered crawling out the window. Even the thought sent a stabbing pain through my leg. Resigned, I carefully stripped off my jeans and sat in the nearest chair, the throw covering my waist to my knees. "Okay," I called.

Dr. St. George came in, a black bag in his hand. He chuckled. "It's a stereotype, but Elma bought it for me the day I got out of medical school." Worn in places, and its leather would never be shiny again, but somehow it made me feel a better. He knelt and examined my knee. "Who doctored this?"

"Andre."

"He did a good job, as he usually does."

"Is there anything he doesn't do well?"

"If there is, he probably doesn't do it." He squint-grinned at me. "Our friend can be a little conceited, but don't tell him I said so."

I grinned back. "You got it. Ouch!"

He stopped moving my leg and gently set my heel back on the floor. "Sorry. I'll put some salve on it, and I can give you some pain killers if you think you'll have trouble sleeping."

"Actually, the ibuprofen I took last night worked fine."

"Good, the less medicine one has to take in life, the better." He pulled a tube of salve out of his bag.

"Dr. St. George…"

"Willard."

"Willard, am I crazy for accepting Andre so quickly? I mean, after all, he's a ghost. They aren't supposed to exist."

He applied the salve before answering. As he screwed the cap back on he said, "Let me ask you this, Tessa. Is it crazier to accept what you know to be true, or to fight it and pretend it doesn't exist?"

"He could be here, listening to us, and we wouldn't even know it."

"But he wouldn't do that."

True. And however pathetic it sounded, I'd never trusted anyone in my life as much as I trusted Andre. Willard left, and I dressed as quickly as my leg would let me. I entered the front room just as Andre finished telling the couple about our intruder. From the amused looks they gave me, I had the feeling my rug surfing had been mentioned.

"I must admit I agree with the consensus," Willard said. "Probably a kid who thought the house empty."

It's nice when everyone agrees.

Elma had fixed everyone breathing a glass of iced tea. I took a sip of mine and worked hard at not making a face. I'd never liked sweetened tea. "I met your nephew," I told her.

"Charles or Buster?"

"Charles."

Elma's smile softened. "Yes, dear Charles, he always tries to do right." Her smile abruptly vanished. "He's a good man." I felt like I'd received a challenge, but for the life of me, couldn't figure it out.

Her husband reached over and patted her hand. "No one has said he isn't."

78

"Simply implied it by your actions. After all that business with Mr. Dockins, Tessa's impression of Charles must be an awful one."

Okay, this I could correct. "Charles was nothing but kind to me, Mrs. St. George. I didn't think twice about him not telling me it was Dr. St. George and Andre who really hired Mr. Dockins to find me. I know he didn't mean to lie."

Three pairs of eyes fixed on me. Two people looked astonished. The third raised an eyebrow and looked curious as to what I might do next.

"I think," Dr. St. George said, "we've come in toward the middle of the story."

Elma's voice went from sunny warm to winter night cold. "Could you please explain what you mean by that remark?"

Oh, to be able to go back in time and crawl out the study window!

"When I thanked Charles for hiring Mr. Dockins to find me, he didn't correct me. He didn't tell me Andre and Dr. St. George actually hired Mr. Dockins."

Elma leaned forward, her hands tightly gripping her knees. "Are you sure that you didn't misunderstand Charles? Did he really say he'd hired the detective, or that Mr. Dockins had been hired to find you?"

I couldn't say what she wanted me to. "There was no misunderstanding. I even asked him if I owed him anything." An inward cringe at that memory. Maybe I owed Dr. St. George?

Elma sank back into her chair and then popped straight up. She thrust a finger at her husband and then Andre. "It's both your faults! It's no wonder Charles feels like he can't make a mistake."

"Why did you, and not Charles, find me?" I asked Dr. St. George.

He studied his hands, the better not to meet the eyes of his wife. "About a year ago, Jimmy left instructions that if anything ever happened to him, I was to lock up his house and keep the key until you'd been found. He also gave me money to hire a detective. He was a good friend, and I honored the promise."

Okay, I didn't owe anybody any money. One year ago… about the same time Uncle Jimmy gave Andre the note addressed to me. What had happened?

"Charles," Willard continued, "didn't take my possession of the key very well. He came over, demanding I give it to him, that as Jimmy's lawyer finding you and handing over the key was his responsibility."

Elma's eyes blazed fierce. "James acted like he was afraid Charles might try and rob the house, or something." She fanned herself with a magazine.

"James had the right to give the key to whomever he wished," her husband said.

"And make sure the whole town knew he didn't trust Charles. That's what it came down to, making Charles look bad." Why so protective of Charles? Maybe her family pride had been bruised?

"Well, Charles did make that remark about conducting a treasure hunt in Jimmy's house."

Willard meant for the remark to lighten the mood, but Elma jumped to her feet. "A joke and you know it! Charles was referring to all the wonderful memorabilia it must hold." She thrust her back toward us and stared out the window.

Memorabilia? Yeah, care for an ugly vase? Cheap?

"Excuse me." Willard hurried to his wife. "I didn't mean to imply he'd been serious." He put an arm around her and they held a whispered conversation.

During all the hoopla, Andre remained silent, detached from the squabbles of the living. Only sight told me he still occupied the couch beside me. No shift in weight, clearing of the throat, or anything that reminds us another human being is near. His otherworldliness hit me hard. Ghost. Dead. Then Andre smiled and my world fell into place again

Elma let her husband guide her back to her chair. She patted her hair and gave me a half-hearted smile. "I'm sorry, outbursts aren't like me."

I felt like a pushy heel, but I had to ask. "How did Charles get the key?"

Now Elma avoided her husband's eyes. "The morning we heard from Mr. Dockins, Willard had left to deliver a baby. So I happened to be the one who took his call. I told him there had been a change of plans. Instead of giving you our phone number, he should give you Charles' phone and address. I called Charles and asked him to come over. I told him what I had done and gave him the key. I'm also the one who convinced Willard not to make a fuss. I guess you can say

I'm the reason he didn't keep all of his promise to your uncle." She lowered her voice. "I'm sorry, Tessa, but your uncle was a bitter man who liked maligning people who weren't strong enough to stand up to him. I'm sure he took great pleasure in knowing how much he would hurt Charles by giving Willard the key. A last game, so to speak, at someone else's expense. A big joke on our family."

"I'm sorry." Information overload and, unfortunately, overload in another way. The tea had traveled straight through me.

"Don't think I'm blaming you," she said.

"I don't." Not quite, anyway.

Dr. St. George hugged his wife. "I'm sorry you've been upset, dear."

Andre leaned toward me. "Are you okay? You're wiggling like a three year old."

"I have to go to the bathroom," I whispered back.

"Why don't you just say so?"

"Right, like a three year old, I announce in the middle of everything I've got to go potty."

"Did you say you have to go to the restroom?" Elma asked. "Here, I'll show you the way. The hall bath is being redecorated, but you can use one upstairs."

"Thank you." I limped up the stairs behind her.

At the top of the landing, a beautifully embroidered family tree hung. Elma noticed me studying at it. She reached out and touched the yarn with one finger. "I made this."

"It's fantastic."

James (D) – Doris (D)
Barney (D) – Sadie   Willard – Elma
Charles   Buster   Alec

"It was a sad day when I had to put deceased beside Barney's name. This is our son's room. You can use his bathroom. Come back down when you're finished." She patted my arm and left.

My family tree would be short and dysfunctional.

Grandma Petey
Uncle Jimmy (D)
Jilly + Creep-of-a-stepfather Larry
David + too many stepmothers to count
Andre, a dreamy, eyes like melting chocolate, ghost

Yeah, normal didn't exactly describe it.

In the doorway, I studied the bedroom. OKC Thunder and Dallas Cowboy posters competed for wall space. A laptop blinked at me from the desk. The bedspread had been pulled tight across the pillow in an attempt to appear made. A comfortable, lived in room. What would it have been like to grow up in a house like this? A pang hit hard. I wanted this so much. This life. This world.

Shake it off, Tessa! You might not get the white picket fence, but … hey, why not? I could have a white picket fence. I could have anything now, thanks to Uncle Jimmy. Except a real family. You can create everything but a family.

Okay, I really had to pee. Open doors kept me from having to choose between closet and bathroom. A used towel was slung over the shower, even though a towel rack stood not a foot away. A sticky note stuck to the mirror said, "Don't forget to take the trash out, Love Dad."

Feeling like an intruder, I did my business and got out. Almost.

A blue-eyed blonde stood in the doorway to the room. He pulled the buds of his MP3 player out of his ears and grinned. "Hey, and it's not even my birthday?"

"Huh?" I answered like an idiot.

"You mean you're not a present?"

"What? Uh, the bathroom downstairs …"

He laughed, showing definitely cute dimples. "Who are you?"

"Tessa, I'm visiting your parents…"

He slipped past me, close enough to make me swallow hard. "How do you know my parents?"

"I'm James Duran's niece."

"James?" He fished in the desk and grabbed a disc. "Hey, I'm sorry."

"Thanks."

Beside me again, he grinned. "I'm Alec, and as much as I'd like to get to know you better, Tessa, I've gotta split." He put a finger to his lips. "Don't tell anyone you saw me, okay?"

"Sure." He loped down the hall to the back stairs. At the top, he grinned again and disappeared.

I seemed to be collecting St. Georges. Of the four I'd met, Charles came off as squirrely, Dr. St. George nice, Elma nice as long as you didn't imply anything bad about the family. And Alec, he might be one St. George worth getting to know better!

As Andre and I left, I heard Elma ask Willard the time. Past someone's curfew? Someone with killer blue eyes?

Later that night, I studied the ceiling. Why did Uncle Jimmy write his letter to me, a letter I wouldn't receive for almost a year? Why did he insist Dr. St. George promise to find me if anything happened? Another question rolled through my mind like the tide hitting the beach. One important to my survival. If Larry really broke in, I'd have heard from Mom by now. She'd have swooped in like an owl, ready to grab the frightened mouse in her claws.

So, where was she?

Had she gone on a genuine honeymoon? When I turned five, she left me alone for an evening. At ten she left me alone overnight and not much older she'd done a weekend flit. So, the fact she'd dumped me in the middle of nowhere didn't surprise me. I knew she'd never let me stay in the house, not without a fight. What are you planning, Mom?

Outside my window, a sunny day greeted me. In the bathroom, I washed my face in the pedestal sink and realized no pimple. My knee felt a lot less stiff even though it sported nasty shades of purple and yellow. The radio forecast called for an afternoon of continued rain, so I decided to put off clue hunting until then. Call me a nerd-ball, but something about pouring rain made hunting for treasure, or even a 'got ya,' note in a big old haunted house seem perfect.

Outside, I stood on the porch and breathed deeply. The comforting smell of burning leaves filled the air. Andre joined me. Did I feel a tingle before seeing him? Or had living with a ghost sent my imagination into overdrive? He'd changed into his white shirt, vest and gray-paint-splattered slacks. I remembered he'd said that it took energy to keep changes in his appearance going.

"I love this season," I said. My eyes lingered on the patched front door. "I'll have to save a long time before I can replace the glass."

"Don't worry about it," he said. Good advice for the broke, so I took it.

A truck with Police lettered on the side pulled into the drive. Andre went invisible. I felt him next to me though, and that wasn't my imagination.

Chief Mason parked and exited her vehicle. "I'm afraid we have something we need to clear up, Miss Kelling." I tried for interested instead of panicked. Some instinct told me this visit wasn't about the break in. "Please go get your mother for me." I swallowed a big lump of fear as I tried to remember what I'd told the Police Chief about Mom. "Is she still on her honeymoon?"

Ah yes, the truth. "Uh, yes, thank you for asking. Do you want me to have her call you when she returns?"

Instead of answering, Chief Mason opened her black notebook and retrieved a pale purple envelope. Mom's stationary, I could smell the lavender scent. Curiosity fought panic. The Chief's narrowed eyes didn't miss a thing. "You recognize this?"

"No." I hated to lie. I'd decided, however, not to admit anything until I knew all the facts.

With a flick of her wrist, Chief Mason tossed the note toward me. My grab fell short. I'd never make it in the major leagues. The note straightened and floated into my hands. Both the Chief and I stood blinking. "Gust of wind," she said.

Thanks, Andre.

"Read it," Chief Mason ordered.

I pulled the matching sheet of paper from its envelope. The words written in dark purple made my eyes widen.

To the law of Ama,

Tessa Kelling is a runaway.

Sincerly,   a concerned friend of the family

Mom's stationary and Larry's handwriting. You'd think one of them could spell sincerely right. I peered from under my eyelashes.

Chief Mason's eyes held their own curiosity."Miss Kelling, "How do I contact your mother?"

"She's on her honeymoon."

The sheriff shifted her sturdy legs. "Are you sure you didn't wander to our part of the country by yourself? Maybe you didn't want to wait for Mama to take care of things, so you snuck off by yourself to see your inheritance?"

Wander? Did I look like a cat? Andre's hand touched the small of my back. I let his touch calm me; remind me of my ally. "Chief Mason, if you'll remember, Mr. St. George met my mother."

She chewed her lip. "That's true. What about school?"

"It's fall break."

She pulled her cell from her pocket and dialed. "Your mother's still not answering her phone."

I turned the conversation to me. "I'm in my house, exactly where I'm supposed to be." That didn't sit well with her at all. Seventeen-year-olds belonged in the bosom of their loving families. I quickly tried a different tactic. "Who do you think wrote this note?"

She took the purple letter and tapped it on one palm, thinking over my answer. "Maybe a little payback from the unsuccessful burglar you scared your first night here. You can buy this stationary at any department store."

"That's true. Finding me here may have irritated him." Wrong thing to say.

She glared. "I don't like your living here all alone, Miss Kelling. When will your mother return?"

"Soon. I promise I'll have her get in touch with you." That is, if Mom can talk after I strangle her.

Chief Mason studied the note and then me. "See that you do, Miss Kelling."

I walked with her to her truck and waited while she swung into the cab. My weird thoughts from the night before caused me to ask, "Sheriff Mason, did anyone ever question whether my uncle fell by accident?"

She frowned. "You mean, you think he committed suicide. Not a very practical way to do it." Her eyes widened. "Murder? No question of that, Miss Kelling. Why?"

I rubbed my shoulders. "Living alone has got my imagination going, I guess."

"Well, I'd try to keep it in check." The truck roared as she turned the key. She did a U-turn in my grass and headed down the drive. I sank down to the top porch step.

Andre materialized beside me. Luckily, he didn't show any sign of having overheard my stupid question. "Do you know who wrote the note?" he asked.

"Mom. Actually, it's her stationary and Larry's handwriting."

"We'll get him a dictionary for Christmas."

I snorted. "Only if I get to hit him over the head with it. I can't believe Mom tried this. I mean, didn't she even think it through? What if Chief Mason hauled me in for my own good?"

"Did your apartment have a landline?"

"No, and I bet Mom won't answer her cell." I leaned forward and gazed at the ground below. "I thought I saw Mom in town yesterday. Going into the post office, in fact." I decided to come clean. "I've even thought Larry broke in to scare me."

"Then we have no worries if I strangle him, because they can't convict a ghost of murder."

I gazed into his chocolate eyes, semi-dark with anger and grinned. "I'd rather you scare him until he pees his pants."

Andre's eyes lightened. "That I can do."

"Charles wanted us to stay at a bed and breakfast in Ama. He said he went by this morning. Still, they might be keeping low."

"You want me to join you on the hunt?" Andre asked.

I shook my head. "No, I can handle the gruesome twosome."

I tried to remember the Red Rose directions. Something about Elm and Ash. At Pine, I kept going. A right turn at Elm and well-kept two-story houses surrounded me. Which way should I go on Ash? Then I spotted it about a block away. A two-story house painted scarlet stood tall above its more sedate neighbors. I'd found the Red Rose.

I climbed the steps and rang the doorbell. My knees trembled like jelly. Get a backbone, Tessa. Mom went too far this time. The door opened and a middle-aged woman wearing a sweatshirt with a scarecrow on it smiled at me. "Hello, may I help you?"

I gave her my biggest wanting-to-please smile. "Hi. I'm Tessa Kelling. I'm looking for my mother."

She frowned. "I'm sorry, dear. We don't have any Kellings staying here."

Think Tessa. "Her married name is Parker."

The frown became a big smile. "Oh, you mean our newlyweds." She chatted away as I entered. "I'm Willa. It's nice to meet you Tessa. I put your parents in the "Til Death Do Us Part" room at the top of the stairs. You can go right up. Knock first." She giggled.

Gag. I managed to thank her without hurling on her shoes then took the stairs two at a time. I'd consider Larry a parent when God himself declared it. And I hadn't heard from Him yet. At the top, I paused. What if they were doing, well, honeymoon things? The shudder ran through me like a freight train through a tunnel. Gross. Gross. Gross! The letter. Focus on the letter, Tessa. That stupid letter could have you taken away from Andre. I pounded on the door.

Larry answered, blinking away sleep. His rumpled clothes told me he'd at least dressed that morning before taking a nap. "Tessa?" Surprise, followed by guilt, played across his face. He grinned. "Living by yourself in the backwoods getting a little spooky? Seeking a little protection from Mommy and Daddy?"

"Where's Mom," I demanded.

He frowned. "She's getting lunch. This place only serves breakfast."

Well, duh, it's a B & B. "The sheriff got your note," I shouted.

He retreated, a wary look crossing his face. "What?"

"You know, yours and Mom's attempt to play games." I saw the protest forming. "I recognized Mom's stationary, Larry. Did either of you remember that she and I talked to the lawyer, Charles St. George, together? He gave us the house key. He knows Mom came with me. How will you explain that one if the sheriff figures out who wrote the note?"

"Oh."

Like talking to a stump. "Why isn't she answering her cell?"

"It died. We left the charger at my place."

And neither possessed the brains to buy another one? I lost

patience. "Did you break into my house, Lar?"

"Huh? Are you nuts?" He frowned. "Someone broke into your house?"

I took a step closer. "Better stay away from my house and me, Lar. Got it?"

He pushed his hands deep in his jean pockets and snorted. "Boy, you sure hold a grudge. Did someone really break into the house?"

"If you want to continue to enjoy your honeymoon, stay away from me." In spite of my tough act, my voice screeched. I realized Willa was gawking at me from the bottom of the stairs. Great. Demented daughter arrives to ruin mom's honeymoon. The police chief would love that one. I lowered my voice. "Got it, Lar?"

"Got it," he hissed.

I fled. Wait. Did Larry say he hadn't broken into my house?

The need to go home to Andre warred with the fear that I'd run the bug into a tree. On Main Street, I parked in the first empty parking space. Andre had mixed some paint samples that either matched or complemented the boudoir set. I grabbed them from the backseat. See, Mom, it's my house. I'm even decorating it.

A few moments later, I stood in the hardware store, staring at rows of paint cans, wishing they'd speak. Anything to take away the sound of Larry's voice.

"Can I help you?" a store employee asked. A definite cutie in my book.

Hands on hips, I tried for faux serious. "Hmm, would you say cotton candy pink or fuzzy wuzzy brown?"

He ran a hand through fashionably cut brown hair. I liked his gold stud earring. "Err, I'm not sure."

Hiding a grin, I faced the paint cans and squared my hands as if framing a picture. "I need something that says, 'all mine.' What color makes that statement?"

He laughed. "I guess not Hoochi Coochi red, huh?"

My eyes widened. "Do you really have a paint named that?" He winked. I laughed. "Honestly, I'm not sure what I want."

"Well, let me show you these. They're colors that came out wrong, or people didn't claim after special ordering them. And they're about half the price."

Definitely cute and most definitely somebody's boyfriend. "Thanks for the tip."

I studied the cans. A nice warm yellow room, nothing too bright, no feeling like I lived inside a banana.

I looked around. Were the gazes directed my way because of gender or because no one recognized me? Unlike the grocery store, a newbie stuck out in this place. Most of the men wore farmer's overalls and moved through the aisles with purpose. Older men gathered around the cash register to talk about crops and the weather.

Okay, okay, time to stop putting off a decision. The pale butterscotch, a slightly lighter shade of yellow than the vase, looked promising. I turned to find the cutie standing at my elbow.

"You look like you've decided," he said.

"You should take your mind reading act on the road."

He grinned. "I'm Buster St. George."

Another St. George. "Hi. I'm Tessa Kelling."

His eyes widened. "You're Jimmy's niece, aren't you?"

I didn't ask how he knew. The town grapevine worked. "You knew my uncle?"

"Yeah, he used to come in all the time. Sorry about his dying."

"Uh, thank you. I've met several St. Georges; Willard, Elma, Alec, and Charles."

"Confusing, huh? Willard and Elma are my uncle and aunt. Alec is my cousin and Charles is my older brother. Hey, can I ask you something about your house?"

"A few bumps in the night."

He grinned again. "That's what my girlfriend said. She works at Ma and Pop's. Here, I'll carry your paint to the register."

Yep, knew there had to be a girlfriend involved. And I'd bet she had red hair. After I paid for the paint, we loaded the cans into the front of the VW. "Thanks for the help," I said.

"No problem. Hey, I forgot to give you paint sticks. Wait a sec." He sprinted inside the hardware store.

"Tessa?" Charles St. George hurried toward me. Alec St. George tailed behind him, giving me a grin and a wink.

"Hi, Mr., er, Charles." I half smiled at Alec who leaned against the wall of the hardware store. Would it hurt him to say hi, or something? He didn't.

Charles grabbed my hands in his and gave them a damp

shake. "I'm glad I caught you. Has your mother returned from her honeymoon?" While talking, he scanned the area as if searching for low flying planes. Worried that Anna, the barracuda, might see us?

I yanked my hands back. "Sorry, not yet." I don't know why I didn't tell him Mom and Larry were at the B & B.

Charles rubbed his hands together. "Are things going okay? No more intruders I hope."

"Nope, not a one."

Alec watched us, his arms folded, amused by the show. Curious about the weirdo who'd moved into the haunted house? I flung open my car door, prepared to leave them behind.

Charles held it for me. His Adam's apple bobbed as he swallowed. "Since you're still alone and living in a strange town, I'd love to take you to dinner tomorrow evening."

"That's not necessary."

"Please. Let me help you get acquainted with Ama."

Sounded sincere. Besides, Anna Gleason's snotty visit stayed fresh in my mind. How dare she warn me away from anybody. "Sounds great."

"Wonderful. I'll come for you at seven."

"Okay."

"Charles." Buster stood next to me with a handful of paint sticks. The little brother stood a head taller than the older and was about twenty pounds heavier. "Hold on a minute."

Charles smiled at me. "See you tonight, Tessa."

Buster shoved the sticks into my hands. "See ya. Hey, Charles, I need some money."

Charles sighed. "Not the right time to ask."

"You're a pain, Charles." Alec pushed away from the wall. "Family's supposed to help family, aren't they?"

"Knock it off, Alec." Charles still held onto my door. Would he notice if I yanked it from his hand to shut it?

"Whatever you say," Alec said. He stuffed his hands in his pockets and moved away.

One good yank, and I could drive away.

"Please, Charles?" Buster said.

Charles sighed. "What do you need?" He looked down. "Oh, Tessa, I'm so sorry."

Freedom. My door shut with a resounding bang.

All families possessed melodrama. At least Mom never played

ours in the middle of town.

Someone knocked on my window. Alec! I rolled down the window. "Sorry about that," he said. "In our family Charles is the fussy one, and Buster is the whiny one." He laughed. "Me, I'm the adorable one." I laughed. Charles and Buster took their argument inside the store. Alec sighed. "I'd better go in case one of them needs a witness." He waved as he trotted after his relatives.

Hmm, I'd look forward to my upcoming "date" if Alec asked me out. Like that would ever happen. The thought brought other feelings, ones involving chocolate brown eyes. Did ghosts date? Wait. Did I really want a ghost to ask me out? And how did that fit into the "normal" life I wanted so desperately?

Deep in thought, I zigged when I should have zagged. The convenience store where I'd bought the peanut butter and crackers came into view. How did they feel about people making U-turns in the parking lot without buying anything? In the parking lot, I spotted a pale green Chevy, whose owner talked on a pay phone. I reversed, rolling down the window.

"Hello. Remember me? I'm the girl with the dead uncle and the boxes in her living room. Well, my dead uncle wasn't in my living room."

Phillip Dockins took one glance at me and dropped the phone. Then he backpedaled. "Hey," I shouted.

He bolted toward the green Chevy, jumped into his car and peeled out, leaving the scent of burning rubber mingling with autumn air. The phone dangled in the wind. I exited the car, grabbed the receiver, and without shame, listened.

"Push it too far, Phillip, and I'll spill all to Charles, understand? Believe me, I'll make you sorry you ever messed with me," a woman's voice shouted.

"Anna?" The phone died. I stared at it, positive I'd recognized Anna's voice. What did Mr. Dockins push? What did Anna threaten to spill? The hate in her voice shocked me. Definitely an unhappy lady. I replaced the phone and glanced up. The spiky haired clerk glared through the window.

Maybe she thought I'd scared off a potential customer? I waved.

"Why," I said over my shoulder to Andre as we carried paint cans upstairs, "did he run away like that?"

"Having never met the man, I can say I don't know. You sure you recognized Charlie's receptionist on the other end of the line?"

"No."

"Then I don't see how it gets us anywhere."

"I didn't say it got us anywhere."

"My mistake."

I would have glared at him, but he was invisible. The main reason he walked behind me instead of in front was that I preferred not conversing with someone I couldn't see. Tired of discussing something that gave me a headache, I changed the subject. "Guess what? I've got a date for tomorrow night."

"With who?"

"Charles St. George."

"Our Anna's boyfriend?"

"Her boyfriend wouldn't ask me out," I replied. Inside the bedroom I deposited the paint beside the fireplace.

Andre did the same. "If you say so."

"What does that mean?"

"Not a thing."

I didn't understand his snippiness and decided to ignore it. The wind blew, and I knew it carried the rain behind it. "You know, it's not really a date. He thinks he needs to take care of me while Mom's honeymooning. Instead of fighting, do you want to tackle the next clue?" No answer came. Andre wasn't just invisible, he'd gone. I spent the rest of the day alone.

The next morning, rain pelted the house. After a breakfast of whole grain waffles and fresh orange juice, I snuggled under the multi-colored afghan and watched streams of water cascade across the living room window. Rhythmic pounding on the roof left me with no urge to stick my nose outside, even though I'd yet to explore the acres that lay beyond the yard. Instead, treasure hunting beckoned.

I searched for Andre and found a copy of O. Henry's short stories floating above an easy chair in the library. Andre appeared, draped over the chair in a manner that said comfortable and not necessarily willing to move. "Treasure hunt?" I asked.

"This weather sure makes you energetic," he grumbled. It sounded good-natured. He placed a bookmark to mark his spot and joined me at the table where we'd left the clues. Together we bent over the second one.

"All art is but imitation of nature," I read. "What do you think it means?"

He leaned on the table. "Maybe it's hidden behind a painting?"

I snapped my fingers. "Your mural."

"What? Wait!"

"It's so obvious," I shouted over my shoulder. I halted before the mural, eagerly trying to scan the whole thing at once.

Andre materialized between it and me. "Tessa, Jimmy never came in here."

"That you know of. What better imitation of nature than your

95

painting? I mean, it looks like a person could step right through and sit on the bench."

"Tessa, I'd have noticed."

"Not if he put the clue in a part you haven't worked on in a while."

The poor guy turned frantic, as if afraid I'd start stripping paint off the walls willy-nilly. "Trust me, I'd have noticed."

I stepped forward with the intention of going around him. Instead, I stumbled, hands flailing, and fell into a startled Andre. A tingling shock, both pleasant and unsettling, discharged through my body. I fell on my hands and knees. Breathless and a little dizzy, I rolled onto my bottom. Andre stood motionless, hands balled at his sides. "Are you all right?" I asked.

He blinked. "Yes." But his voice sounded strange.

"I've never experienced a sensation like that before," I babbled, still feeling a little lightheaded. But not in a bad way. He didn't answer. "Andre, everything okay?" It felt weird worrying about hurting a ghost.

"Yes." He made a clear effort to pull himself together. Those brown eyes gazed into mine and, for a moment, I fell in a different way. "That was very intimate for a ghost."

The familiar flush climbed my neck. "I'm sorry."

He smiled. "Don't be. Did you get hurt?"

"Aside from my pride, no."

Andre crouched in front of me. "Are you sure?"

No new blood, although my knee throbbed. "I'm sure."

"I don't think there's a clue in here, but check if it'll make you feel better."

"Please. I promise not to touch."

He grinned.

"The mural," I choked out.

"Of course." He stood and offered his hand.

"How long can you remain visible and solid?"

Andre shrugged. "I'm not sure."

"Have you ever tested your limits?"

A whisper. "Yes." As if he found the words painful.

"When?"

"When I found Jimmy at the bottom of the stairs. After alerting Willard, I returned and stayed visible and solid. I wanted Jimmy to know he wasn't alone."

Feeling like I couldn't hurt him more if I prodded a wound with a knife, I still asked, "How long did it take?"

"I don't know. Twenty or thirty minutes maybe." Andre gazed at the mural. "I left him after they put him in the ambulance. I had to rest. So, I wasn't with him when he died."

I also studied the painting. "Where do you go when you rest?"

"Nowhere."

"Nowhere?"

He sighed. "It's hard to explain."

I accepted that. We reached the end of the mural and I groaned. "Guess nothing's hidden here."

"Lots of places to search."

I snapped my fingers. "The fruit magnets on the fridge. I saw a piece of paper behind one of them."

"Which I put there. It's the new grocery list."

"Oh."

We searched behind pictures and under furniture until lunch.

"You know," Andre said as I enjoyed a grilled cheese sandwich and homemade vegetable soup, "some people call those books Jimmy kept under his mattress art."

"Do you think they might hold another clue?" I asked.

"I don't think so, although you're welcome to check."

"No thanks." I hoped my pouting didn't show.

Maybe it did because he said, "Let's forget hunting for clues. Come with me."

"Why?"

Andre put a hand on either shoulder and pushed me toward the door. "Come on." He led me to the landing, stopping in front of the narrow door I'd peeked behind the first day.

"The attic?" I asked.

"There's something you should see."

I wrinkled my nose, remembering the musty smell. "Show me something in a cheerier part of the house."

"Open the door."

I resisted the urge to stick out my tongue and opened the door, on the lookout for spiders. I know it's all "girly girl" to fear the creepy arachnids. So what? I've never liked anything that might creep under my covers. And even if they've debunked the myth that spiders can crawl into your mouth while you sleep, I still don't like the thought of them spinning webs above my open mouth.

Trying to act brave, I searched for a light switch. If anything creepy crawled over my hand, Andre could stand on that landing all by himself. "I can't find the light."

"It's at the top of the stairs."

"What idiot puts a switch at the end instead of the beginning?"

"On the way back it's at the beginning." That meant walking in the dark. I planted my feet sideways and climbed the shallow wooden steps. I hoped Andre could go solid pretty fast in case I missed a stair and tumbled backward. As if wondering the same thing, he warned, "Be careful of your footing."

A thin, sticky thread brushed my cheek. Gross. I wiped it off. I'd keep the dark. If thousands of webs hung over my head, filled with their owners, I didn't want to know.

"Hit the switch on your right," Andre said.

I found it and flicked it on. A single, bare bulb shone from the middle of the long room.I examined the maze of webs and dust that covered dark objects the light half-illuminated. "I don't suppose anything of value is stored here?"

"It depends on what you call valuable."

"That means no."

He ignored my observation and ordered, "Walk straight ahead."

Still on the lookout for kamikaze spiders I complied, stopping at the far wall. A shaded window faced the front yard. "Now what?"

"Down by your left foot."

I peered at a tattered cardboard box. "Your big surprise? What's written on the top?" I knelt for a better view.

"Here." He reached over my head and drew the shade. It creaked in protest, as if it might turn to dust and crumble at our feet. Andre managed to get it halfway up. "I think we're going to have to make do with that."

The writing on the box spelled a familiar name. "That's my mother's name," I said.

"It belonged to her."

"That means she left it here." I sat cross-legged on the floor, temporarily forgetting about spiders.

"It means it's something left from the time you lived here."

My words to him. He'd remembered. "Yeah, I guess it does." He sat across from me with his long fingers clasped around one of his knees. Blurry edges told me he wasn't solid. I reached for the lid and stopped.

"What's wrong?"

"It's not my box. It's my mother's."

"I believe it may also contain a few of your possessions."

"Really? Well, I can peek, right? I mean, it's my stuff." He answered with a grin. I pulled a flap. "Crap!" Jumping to my feet, I frantically brushed at my clothing.

Andre stared, astonished. "What's wrong?"

"A spider jumped out of the box." I whirled around like a puppy chasing its tail. "Can you see it? Did it land on me?"

"You mean this little guy?"

I saw the daddy long-legs in his solid hand. "Don't hold it, smash it."

"Believe me, it can't hurt me. It can't hurt you either. Its mouth is too small." He placed the spider on the floor and it took off in the direction farthest from the crazy lady.

I sat, refusing to meet Andre's eyes. With one index finger, I reached and pulled back the rest of the flaps. I squealed at the first item revealed. With both hands, I grabbed the worn teddy bear. He possessed one black button eye and a faded red ribbon around his neck. A suspicious purple stain circled his mouth, as if someone might have tried to give him grape juice. I laughed. "Wally. It's you."

"Introductions?" Andre said.

I paused in the act of inspecting my beloved friend. "Andre, meet my best friend, Wally. Wally, meet Andre. He's my ghost."

"I remember him," Andre said. "You used to read to him while sitting under the oak tree."

I blushed, feeling a little confused at the thought of Andre watching me all those years ago. Kind of like a guardian angel without wings. A tear snuck into my eye and I hastily wiped it away. Then I ran a finger along Wally's good ear. "I thought I put him in the backseat of our car when we left. But he disappeared. I remember crying and begging Mom to go get him, but she said no. I guess Uncle Jimmy found Wally and put him in this box." A thought hit me. "I guess Jimmy knew how much Wally meant to me."

Andre didn't say anything, his eyes didn't meet mine.

"What do you know?" I demanded.

"Your uncle did know how much your bear meant to you,

Tessa. He didn't pack Wally away. Your mother did."

"What? Mom left Wally behind?"

"I saw her packing the box. When she finished, she left it sitting in the middle of the upstairs hall."

"Why?"

He shrugged. "When Jimmy found the box, he cried. He sat on the floor rummaging through it, tears running down his cheeks. He carried it here and never touched it again."

"And he never said anything?"

Andre shook his head.

I nestled Wally against my tummy. Time later to dwell on the fact Mom snuck Wally out of the backseat. For the time being, a far more interesting mystery loomed. What in the box made my uncle cry? "He wanted to get rid of us. I mean, that's what Mom said."

"That's what he always told me."

"He really cried?"

"Yes."

I reached into the box. This time I retrieved a scarf. It hadn't fared as well as my teddy bear. Tattered and stretched, it existed more as holes than fabric. "Uncle Jimmy gave this to Mom the Christmas we lived here. It's real silk." I laid it aside and pulled out a silver tray, tarnished with age. "Uncle Jimmy's wedding present to my parents." My fingers brushed its surface. "Mom made the dent when she hit Dad over the head."

"Ouch," Andre said.

The tray took a place beside the scarf as I dug deeper, still mindful of creepy crawlies. "Check these out." I held out the booties for Andre to inspect.

He fingered the toes. "Yours?"

"Yes. Mom used to keep them on her dresser. They're hand-crocheted and a baby gift from Uncle Jimmy. Andre, do you realize what all this is? Jimmy gave us everything in this box."

"Including Wally?"

"Yes, along with the booties. Mom didn't pay any attention to scares about babies smothering, so Wally slept in my crib with me. I teethed on his left ear. For some reason, I never liked the taste of the right ear. I used to celebrate Wally's birthday right along with mine. I even insisted he have his own piece of cake, which of course I helped him eat."

"Maybe your mother left Wally and everything else to tell Jimmy he didn't belong in her family anymore."

"And that made him cry."

"Yes."

"Maybe he liked us a little more than he let on."

"That's my guess."

I stood and brushed off my rear end. "I want to take these things downstairs, so I can study at them in better light."

"I'll carry them."

"Wait." I put my hand out, stopping short of touching his arm. I liked the illusion of solid. "You're using a lot of energy."

"I intend to go down the stairs invisible."

"Then you definitely go behind me."

At the top of the stairs, I hesitated before shutting off the light. Did the musty attic hold anything else of mine? I'd explore another time. I flipped the switch and slowly headed toward the welcome light of the landing. Mom hated her brother so much she left behind the teddy bear I adored. My uncle's anger at Mom forced us to leave, even though it hurt him. Dysfunctional anyone?

Andre stayed invisible until we reached my room. He reappeared, lit the fire, then disappeared. Not literally disappeared. He exited the door. A normal exit for my benefit? I'd have to get used to his ghostly ways. Disappearing was for him like breathing is for me. Actually, no. In and out, that's the way the air went. Walking or sleeping might say it better. I walked to get where I wanted to go. Andre disappeared and reappeared. He rested after staying visible and solid. I slept or got cranky.

So, I'd have to stop gasping and staring like a hick every time I saw a floating object.

Head hurting, I retrieved memories from the box and scattered them into a semi-circle. They lay about me, as if I'd called them to a meeting. First, Wally went on my pillow. However, a closer inspection revealed a couple of holes in his fur. Not knowing what creature made them, I'd repair him and clean him before snuggling. In addition to the teddy, scarf, booties, and tray, I found a silver cigarette lighter and a gorgeous pearl brooch.

Mom left our things behind, even the lighter. And the brooch looked to be worth some money. As a child, I remembered Mom snapping, "don't touch," because it was very old. Why hadn't she sold it? Because leaving it hurt my uncle a lot more? Apparently when she said she hated Jimmy, she meant it.

The scarf appeared beyond repair so I stuffed it back in the box. I'd clean the tray and put it on the coffee table. Mom would never forgive me for using what she'd tossed in my uncle's face. Did she expect him to keep it? What would she think of that?

One of the booties had a hole in the heel. Nestled beside the cracked vase you couldn't see the hole. I pinned the brooch to my sweater. The pearls shimmered in the firelight. Antique or not, I wouldn't part with anything from my past. Mom and I moved so much that I only kept things easy to carry. No family heirlooms. Heck, not even family junk.

I crossed my legs and watched the fire. Mom wouldn't understand my feelings, much less answer any questions. A deep sadness washed across my mind. It certainly wasn't a trusting mother-daughter relationship.

"Hey." Andre stood in the doorway. "Are you okay?"

"Yeah, just licking old wounds."

He leaned against the door jam, hands in his pockets, one lock of dark hair falling across his forehead. "Anything you want to talk about?"

"No thanks." I stretched. "Right now, I really want to take a long, hot bath, preferably while reading a good book."

Pure shock radiated from him. "You read in the bathtub? What if you drop the book and ruin it?"

I raised my right hand. "I promise I'll harm no books in the taking of my bath." I'd scanned the library for reading material earlier that morning and noticed most of the books were first editions. I didn't dare read them anywhere near water. But I'd found a Louis L'Amour paperback called Haunted Mesa. It sounded perfect for a rainy afternoon of reading and soaking.

I filled the claw-footed tub with vanilla scented bubble bath. For atmosphere, a candle went on the edge of the sink. The warm water slipped around my shoulders as I opened my book. Delicious. A box of chocolates would have made it perfect. I'd have to buy some, even if they weren't on his royal highness's list. Surely I could squeeze chocolates onto it somewhere. Of course, my baby-sitting money would only go so far. I lived on my own. Did I really have to eat all my veggies?

The water grew cold and I'd pruned by the time I emerged. Despite the paint cans sitting in the corner, my room had become a refuge. The rest of the house might still reflect Jimmy's personality, but I belonged here. I snuggled in the bed, listening to the rain hit the windowpane.

My feelings for Andre continued to grow. The fact that he wasn't a flesh and blood hottie didn't matter. I empathized with Sleeping Beauty. I needed a kiss, one kiss from those full, gorgeous lips. The ache for that kiss gave me an almost physical pain. My eyes grew heavy. Maybe I'd get my kiss in my dreams. I let myself slide into sleep.

Larry's leering grin floated in front of me. "He's pretty."

"You've always did have a dirty mind," I snapped.

He snorted. "Remember, I like family to stay real close."

I bolted upright, heart racing. No Larry. The dream melted into a nasty afterthought. A description, I realized, that fit my new stepfather. "Stay away," I whispered.

Dark shadows filled the room. In a panic, I glanced at the clock. My heart slowed. Only five thirty, not time for Charles to pick me up. What to wear? I didn't expect Charles to take me to a fancy restaurant. Still, I didn't want to embarrass the nice lawyer by dressing up for the nearest fast food place; worse yet, a drive thru.

I'd packed two pair of jeans, a pair of tan slacks (already rumpled from the day before and not fit to wear again until laundered) and two skirts. No fashion plate here. I focused on the skirts. One, a long denim, and the other a swingy, flower-patterned number in dark blues. I laid them side-by-side on the bed. My flats went with either.

I owned three sweaters, several long sleeved-tee shirts, and one nice button-down-the-front blouse. I chose a light blue sweater and the flowered skirt.

Usually I wore my hair tousle and go. Not this time. Instead, I took great care with the curling iron. The resulting waves framed my face and looked okay even to my critical eye. Makeup, no matter how carefully applied, still made me feel like a little girl playing grownup. Jewelry presented no problem as I owned almost none. Small diamond earrings, a gift from Grandma Petey, went into my lobes. As I fastened my watch, I remembered another piece of jewelry I owned. The pearl brooch completed my outfit.

At 6:45 I slipped into my flats, ready for my sort-of date.

Andre greeted me at the bottom of the stairs. "Wow, aren't you all dolled up."

"Thank you." Warmth filled my cheeks. The kiss hadn't really happened, right? Only a thought before before going to sleep? Definitely glad ghosts don't read minds.

"Are you okay?" he asked. "You don't look quite ducky."

Nothing a kiss wouldn't fix. "Uh, I'm still trying to wake up."

"You're a little flushed, do you feel alright?"

Oh my, if he actually touched my forehead, I'd die. I took a step backward. Thank God for doorbells.

"Sounds like your bespectacled prince has arrived," Andre said before disappearing.

Out of habit, I pasted on my ready-to-please smile and opened the door. "Hello."

"Hello." Charles stood with a ready smile of his own. "You look very nice tonight."

"Thank you." Had he expected jeans and a stained tee shirt?

"I especially like the brooch. It looks like an antique."

"I'm not sure, although I know it's old."

He chuckled. "I imagine at seventeen everything seems old. You and your mother should take it to a jeweler to have it appraised."

"Uh, sure, we'll do that." Why did all grownups think teenagers are idiots? I mean, when you make stupid generalizations, who really looks like the half-wit? Besides, Charles wasn't much older than me, just prissier.

He helped me on with my coat. "I've looked forward to this," he said. A lie, for sure. But a nice one. It almost made up for the seventeen-years-old remark. Outside, he paused to touch the wood covering the hole in my door. "I'm glad you're okay."

"Thank you."

"Is your knee doing better?"

"It's not so stiff." Before closing the door, I gave a covert wave to the inside of the house. It made me feel better about not saying goodbye to Andre. Yelling a cheery, "see you later" to an empty house might make Charles think me slightly crazy.

Out in the car a surprise awaited me. Alec sat in the backseat. "Hi," he said as Charles held my door for me.

"Hi." My fickle heart raced.

"I thought you and Alec might have more in common, so I asked him to tag along," Charles said.

How embarrassing, a pity date. My day got worse.

As we drove, Charles chattered on about local attractions, like an uncle trying to entertain a niece he didn't see very often. "I thought we'd take you to The Station," he told me.

"The Station? I guess you're not talking about a police station or firehouse?"

"Actually, our fire chief is a gourmet cook. Although, that's not the type of station I mean. It's a true station from when passenger trains still ran through this region. A few years ago, someone started a movement to tear it down. Of course, that sparked protests to declare it a historical site. Before the city council ruled, a couple from Tulsa bought it and made into one of the best restaurants in town." He grinned. "Guess it's Ama's first theme restaurant."

"How about Ama's only theme restaurant," Alec said in a monotone.

Charles glared at him from the rearview mirror. "I asked if you wanted to go someplace else."

"Nah, The Station's got great burgers," Alec replied.

Charles smiled at me. "Do you know what Ama means?"

"No."

"It's Cherokee for water."

I laughed. "That's sure appropriate for this week."

His cell phone rang. "Excuse me. Hello?" Charles frowned as

he listened. "Well, isn't your nurse helping? Did she give you your medication?" He listened some more and then hit the button to end the call. "Sorry about that."

"No problem."

"Is Grandma okay?" Alec asked.

"She's fine. Nothing her nurse can't handle." Charles grimaced at me. "I'm sure you understand how family can be." Did I ever. "I own a condo here in town. However, life can get so hectic," Charles continued. "I'm thinking about buying a place in the country."

Hectic? Ama? With only two traffic lights on Main Street?

A snort came from the backseat. "People here consider it a traffic jam if more than two cars stop at a red light," Alec said. Our exchanged grin felt like a private joke.

Charles didn't seem to get the joke. "I've mulled over making an offer on your house," he said.

"My house?" I stopped grinning.

"Yes. Maybe renting it until you're able to sell. However, Ms. Gleason told me you're considering staying in Ama."

"That's right."

"Maybe I should have this conversation with your mother?"

I kept my voice even. "Why? It's my house."

"You're right. Please accept my apologies."

"No problem." What a jerk. Wasn't my lawyer supposed to help me keep my house?

"Don't let him push you around, Tessa," Alec said.

Charles' jaw tightened. "We're here."

The Station nestled beside a small section of unused railway track. A sign attached to an old hand car instructed prospective diners to Come Aboard for Good Food. The wide porch ran the length of the front. The ticket windows at either end held geraniums. Inside, railway memorabilia covered the walls.

"Nice," I told Charles.

"I'm glad you like it. Our other restaurant, The Homey Buffet, comes complete with screaming toddlers."

"Sounds like a place I used to take the kids I babysat. Dried ketchup smeared the tables, and stuff you don't want to know about covered the bathroom floors."

"Sounds yummy," Alec said. He stood near enough I got a whiff of his shampoo. He had nice, thick hair, perfect for running fingers through. I inwardly blushed. Good grief, what was wrong with me?

"Be with you in a sec," called a waiter carrying a loaded tray.

Charles' phone rang again. "Excuse me." He walked to the far end of the lobby, one hand cupped over his ear.

"Ever since Uncle Barney died, Aunt Sadie's depended a lot on Charles," Alec explained.

"Tessa!" I followed the voice to an eagerly waving hand and spotted Chloe from Ma and Pop's. She sat with two other girls, Buster's arm slung around her. A prick of jealousy hit. I'd never hung with friends. Always too busy fitting in as the new kid. Pasting on a smile, I waved back.

"Hey, Alec," Buster called.

"Hey."

Happily he didn't walk away and leave me standing by myself.

Charles reappeared. "I'm so sorry, Tessa. We're going to have to leave. There's a family problem."

Chloe joined us. "What's going on?"

"Grandma probably battling with her nurse again," Alec said.

Charles glared at him. "Some domestic problems have arisen, yes."

"Well, why don't you guys join us?" Chloe asked.

"Sure," Alec said. "We can hitch a ride home with Buster."

Charles frowned. "What do you think, Tessa?"

"Are you sure your friends won't mind?" I asked Chloe.

She dismissed that idea with a wave of her hand. "Nah."

"Then, great, I'd love to stay." Not really a date with Alec, but I'd take it.

"Tessa, I'll call you later," Charles said. "Chloe, tell Buster to drive safely, especially in the country at night." He exited almost at a run.

She rolled her eyes. "What a worrier."

"That's our Charles," Alec said. "Come on, Tessa. Meet the group."

Chloe linked her arm in mine and we followed him. At the table, she pointed to a blonde. "Misti."

"Hey," Misti said with a smile.

"Hey," I replied.

"And this is Vera." She wore a blue dress with white polka dots. She wore her curly brown hair pinned in a bun. Think Lucille Ball with a daisy tattoo on her neck. She winked. "Howdy."

"Hi."

"This is Tessa." Chloe concluded the introductions. "Buster, let Tessa, scoot on in," she ordered. Buster stood and I scooted. Chloe plopped in the booth beside me, and Buster sat on her other side. Alec grabbed a chair from another table and sat backward in it. Chloe leaned in and dropped her voice. "Tessa is James Duran's niece. She lives in, you know, the house."

So, nosey curiosity prompted her invite, not friendship. I fought a sudden urge to elbow her onto the floor.

Then Vera laughed. "You'll have to invite your ghost to the next youth group meeting at church. We need a few more guys, even dead ones. He's single, isn't he?"

"As far as I know." Good grief, get a grip, Tessa. Andre doesn't live in a vine-covered cottage in the clouds with a Mrs. Ghost and little ghosts running around.

"Hey, she's got a sense of humor," Vera said.

Chloe reached over and squeezed my arm. "Well, with or without your ghost, you're welcome. Anything you need, anything at all, I'm here for you."

"Thanks." I relaxed a bit.

Vera snorted. "Hey, Chloe, when did they make you the Welcome Wagon?"

Chloe glared at her. "Hey, I'm being friendly. Tessa needs a friend. She needs—"

"—food," I interrupted. "Tessa needs food." We all laughed and then ordered. I got a half-pound burger with bacon, the "Day Trippin' Special."

"We can share fries," Chloe explained. "They're huge." She took a drink of her soda. "I hope everything is okay with your grandma," she said to Buster and Alec.

"Problems?" Misti asked.

Alec slurped his drink. "Same old drama."

Buster punched him in the arm. "Jerk. You know she gets confused."

Vera rolled her eyes. "Another day, another St. George drama."

"Not unusual?" I asked, feeling nosey.

"Ama's filled with St. Georges," Chloe said. "You know, they're not the only ones with relatives. You've met my aunt."

I gazed at her red hair. "Let me guess, Chief Mason?"

"Yep."

Vera blew the paper off her straw. "Is Snotty Gleason still trying to get in Charles' pants?"

Misti choked on her coke. "Vera."

Chloe snorted. "Always."

"And they say guys are crude," Alec remarked.

"Sooorry," Vera drawled out.

Personally, I approved of the nickname for Anna. "Charles doesn't like her back?" I asked.

"Oh, where to start," Chloe said. "Nobody knows who Snotty Gleason's dad is. Her mother raised her in Oklahoma City. Too bad she didn't stay there. She moved to Ama a few years ago to take care of her aunt. And that's the only good thing you can say for her. Anyway, Charles' mother insisted he hire Anna, and he's regretted it since. Can you believe she's actually attends St. George family get-togethers? Somehow, she always manages to get an invitation from Sadie."

"Thanks so much for discussing our family like Buster and I aren't even sitting here," Alec snapped. "Why don't I leave and make it easier for you." He shoved his chair back and stalked off toward the video games.

"Alec," Buster called after him. He groaned. "Is it his time of month or something?" He took off after his cousin.

"Ouch," Misti said.

"Sensitive much?" Vera said.

I didn't really blame Alec. I might gripe about Mom. But, it would irritate me to listen to others list her shortcomings. "Anna warned me away from Charles," I said. All movement stopped as they gawked at me.

"Give," Chloe demanded.

I told them about Anna's visit.

"Can you believe it," Vera said when I'd finished. "It sounds like Snotty finally chugged her train around the bend."

"She's jealous of you," Chloe teased.

Vera eyed me. "Maybe she's got reason. After all, Mr. St. George asked you out."

"No, he didn't." Oh, great, let that get all over town. "He's just nice."

"Suuure," Vera said as Chloe and Misti giggled. "Or maybe it's Alec you're on the date with?"

Okay, a nightmare come true.

Luckily, our food came and the conversation changed. Alec and Buster returned, Alec still looking thunderous. Everyone acted normal. I stayed quiet and listened. Talk flowed around me. I didn't know any of the people they talked about. Didn't get any of the inside jokes. What if I actually enrolled in Ama High School? Would these girls stay my BFFs if I arrived on the school doorstep? Or head for their own groups, leaving the new girl to stand all by her lonesome? Already done that, not doing it again.

At the end of the evening, Buster, Chloe and Alec drove me home. In the dark backseat, Alec leaned close, making my heart thump. "Sorry about the drama."

"No problem." Breathe, Tessa, breathe.

"I promise a St. George-crisis-free zone next time."

"Sounds great." Next time? How did I feel about that? Alec leaned away and my breathing slowed to normal.

As we pulled into the drive, Chloe asked, "What do you do all day?"

I shrugged. "Mostly work on decorating my room."

"Really? I painted my room three different colors of purple. It turned out so cool."

The truck lights shone on my front door. "Is that the window the creep broke?" Buster asked.

"Yes."

"I'm glad you weren't hurt," Chloe said.

In the back, Alec squeezed my hand. "Me too. Hey, let me get the door for you." He held the door, and I slid across the seat to follow him.

Chloe hung over the backseat. "Be serious, have you ever found anything strange here?"

"What do you mean?"

"Chloe thinks ghosts exist," Buster said. He reached over and tickled her neck.

"Eek, stop that," Chloe yelled as she smacked his hand away.

Both the guys roared with laughter.

"Is your room the one with the painting in it?" Chloe asked.

I shook my head. "No."

"What's with all the questions?" Buster broke in again. "Are you practicing to take over your aunt's job?"

She slapped his arm. "Shut up."

"I'll walk you to the door," Alec said.

"No, let me," Chloe said. She scrambled out of the truck. "I've got to pee."

Darn.

I waited while she used the bathroom under the stairs. Finished, she hung around in the foyer. "Hey, I want to see your room."

"Uh, okay. What about Alec and Buster?"

"Those guys can entertain themselves for a while." Upstairs, she plopped onto the bed. "You must feel weird living in the house where your uncle died."

I shrugged. "I've lived here before."

"You lived here? In this house? In Ama? When? I don't remember you in school."

"I was five, and we only lived here a month."

"Wow." She glanced at her watch and groaned. "I've got to go. Aunt Josie'll have her deputies searching for me."

"Thanks for bringing me home."

"No prob."

I grinned. "You're a cheerleader, aren't you?"

"Wow, yeah. How'd you know?"

"Lucky guess." I headed for the stairs. She didn't follow. Chloe?" Her face turned pale as a, yeah, a ghost. "Chloe, what's wrong."

"Clumsy me, I almost tripped on your rug."

I spied a loose piece at the baseboard. "I am so sorry."

"No harm." It came all breathy.

I answered the unspoken question, "Yes, my uncle tripped in this very spot."

"Get me a hammer and I can fix it," she burst out. "I'll wait here until you get back."

"No, I can do it later."

"Please, let me help." She knelt by the loose piece. "Really, go get a hammer and a nail."

Okay, this went beyond friendship or voyeurism. "Chloe, don't

114

you have to go? You know your aunt's deputies and everything. Not to mention Buster and Alec will start wondering where you went."

She blushed from her neck to her roots. "Tessa, I'm so sorry. Wow, you must think I'm a dork."

"Don't worry about it." Get out. We descended the rest of the way in silence. Was she trying to figure the most dramatic way to tell the pep squad how she tripped in the exact spot as Jimmy Duran?

"Cool," Chloe exclaimed. She pointed to my front door. "Did you paint it? Why haven't you done the outside?"

I gasped. Wood covered the hole. Yellow stars scattered against a purple background decorated the wood. In the middle a Janus-type figure grinned at me. The left half, in greens and yellows, represented the sun. The right half, painted a pale grayish white, clearly stood for the moon. The paint looked wet in places.

"Maybe you can do something like that for me sometime?" Chloe said.

"Uh, maybe." I yanked open the door.

She paused before continuing. "Tessa, I lost my mother when I was seven. So, I know what it's like to feel different. I love my father and my aunt. But it's not the same as having my mother. I hope you'll count me as your first friend. Promise me that you'll ask me for help if you ever need it."

"Uh, thanks, and sure." Even though she'd lost her mother, she had a real family and a lot of friends.

Chloe gasped and touched her left cheek. "Somebody kissed me."

"I guess my ghost likes you." With a laugh, she ran to the waiting truck. I shut the door.

Andre materialized behind me, so close breathing became difficult. "I didn't have time to do both sides. Besides, even our Charlie might notice an outside change when he brought you home. Um, what happened to him?"

"I'm going to hug you," I warned. A little shimmer and he went solid. I wrapped my arms around his waist and squeezed. "Thank you."

"You're welcome. It will do until we can replace the glass."

No way would I ever replace that beautiful artwork, no way. "You realize that I'll get the credit?"

He stuck his hands in his pockets and shrugged. "I think I can live with that." He grinned. "Or not, as the case may be."

"Charles left to take care of his mother."

"So, Chloe and those two lollygagger's brought you home."

"Huh? Oh, yeah. Buster St. George and his cousin Alec." For some reason, I didn't want to talk about Alec with Andre. As we walked upstairs, I repeated Chloe's gossip about Anna.

"Sounds a little obsessive," Andre said.

"You got that right."

Later, as I lay in bed, thoughts of blue eyes won out. Alec hadn't acted in any way romantic. Still, he'd hinted at going on a real date. I snuggled a bit further under the covers. Imagine growing up with Willard and Elma as parents. I bet the whole St. George family gathered around the table at Thanksgiving. And at Christmas, a real tree decorated their front room. As for the drama I'd seen at the station, well, all families fought, right? Then blue eyes blurred and colored brown. Andre, sexy, gorgeous Andre. I still wanted my kiss. A cocoon of sleep took over.

I slept deeply until around 2:00 a.m. when Larry made another appearance. The dream turned to nightmare as he leered from above my bed. "Tessa, you're in over your head. Everyone's laughing at you."

I sat up, pushing against the headboard. His face lingered way too close. "Go away," I yelled at him. He faded, his leering smile disappearing last, just like the Cheshire cat's.

I woke gasping. "Slow down," I told my racing heart. Mom's marriage brought back an old, nasty memory. Maybe, I'd never get dear old stepdad out of my dreams. Turning eighteen would help. No one could hurt me then. Larry…Larry would never spend a night in my house.

I focused on the glowing embers in the fireplace and pushed my thoughts in other directions. An awful lot of people seemed determined to either get into, or take possession of, my house. Charles wanted to buy it. Anna wanted to move in, at least for a night. Not to mention an intruder who might or might not have been Larry. Why? Dr. St. George said Charles wanted to go for a treasure hunt in my house.

The same treasure hunt Andre and I followed? 'If the both of you are smart enough to follow the clues, you'll get the payoff…a payoff that'll continue for as long as you've got the guts to use it.' I hugged my knees. The hunt I'd thought fun for a rainy day suddenly held sinister twinges. What would Andre and I find when we solved the last clue? And how many people were playing this weird version of hide-and-seek?

Slipping into my robe, I hurried to the mural room. No answer to my knock. A peek inside told me no books floated in the library. Great, I'd decided we might have a real mystery on our hands, and he'd disappeared. In the hall I stopped, awed, as the moonlight caught the stained glass flowers of the hall window. Half in dark, half in light, the dark red took on an otherworldly quality, except for the blotched repair. Even in the dim light the pattern didn't flow. I'd ask Andre to fix it.

I walked on in the dark, enjoying the soft flow of the moonlight. I didn't see the intruder, and he apparently didn't see me, until we bumped into each other in the entryway. He shoved me hard and made for the front door.

Oh, no. Not this time. I scrambled to my feet, grabbed the ugly vase, and swung. Missed! The vase bounced off his back. He muttered a curse, stumbled, and landed on all fours. I jumped on him, pounding his head and anything within reach.

A burst of energy got him to his feet, throwing me off in the process. He bent and yanked the carpet. My feet went airborne and my head hit the floor with a resounding whack. He stood over me for a split second then ran.

I sat up, rubbing my head. I'd burn that rug. No, I'd chop it into little pieces first. No …

"Tessa?" His arms went around me.

"No." I pushed and Andre stepped back.

"What's wrong? Why are you sitting in the dark?"

"Where were you?" I shouted.

The lights came on. Andre knelt in front of me. "Are you okay?" His eyes blazed with such concern I relented.

118

"I'm fine."

He touched the top of my head. Strands of his hair brushed my face. "You have a small knot."

I tried for bravery. "Nothing a little ice won't fix."

"Are you sure? You might have a concussion."

I started to shake my head and thought better of it. "No, it wasn't that hard of a hit."

"Here you go, sweet girl." I stared, open-mouthed at the chubby-cheeked, balding man who held a baggie full of ice. Since Andre still knelt, arms encircling me, I realized the man posed no danger.

My yell died in my throat and I took the ice. "Thank you."

"I'm afraid Andre's absence when you needed him was my fault." In his left hand he held a whisky glass a little over half full.

"Tessa, meet Paul, one of my, er, oldest friends. Should I get Willard?" Andre asked.

"No."

Each man took a side and I soon found myself seated in the corner of the couch, holding the bag of ice to my head. Andre covered my legs with the afghan and sat next to me. I pulled the cover around me, glad of its comfort. The guy with the drink loitered in front of the fireplace. "I didn't know we had any liquor."

"You don't." The hefty man chuckled and lifted his glass in a mock toast. "That's why I brought my own." He took a sip and wandered toward the foyer. "I'm afraid your vase is destroyed," he called back.

"I'm sorry. I never thought about you having a social life," I told Andre.

He rubbed his eyes, something he must have done a lot in life (or maybe only since meeting me). "It's okay. Tessa, what happened?"

"While looking for you, I surprised another prowler."

He frowned. "I can't believe it's a different looter. Which means the first break-in wasn't about an empty house. Who wanted in badly enough to risk coming back and getting caught?"

I leaned forward, careful of my head. "Think clue." Realization dawned in his eyes.

Paul wandered back. "I'm afraid you have a rather big, orange mess on your doorstep."

"My pumpkin." I groaned.

"Better it than your head." He shoved his hand almost under my nose. "Yours, sweet girl? Or your recent visitor's?" He held the only pair of wooden glasses I'd ever seen. The thought of Charles breaking in made my stomach roll.

Andre also recognized the glasses. "Charles St. George broke in? He's the one who hurt you?" The harsh fury in his voice made me blink in surprise. His dark eyes had changed, resembling cold, hard stones more than soft chocolate candy.

"I'm not sure. I'm positive it has something to do with …" I stopped.

"It's okay. As I said, Paul's a friend," Andre said. Did I imagine it, or did Andre pause before the word friend?

Paul took a deep drink, and wiped his mouth with the back of his hand before extending it to me. His fingers engulfed mine in a hearty shake. "Hello."

"Hi. Did you know my Uncle Jimmy?"

He held his drink high in a half-salute. "To my pleasure. What a rascal. Sorry he's gone." He took a large gulp. And the glass remained half-full. I studied his clothes. He wore a coat with large patch pockets, a pair of plaid golf knickers and boots. I arched an eyebrow at Andre who nodded.

"Paul is one of my otherworldly friends." The gentleman in question bowed at the waist, tottered a bit, then managed to straighten himself.

"Nice to meet you." I'd already fainted when meeting Andre. I'd accepted one ghost, why not another?

"You too, sweet girl."

Andre rose from the couch and paced. "You think Jimmy's clues have something to do with the attempted break-ins?"

"Yes. What if someone knows a secret they don't want us to discover?"

"It sounds very, very dangerous for you," Andre said.

"What clues?"Paul asked. I explained. Paul watched the ice in his glass for a moment then said, "Sounds like the real McCoy to me."

"Report everything to the police chief. Take those glasses." Andre waved his hand in their direction. "Let the authorities question Charlie."

"Not yet. I want to solve the rest of the clues first."

He shook his head. "We don't even know how many clues Jimmy left. He could have hidden them all over the house."

When I stretched my legs to stop my knee from hurting, my head ached. When I tried for a position that my head liked, my knee protested. "I don't think so. He wanted us and no one else to find what's hidden. Let's keep trying. We really don't have any proof that the break-ins and the clues are connected. Chief Mason certainly isn't going to play hunt-the-treasure with us."

"Don't know the lady. However, I imagine that's very true." Paul said.

Andre glared at him. "Okay, one of you please give me another explanation as to why Charlie keeps trying to break in here?"

"He's hunting for treasure," I whispered. I cleared my throat. "I don't think there's any real danger from Charles." They both stared at me. "Well, I don't. And another reason I can't go to the Police chief—she thinks Mom will return any day now."

Andre tilted his head. "And she's not?"

The softness in his tone almost made me lose the little composure I had. "Not if I have anything to say about it." I rushed on. "Can we wait until tomorrow to make a decision? After all," my voice faltered, "you're not planning on leaving again tonight?"

"Of course not."

Paul smiled at me. "I'll stay too, sweet girl."

"Tessa."

"Beg pardon?"

"Please, call me Tessa."

"Will do, Tessa." His grin showed tobacco-stained teeth. If a ghost could change his clothes, couldn't he fix his teeth?

I faced Andre. "Then it's settled."

He shrugged. "For now, I'll comply." Okay, not a happy agreement, but I took it.

I laid the ice bag on the floor. "Why did Uncle Jimmy make this such a big mystery? Why create the clues? It's almost like insurance in case something happened to him, like he knew he was in danger."

Andre looked shocked. "I'd never thought of that. But if so, why didn't he tell me? Why didn't he let me protect him?"

"I don't know," I said softly.

"Also, why didn't he go to the police?"

"Because whatever got him into trouble wasn't something he wanted to share with the law," Paul suggested.

"No!" The word exploded from Andre, causing me to jerk my knee. A bolt of fire pulsed through it. Andre shimmered around the edges. With his intense anger Andre lost some control of his visibility.

"You're talking about my friend. Jimmy wasn't always the nicest person, but he wasn't evil." The fireplace lit. The flames crackled and leapt so high I imagined them shooting out the top of the chimney. I shrank against the sofa and gripped the edge of the afghan, feeling the yarn pushed into my palms.

"Andre, it isn't nice to frighten a lady." Paul's hand rested on his friend's shoulder.

My housemate blinked, closed his eyes, and willed himself completely visible again. To my relief the flames died down. "I'm sorry," he said.

The raw emotion made me feel guilty. Jimmy's guilt wouldn't surprise me in the slightest. But, he'd been Andre's friend. "Andre?" My voice squeaked. I coughed and tried again. "We need to find what's at the end of the clues." For an instant, our new, emotional friendship hung suspended.

To my deep relief, he said, "I agree." He returned to the couch, not happy, but willing to listen.

Although Andre looked young and gorgeous, he lived the un-life of an old, confirmed bachelor. Andre's knowledge of anything past the 1920s came from his friends. My uncle wasn't worth your pain. No matter what happens, I won't let what he did destroy you. You're too important to me.

We needed a change of subject, something neutral. "How did you two meet?" I pointed at Andre and then Paul. "Was it in life or death?"

Okay, not witty. Still, it didn't deserve the silence that greeted it. Paul gazed at Andre. Andre stared at the space between his feet.

"Well now," Paul said, "we don't need to hash through that story again."

"Stop protecting me." The anguished voice sounded so unlike my self-assured housemate's that I automatically reached for him.

A quick shake of Paul's head stopped me. Andre wasn't solid."- So many moments can define our lives," Paul remarked. "Why do we always choose the bad ones?"

I should have never asked the question.

"Paul and his wife hired me to paint a mural for them. Paul was a banker and gone most of the day. I had an affair with his wife." A blink and Andre stood at the bottom of the stairs. "And now you know the horrible person I was in life."

He vanished.

Paul took Andre's vacated place on the couch. "Would you like to hear the long version?" Stunned, I nodded. "We did hire Andre to paint a mural for our dining room. We loved the exquisite sketch he showed us of an enclosed garden." He paused. "I'm sure you've seen its copy upstairs. Breathtaking isn't it?"

"Yes it is."

"He and Maria did have a one-night affair."

"You don't sound upset about it."

He snorted. "It happened over seventy years ago, and if I did carry a grudge it wouldn't be against Andre."

"Maria?"

"He wasn't her first. And he felt guilty after it happened. Now, I'm not excusing the behavior. You should keep your hands off another man's wife. Still, I'm realistic enough to know who did the seducing. Andre broke it off. It infuriated Maria that some wandering artist rejected her."

I wrapped my arms around a throw pillow and leaned my head on it. "What did she do?"

"Served the both of us poisoned mushrooms for dinner. Her way of getting both revenge and rid of the husband she'd grown tired of." He laughed at my horrified expression. "Personally, I found it a bonding experience. Andre, however, still carries the guilt. Not only for sleeping with Maria but for getting me killed."

Had I discovered Andre's reason for becoming a ghost? Guilt over something he could never make right? "Do you have any unfinished business?" I asked Paul.

He raised his glass to me. "To live, Tessa. To live."

"Fair enough. Paul, do you mind telling me where you lived when you died?"

"Not at all. Our fair state capital, Oklahoma City."

Goosebumps crept down my arms. At one time, Andre roamed the same city I'd lived in. Someday I'd ask him what part. Maybe we'd visit together and see the changes. "Thanks for telling me what happened," I said.

"You're very welcome."

Leaving Paul happily sitting in front of a fire, sipping his ever-full drink, I went in search of my tortured housemate. He stood in the mural room, staring at his painting.

"I shouldn't have tried to paint it."

"Why?"

"I don't deserve to see it finished. I don't deserve something that makes me so happy."

The pain in those brown eyes almost undid me. "Andre?"

He took my shoulders and whirled me around to face the door. "I've extended a lot of energy tonight, Tessa. I really need to rest. Don't worry. I won't go anywhere that I can't hear you." I'd been charmingly tossed out.

Before going to sleep, I stowed Charles's glasses in the drawer of my nightstand. Tears streamed across my cheeks and onto my pillow. So much hurt, I even wanted Mom. How come sweet-although-stuffy Charles turned into a jerk?

A soft knock sounded at the door. "Tessa? Can I come in?"

"Yes."

Andre's weight creased the mattress. His arms slipped around me. He didn't say anything, just held me. I closed my eyes tight, afraid that even in the dark I'd see nothing. And I needed the reality of that touch.

He stayed until I fell asleep.

Morning light streamed through the windows. Unfortunately, I could barely breathe through my stuffy nose, or see through puffy eyes. And my head hurt. I groaned and swung my legs over the side of the bed. A bathroom trip confirmed I looked as scary as a celebrity mug shot. I pulled on my jean skirt and the blue sweater from the night before and dragged my butt downstairs.

No breakfast greeted me. Feeling pathetic, I managed to make a couple of pieces of toast without burning them. I slapped on some peanut butter, poured a glass of milk and sat at the table.

"Gross." Andre materialized across from me.

"What? A lot of people eat peanut butter on toast," I muttered.

"A lot of people put ketchup on eggs. That doesn't make it right." He leaned in the chair and stretched his legs, perfect from head to toe. In this story, he definitely played Beauty to my Beast.

"Where's Paul?" I asked.

"Gone. Don't worry, he always comes back. For some reason he likes it here."

"He likes you. He considers you a good friend." Dying together might do that.

He changed the subject. "Are you going to see the Police Chief today?"

"No."

"Do you want to tell me about your mother?"

Be cool, you're a big girl, remember. My I-don't-care-shrug didn't quite come off. "Like I said, she's on her honeymoon.

"Is she coming back?"

"Mom left with a plan. She figured she'd leave for a couple of days and when she came back, I'd sob and beg her to take me to Oklahoma City."

"She doesn't know you very well, does she?"

"Never has." The knot in my stomach loosened as I talked. "Like I said, for a while I thought Larry might have broken in the first time."

Andre frowned. "With or without your mother's consent?"

"Oh, definitely with it."

"What makes you think your mom and Larry might not come back?"

"Except for that stupid letter they sent the Police Chief, they've left me alone. I don't understand it. They stayed in Ama, so they're planning something. Mom's not the type to give in if she thinks there's easy money she can grab."

"What about Larry?" The knot in my stomach tightened so hard and fast I thought I'd either upchuck or stop breathing. "Tessa?"

Mom hadn't believed me. Would Andre? "Once upon a time, Larry crawled into bed with me."

"What?" Andre's anger raced around his edges in an electric crackle. He closed his eyes, concentrated, and the charge faded. "I'm sorry." A slight shift told me he'd gone solid. He offered his hand.

I determinedly kept mine in my lap. I couldn't tell this while touching him. "It happened last year. We lived in a one bedroom apartment and Mom slept in the bedroom. I slept on the living room couch. One night Larry climbed on top of me. He wouldn't get off even when I yelled. My knee in his crotch sure stopped him though. That's when *he* started yelling."

The crackle ran along Andre's edges. "What did your mother do?"

"She came running in, demanding to know what I'd done to 'Sweetie.' To make it short, he claimed he was too drunk to recognize me, and thought it was Mom waiting on the couch. She believed him."

"And?"

I glared. "He wasn't that drunk." Deep breath. "Or maybe he was, I don't know. I do know if Mom tries to make me sell this house, I'll turn Larry in to the police and let them sort it out."

"I have a few things of my own I might do to him. I mean it,

Tessa. No one will hurt you again if I have anything to say about it."

I might have muttered a half-hearted, 'I'm a big girl', but all thoughts of protest left as soon as he stood and pulled me to him. Staring into those chocolate brown eyes, I knew, absolutely knew, I'd get my kiss. Take that, Sleeping Beauty! His arms went around me, hands pulling me closer. His lips brushed mine, feather soft, then, hard and searching. I threw my arms around his neck, letting him know I didn't object. My mind stopped working when he rubbed my back, and the frantic kiss turned slow, more deliberate. Dang. The need to breathe collided with my desperate desire for the kiss to never end. I pulled back slightly, enough to get some air.

Andre let go and stepped away. "I'm always here for you, Tessa. I promise."

"What? Thanks." My mind reeled. He disappeared. "Andre?" Heat flushed my cheeks. "Hey, I'm not that bad a kisser am I?" My laugh sounded loud in the kitchen where I stood. Alone. And it hit me. Andre kissed me out of pity. Because if he liked me, he wouldn't have disappeared.

And the only thing worse than no kiss was a pity kiss.

I ran, out of the house, down the steps and to my car. It took three tries to get the key in the ignition. I drove the bug too fast, gravel flying across the drive. Skidding, I barely made the road instead of the ditch.

Everything was going wrong, wrong, and wrong. Everyone appeared intent on taking my home away from me. The cute guy I'd kissed had a fatal flaw. He was a ghost, and he thought me a pathetic sob case.

Not paying attention, I soon found myself near downtown. A pay phone next to a bank gave me an idea. I fished out my calling card and phoned the most special person in my life. That is, the most special alive person. The phone rang, one, two, three, four, five times, enough rings to let people know you had better things to do than answer the phone, but not long enough that they'd hang up. "Hi, Grand."

"Tessa, it's so nice to hear from you." No questions, no rambling, just a heartfelt greeting.

I told Grandma Petey about everything except Andre. Even a doting grandma's love and acceptance might falter over talk of your friendly neighborhood ghost. I also forgot to mention the intruders.

"The Lord works in mysterious ways."

You don't know HOW mysterious, Grandma.

She called my mother a not nice word.

"Grand."

"I don't apologize. Your mother never did have any sense. Now, what do you plan on doing? Will you enroll in the Ama high school after fall break?"

"I'm not sure what I'm going to do about school. Grand, I don't know if I can handle another new place and worse, new faces. I do plan to hold onto the house before and after I turn eighteen. After that, well, I haven't gotten that far yet."

"Let me know if you need help reinforcing the barricades."

"I will."

"And Tessa, think about school. I know it's hard. You know it's worth it."

"I'll think about it."

Knowing my grandma would get on a plane and fly all the way to Oklahoma from Florida to help me kept the tears from flowing. But I needed to fight to keep my house, to stand on my own two wobbly feet. I could rationalize Andre's helping me. After all, he lived there too. Of course, after today I could never look my housemate in the eye again. Might make things more than slightly awkward.

Feeling slightly better, I hung up. That's when I noticed that unlike every public phone in OKC, this one possessed a phone book. That gave me an idea. I found Charles St. George and copied his home address. He knew where I lived, and I knew where he lived. That made us even.

No going home and facing Andre yet. I drove until I located the condos where Charles lived. Driving through Ama's neighborhoods helped clear my head, if not my heart. The White Horse Condos flowed along the edge of a wide creek. Their colonial pillars mocked, "You couldn't afford to live here even as the maid." I parked in front of the clubhouse, fighting the temptation to confront Charles. I remembered I hadn't brought his glasses, and I wanted to throw them in his face when I demanded to know why he'd roamed around my house.

No use loitering in the parking lot. I might as well go home and face Andre. I barely noticed the fall colors on the drive home as my mind struggled to ignore the kiss and concentrate on the mystery. As a detective, I blew big time. People kept breaking into my house. Why? Did the clues lead anywhere? And what would have happened if I hadn't arrived earlier than expected?

No answers.

Heart and head weary, I arrived home. On the porch, I drew my dignity around me and wore it like a protective cloak.

Inside, Andre paused while watering the plants and gave me a friendly grin. "Have a nice drive?"

"Yeah." Okay, so he wanted to act like the kiss hadn't happened.

"Are you okay?" he asked. He didn't meet my eyes.

"Sure."

"Good." He started for the stairs.

"Hey."

Andre gave me a wary gaze. "Yes?" Did he think I'd demand to know what his intentions toward me were?

"You forgot to water the plants in the entryway."

His look of relief ticked me off. After all, I hadn't asked him to kiss me. "They're plastic," he explained.

"Really? Oh. Any other fake plants in the house?"

"Honestly, your uncle didn't like them. But every living plant he placed in that spot died."

"All art is but imitation of nature," I quoted. "Maybe he hid a clue in one of them."

"Perhaps, though I wouldn't call them art."

"Snob. But they are imitations of nature."

We practically destroyed the plants, even prying the bases apart. Nothing. I stuffed a few stray leaves back into the pots. "So much for that."

"A good idea."

"You mean stupid idea. Of course, I'm the idiot who thought of it." Low self-esteem anyone?

"Come on," he ordered. "You've got to leave this house. You're going loopy."

"But I just got back."

He half dragged me through the kitchen. For once his touch didn't do things to my breathing. Apparently feeling numb had its advantage. I hadn't inspected the backyard since searching for Andre the first day. And then, I'd only paid attention to the tree. We walked onto the brick patio. The mowed yard stretched about fifty feet before the woods took over again.

I pointed to the oak. "It should look smaller now that I'm

grown. It doesn't."

"You're not that big."

"You know the saying, 'great things come in small packages.'"

Silence. Apparently one kiss equaled tons of awkwardness.

I pointed again. "What grows over there?"

"My kitchen gardens."I followed Andre to a brick path. "Here," he gestured left, "is where I plant greens, potatoes, tomatoes, onions, cauliflower and asparagus. At the fence, I grow corn and beans. On this side, I plant cantaloupes, and in the back, watermelons. You do like vegetables, don't you?"

"Sure, except the cauliflower."

"I'll keep that in mind."

A white picket fence separated a small area. "What do you plant there?"

"That's where Jimmy grew his strawberries. He did all the weeding and watering. Funny thing, he was allergic."

"Then why did he grow them?"

"Because everyone told him it was foolish." Uncle Jimmy took stubbornness to new heights.

"What will you do with that part of the garden now?"

"What do you want me to do with it?"

"Have you ever thought about growing pumpkins?" I asked.

"Sure, if you'd like. I already have a list of seeds we'll need."

Some ghosts liked rattling chains; lists made mine happy.

"Add them."

Needing a little distance from Andre, I wandered to the front of the house. The stone pond would need a good cleaning before my dream of goldfish swimming in it could come true. Uncle Jimmy grew wild strawberries by the pond and in the garden. For someone who couldn't eat them, he sure grew tons. But for me, thoughts of spending lazy summer evenings communing with the fish and eating juicy berries were welcome.

The sound of a car's engine startled me. A blue Mustang inched its way across the gravel. Wouldn't want to mess up that paint job, would you. It pulled to a stop, and I realized Alec drove. How did that make me feel, especially after that kiss? Happy? Confused.? Yep, confused covered it. I walked over to the driver's side. "Hi."

"Hi." He swung out holding a paper bag. "Mom sent some pies. She said to tell "You-Know-Who" not to try and guess the recipes. Whatever that means."

"She's probably talking about my mom." Like Mom would be anything but horrified at the thought of anyone expecting her to cook, much less bake a pie.

He handed me the bag and then stuck his hands in his back pockets. "Mom's kind of protective of her recipes. She's won a couple of blue ribbons and thinks she's the local Martha Stewart or something."

"I can't wait to taste them. Give me a minute to put them in the kitchen." He followed me up the porch steps. At the front door, I had this unreal vision of finding Andre in the kitchen and introducing them to each other. "You can wait for me on the front porch," I said.

He raised an eyebrow, shrugged and plopped down on the top step. Did he think me leery about being by myself in the house with him? Go with it, Tessa. In the house, I put the bag on the kitchen table.

No Andre.

Back at the front door, I took a deep breath before going outside. Being breathless might give Alec the wrong impression. "Thanks for bringing the pies." He scooted to the side for me to sit. "And thank your mom for sending them."

"Will do."

Awkward silence.

I tried to rub my arms without making a big deal of it, since it had been my idea to sit outside. "So, this is you drama free."

"Huh?"

I counted on my fingers. "The first time I saw you, you were sneaking out of your house. The second time, Buster and Charles were quarreling outside the hardware store. And, well, you kind of lost it at The Station. Over Anna, or at least that's how it had seemed."

His sheepish grin made me melt. "Yeah, I kinda blew up, didn't I? Sometimes people don't know what they're talking about. Take Anna, she's had a rough life. She's had to handle a lot of crap that those jerks don't know about. You know?" Hadn't a clue but nodded anyway. Being sympathetic toward Snotty Gleason wasn't high on my to-do list.

"Anna doesn't have anyone else to stand up for her."

"I guess I can see that." But who made you her knight in shining armor?

Alec reached out and put a hand on my knee, right above where I'd hurt it. The warmth of his touch instantly warmed a lot of other places. "You got a boyfriend in The City?"

I shook my head. "Not a one."

"The guys there must be idiots."

"I moved around a lot."

He inched closer. "That must have been hard."

"Sometimes." *Want to be my knight in shining armor?* His breath smelled of peppermint and a little bit oniony. Warring emotions filled me. Would Alec's kiss be anything like Andre's?

132

Alec leaned in, his lips brushing my hair. He whispered, "So, you know what it must be like for Anna, not belonging anywhere." What, huh? I would have jerked back, but his hand had gone from my knee to around my shoulders. "I'd really like a tour of your house sometime, Tessa." A soft kiss, sweet and way too short. Before I could react, he'd bounded to his feet. "Gotta go, I'm supposed to help Dad rake leaves this afternoon." At his car he stopped and grinned. "No boyfriend, huh? We might have to do something about that."

I came out of my idiot stupor. "I'll let you know when I'm taking applications."

He laughed and was gone.

I whirled. Had Andre seen the kiss? Would he have cared if he had? Did I want him to care?

The way my emotions warred with each other, going into the house wasn't an option. Instead, I took a walk. Maybe I'd visit my neighbors at the cemetery. That couldn't be any more crazy then the rest of my wacky life. Let's see…

- someone kept breaking into my house;
- the fun treasure hunt Andre and I had been conducting might be real;
- I'd been kissed by a ghost (fantastic!);
- I'd been kissed by the cute guy who had the life I'd always wanted (pretty good).

Yep, crazy covered it. At the mailbox, I grabbed the junk mail. If the ghosts at the cemetery weren't feeling chatty, then I could read it.

A rusted iron canopy proclaiming Eternal Rest marked the entrance to the cemetery. From beside the fence, I tried to determine which grave was Jimmy's. I had no desire to enter the graveyard. What if someone really rose up and introduced themselves? After all, Jimmy claimed to have friends among the inhabitants of Eternal Rest.

"I'll come back and pay my respects another time," I told him.

Yet for all my heebie jeebies, a peacefulness hung in the air. No weird clues, intruders, or potential boyfriends here. I crossed my legs and sat with my back against a fence post on my side of the road and fished through my mail. A brochure from nearby County Vo-Tech lay on top, all glossy, with happy people making happy lives plastered on the front. "Study for Your GED" caught my eye.

Huddled inside my house with Andre, I had all the life I wanted. Except maybe for Alec...But, what if Andre got tired of feeling sorry for me and moved on? And even if he didn't, could I make a life around a ghost? What kind of future did I envision with Andre? A strong chest just right for leaning on? Tousled dark hair that tickled my cheek? Melting chocolate brown eyes? All an illusion, but I could really fall for that illusion. Scary. Scary and stupid.

I jammed the brochure under the rest of the mail. No use thinking about the future until everyone trying to screw up my present had been dealt with. And, I couldn't forget my goal of a normal life. Alec had a normal life. If I became his girlfriend, I would be close to my dreams, closer than I'd ever been.

Okay, sounding a little stalkerish, Tessa.

I pulled a long, white envelope out of the pile. No writing on the outside and it looked like it had been crammed in somebody's pocket before finding its way to my mailbox. "Curiosity may have killed the cat, but satisfaction brought him back." I ripped open the envelope and found a torn piece of notebook paper. The pasted letters of a magazine were like something out of a bad, late night movie. I screamed anyway. "Andre! Andre!"

I hobbled down the road as fast as my injured knee would allow. In a hurry, I left the driveway and cut across the yard, narrowly missing the stone pond. At the top of the steps, Andre leaned against the railing. "If you and that pond get into a shoving match, it'll win."

"Not funny," I gasped. Both my lungs and my knee protested. Partly bent over, I lifted my arm and waved the letter in Andre's general direction. "You've got to read this!"

He stepped back. Maybe even ghosts don't like getting poked in the eye with the corner of a sheet of paper. I watched and knew the exact moment his hand went solid enough to take the note from me. He walked down the steps. "Is this a joke?"

By going up a couple of steps, I could peer over his shoulder. "I don't think so."

"It looks like a cheesy ransom note."

"Only it's not. Besides, we don't know anyone who's been kidnapped, do we?"

Eyes still on the note he shook his head.

Want answers? Want to know what really happened to your uncle? Meet me at the Café at 8:00 tomorrow morning. Do not be late.

134

Apparently unable to find an eight, the author had closed a red three in with a black magic marker.

"Do we want answers?" Andre asked.

"You bet we do."

"Don't you think there might be some danger?"

"It's a public place, so I think I'll be safe. Besides, you'll be hanging around. Surely you can stick out a ghostly foot if someone tries to chase me."

His chocolate eyes grew determined. "You can count on it."

"I'll meet you at the cafe," Andre said the next morning.

I stopped in the act of opening the car door and studied Andre's face. Set lines said this time he'd out-stubborn me. "Okay, see you there."

Eight o'clock in the morning found the town already bustling. I had to park several spaces down from the Cafe, in front of Loans for Less. I needed a loan too much to get one, so had no temptation to go in. The butterflies in my stomach started as soon as I left the car.

"Andre?" I whispered.

"Right here," said a voice to my right. In spite of expecting it, I jumped. A lady walking past gave me a funny gaze. I moved on. "Are you sure you want to do this?" he asked as I put my hand on the door.

"Yes." I yanked it open, sending the attached bell into a frenzy. Several people glanced up from their coffee and eggs. I smiled apologetically, lightly closed the door and stopped dead.

Anna sat in the first booth. Had she sent the note? Judging by the way she glared from me to the door and back again, I'd say not. Her grimace told me I was the last person she wanted, or expected, to see. Not knowing what else to do, I said, "Hi."

That shark smile could've killed. "Hello."

"Do you need your own table or are you joining her?" the waitress asked. I didn't know how to answer what must rank in the top ten of simple questions.

Anna shot another glance at the door. "Sit." She must've decided better company wasn't coming.

Frankly, I thought my chances of meeting my pen pal had also flown. "Sure." I slid into the seat. The scent of her musk perfume fought with the bacon and eggs.

"What can I get you?" the waitress asked, pen poised.

"Juice please." Mindful of Andre nearby, I decided a glazed donut wouldn't be worth his sulking. "And a banana nut muffin."

"You got it." She hurried off.

Anna sipped her coffee. "You haven't been bugging Charles again have you?"

"Actually we went out to dinner last night." Didn't have dinner, but that wasn't her business. The nickname 'Snotty' really did fit her.

Anna's eyebrows shot up. "He's way out of your league." She sneered.

I bit back a nasty answer as to satisfy curiosity. "More your type?"

Anna laughed. "What an idiot."

How did I reply to that? Maybe you like them younger? A hasty mental shove pushed the picture of her and Alec together out of my head. Anna wiped her mouth, slid out of the booth, and strode over to the cash register without even a goodbye.

Didn't hurt my feelings.

Donna brought me my juice and muffin. "Thank you." I gazed at its crusty top, making no attempt to eat it.

"What are you thinking?" Andre's voice, right next to my ear, made my chest tingle.

"That she was waiting for someone."

"Do you think anyone else is going to show?" Andre asked.

"No." The weight around my shoulders had to be his arm. I resisted leaning my head on his shoulder. What he probably meant to be comforting had a whole new meaning after that kiss we'd shared. "Let's get out of here. I want to be able to talk without getting hauled off by the men in the white coats for answering myself."

His arm moved. "Sure. I'll meet you back at the house."

"Okay. But don't get alarmed if it takes me a while. I have a stop to make."

"Where?"

"It's my turn to be mysterious."

He didn't answer. Had he really gone without an argument? As I slid out of the booth, I spotted a piece of notebook paper on the floor and picked it up. It smelled of musk. Snotty must have dropped it. I stuffed the paper in my jeans pocket. I had another task to tackle first.

Anna's attitude irritated me. Too many people were trying to tell me what to do. My irritation added fury to the thought of Charles pulling that rug out from under me. I'd shoved his glasses into my purse before leaving the house. A deep urge to show them to their owner rose.

I drove to his condo, pulling into the first parking spot I found. My watch said 8:30 a.m. The law office wouldn't open for a full thirty minutes. I hobbled up the stairs to # 27. A neighbor juggling two grocery bags looked curious as I banged on the opposite door. He ducked into his own apartment when I leaned on the railing and used my good leg to kick the door.

The door opened and Charles's startled face peeked around the corner. He sported an egg-sized shiner over his right eye. "Miss Kelling?"

"What happened to Tessa?" I growled. "I thought we were friends?"

"Of course." He licked at his lips. "Uh, Tessa, you must excuse me, but I'm not feeling very well. Is this something that can wait until tomorrow morning?"

"No." I pushed past him, wondering if his neighbor was at his peephole, phone in hand, ready to dial 911. Charles' neutral beige and white décor allowed nothing out of place, not even a magazine or a book. And I thought Andre a neat freak. Charles was anal.

"Tessa," the lawyer tried again, "I can see something is upsetting you."

"New glasses?"

His hand fumbled at the smaller, much plainer wire frames. "Actually older. I broke my other ones."

"How did you hurt your eye?"

"If you must know," he snapped, "I ran into a door."

"Yeah, my door." I reached into my purse. It would have been quite a "ta da" moment, but one earpiece got tangled on a strap, and I had to pause and untangle it. Then I held out my palm, the mangled eyewear lying across it.

Charles licked his lips at a frantic pace. His eyes shot toward the door. Where did he plan to run? How long would it take for him to realize he'd left me standing in his condo? "I knew you'd find them," he said faintly. "I'm sorry."

"Sorry that I found them?"

"No, just sorry." It actually sounded genuine. "Why did you break into my house?"

Sinking into the nearest chair, he covered his face and moaned. "Desperation. Breaking in wasn't my first plan. I wanted to get in legitimately. But you and your mother arrived." His voice trailed off.

"Why didn't you break in right away, after Jimmy died?"

He hung his head and I could barely hear his mumble. "Stupidity and bad planning."

"What do you mean?"

He refused to elaborate.

"Why shouldn't I tell Chief Mason?"

He gaped at me from dark circled eyes. "Because your uncle was blackmailing me."

I'm sorry, Andre. I plopped on the couch. "Explain."

"My grandfather made his money in oil. A lot of people lost everything in the oil bust of the '80s, but Grandfather invested wisely and continued to make quite a tidy fortune. When my father died, I should have become a wealthy man. Mom would get her share, of course, but the bulk of the estate should have gone to me, and then I'd take care of everybody. Just like Father always took care of the family."

"Why didn't you? Inherit, I mean."

"Because Father left no will, or so we thought."

"Can't you split the money?"

"Why should I split my rightful inheritance?" He wiped a string of spit off his chin. "I'm the legitimate heir." He shook his head.

"What about Buster?"

"Buster is actually illegitimate. The product of our father and my nanny. His mother died during childbirth and Mother insisted Father bring Buster home."

"Oh." Suddenly, the St. George family didn't seem so perfect. In fact, skeletons were falling out of the closet faster than I could count. Then I felt Andre, right beside me in the room. "Charles, what has all this got to do with you breaking into my house twice and Uncle Jimmy blackmailing you?" That should catch the ghost up to speed.

"Twice?" Charles looked confused. "I only broke in once."

"Last night?"

He nodded. "I've no idea who broke in the first time. Chief Mason was probably correct about it being kids."

Lying or not lying? Making my brain ache over it wouldn't help. "Okay, answer the second half of the question."

"James claimed he had possession of my father's will. He refused to tell me the name of the heir, but hinted that it isn't me."

"Have you ever seen the will?"

He shook his head.

"Then how do you know it exists?"

"I couldn't take the chance," he whispered.

"So, you've been paying my uncle's blackmail in case he was telling the truth?"

"Yes." I stood. Charles fumbled his way to his feet. "Could I please have my glasses back?"

"Sorry. I may still take them to the Police Chief. And next time, stay out of my house." Charles' Adam's apple bobbed as he swallowed and took a step forward. My hold on the glasses tightened. "I'll tell," I warned.

The fight fizzled out of him as he slumped back onto the sofa. Right before I stalked out he moaned, "She was going to get us in. It would have been so much easier if she had."

The light went on in my head. Anna trying to worm her way into spending at least one night under my roof made sense. As I walked past the neighbor's apartment, I waved toward the peephole. At my car, I spoke to the air, "Did you get all that?"

"Yes."

"Do you think there really is a will?"

"I think we both know where the clues are leading."

It was like speaking with a sexy-sounding wind. "I agree. But I still don't understand why the head honcho of the St. George clan, loony as they're turning out to be, would give his will to Uncle Jimmy."

"Well, they were card-playing buddies. Barney liked practical jokes as much as your uncle did. And when it came to the will, he knew it would irritate his family to have to deal with Jimmy."

"Do you think Barney knew Jimmy would blackmail them?"

"I don't think so. He believed money should stay in the family. I think he expected Jimmy to give the will to his family, when their panic had reached its pitch."

"Andre, do you realize that Jimmy wrote his note to me about the same time he started blackmailing Charles."

"Yes."

"I'm sorry, Andre."

"About what?"

"About Jimmy messing around in something he shouldn't."

"Me too." He sounded like he was starting to fade away.

I tried to keep him with me. "Hey, how did you find me?"

"I told you, Dr. St. George—"

"—No, right now. Did you tailgate?"

"I've formed a connection with you."

"Really? Well …" A woman walking her dog gaped at me talking to the air. I pretended to try and find the key to my car, which should not be a hard feat since I only had two keys on the ring. After she'd passed, I turned to tell Andre to materialize, but I realized he'd gone.

At home, he waited on the front steps. I hurried past, jealous that the wind didn't mess up his hair in the slightest. He followed me inside.

"How did I know when you entered Charles' apartment?" I demanded as soon as I'd shed my coat.

"It happens sometimes."

"Happens?"

He searched for a word. "You also have a connection to me."

"Connection?" Was it me, or did I sound like a parrot?

"You can sense me when I come into a room."

"Can I do that with all ghosts?"

"Apparently not," said a voice at my elbow. I shot up about three feet and then glared at Paul, who stood grinning at me, drink in hand. "Connecting," he added, "as Andre calls it, is very rare, and usually takes months if not years to happen."

"So why am I so special?" I snapped.

"Maybe it's not why you're special, but who you're special to."

That stopped me, but not Andre. I felt him leave.

Paul ignored Andre's departure. "What's the uproar? What have I missed?"

I flung myself on the couch and filled him in.

Paul took a deep drink of his never-ending Scotch, and then whistled. "So, we need to find that will?"

"If I want people to stop breaking into my house in the middle of the night, yes, we do."

"Well then, let's go retrieve Andre from wherever he's sulking and get started."

"He won't be in the mural room."

"Why not?" I quickly explained that development. He hit his forehead. "The two of you are certainly in need of someone to take care of you." Since he'd included Andre among the incompetent, I didn't take offence. Paul wagged a chubby finger. "Let me think on this one."

"Gladly."

We headed upstairs and found Andre kneeling at the spot where Chloe had tripped. He had a hammer and a couple of carpet tacks. "I thought I'd better fix this."

"Do you think that's why Uncle Jimmy fell?"

He frowned. "It could have been. He never said anything about this being loose. I should have noticed."

Oh, boy. "It's a little spot. I've walked these stairs dozens of times since I got here and never noticed it. It could've even come loose when Jimmy fell. Or his fall might not have even had anything to do with the carpet. Did Jimmy have dizzy spells?"

"No."

Aware that I talked about his friend, I asked cautiously, "Did Uncle Jimmy ever drink too much or take anything to help him sleep?"

"No," Paul said, waving his glass to an imaginary beat. "I'm the only drunk around here."

"Jimmy," Andre said in an even voice, "was a teetotaler. Never took a drink. We had quite a job getting him to even take an aspirin. Don't you remember that full bottle of sinus medicine? We'd had it for years."

Hmm, had Snotty Gleason been given out-of-date medicine? I hoped so. "So, Jimmy didn't have any health problems that might cause dizziness, and he didn't drink or even take pain medication. Andre," I said, "what if someone pushed my uncle?"

He shrugged, obviously frustrated. "I've been thinking that same thing. Maybe someone got tired of being blackmailed? After all, we don't know that Charlie is the only one, do we? "As he talked, he pulled the loose edge of the carpet taut. Something rolled.

"Andre."

"I see it." He picked it up and held it out. A diamond earring.

"I take it from your startled face the earring isn't yours?" Paul asked.

"No, it's not." I pushed back my hair. "These are the only diamond earrings I own, and they're round, not heart-shaped. Andre, do you know whose it could be? And how long do you think it's been hidden under the rug?"

"This runner has haunted this house longer than I have," he replied.

"And the answer to the first question?" I asked.

"No."

"A lot of women own diamond studs, even heart-shaped ones. And Chloe was so eager to fix the rug."

"Tessa." Andre's liquid eyes stared into mine. "I'm sure Chloe was simply trying to be helpful. She comes off as a sweet tomato."

"You don't know her very well?"

"Never met her until she came to see you. She's not exactly Jimmy's type of visitor."

But Chloe had mentioned the room with the painting in it. Hadn't she?

"Chloe?" Paul asked.

"Little cheerleader who wants to be Tessa's best friend," Andre answered.

"If we don't want it to be her," Paul said, "then let's think of someone else it could be."

"Anna came nosing around the other day," I said.

"Even if she lost the earring, it's still not proof of foul play," Andre pointed out.

"I don't see how she could have lost it," I said slowly. "Besides, she'd have yelled bloody murder as soon as she noticed it missing. Heck, she'd probably accuse me of stealing it. That lady really doesn't like me." I sank to a sitting position. "I think she's who Charles meant."

"Charles?" Andre repeated.

"Charles said that 'if she could have gotten them in, then everything would have been easier.'"

"He said that to you?"

"He mumbled it to himself. The door hadn't quite shut behind me. You must have already gone to the car."

Andre rubbed his neck. "Maybe Charles and Anna have joined forces to get the will."

"My suggestion is to get on the trolley and solve the clues," Paul said, taking a drink.

"He's right." Andre pushed the carpet back into place. "I think I'd better leave this like we found it. But be careful taking these stairs. Let's take another gander at that second clue." He handed me the earring. "And I suggest putting this someplace safe."

I held up the glasses. "We're getting quite a collection." No one answered. I followed Andre to the library. Paul floated behind me. "Okay, we know Charles was being blackmailed, so I'll bet he didn't cry too hard over Jimmy's death," I said.

"And Chloe?" Andre asked.

"I have no idea what her motive would be, except that she's dating Charles' younger brother, Buster. Maybe they think the will names him. We also have Willard and Elma." I didn't mention Alec.

"No." Andre shook his head. "They wouldn't do this."

"And Anna?" Paul asked.

"We have to consider her," I said. "Wait!" Ding, dang, duh! How could I have forgotten? They waited while I dug into my pocket. "I think Anna dropped this when she left the booth this morning." Three heads, one breathing, crowded around the pasted note.

In case you think I'm stupid, come to The Café at 8:00 Monday morning. You'll see how I can hurt you if you don't cooperate.

"Same as yours," Andre said.

A chill, not caused by the presence of ghosts, ran across my neck. "I'm the way this somebody could hurt Anna," I said. "According to Charles, he didn't break in the first night."

"Could it have been Anna?" Paul asked.

"I don't know. They're about the same size." Alec, Anna's champion, had more bulk. But my sizing could be confused. After all, I'd thought it could be pot-bellied Larry.

"Charles could have hired someone else," Paul said.

"Not to mention there are other members of the family who might be involved," Andre added. "As you said, there's Buster."

The cute guy who'd helped me in the paint store…I wanted to believe Buster's friendliness had been genuine and that no way were he and Chloe involved in this mess. "Buster wears an earring. It's a gold stud, but that doesn't mean…anyway, as you pointed out, we won't find any real answers until we find the will. And that means we have to solve Uncle Jimmy's clues." We gathered around the library table. "All art is but imitation of nature," I read. "Well, we know he didn't mean plastic plants."

"It wasn't a bad idea," Andre said.

I shrugged and rubbed the back of my neck. As I did, I gazed down the hall to the stained glass window. The botched rose…A light went off in my brain. "Andre, how long has that window been broken?"

"That happened in a storm about a year ago. A tree limb struck by lightning crashed through it."

"Did you repair it?" I asked, knowing the answer.

"Jimmy did. He'd never let me fix it, even though it looked awful. Believe me I would have…" He stopped.

"I spy the answer to a clue," I whispered. The ghosts followed my mad dash to the window.

Andre floated upward until he came even with the rose then paused. "Perhaps you'd prefer we got a ladder and you did the honors?"

"Hurry," Paul and I shouted.

He reached through the globs of paint. Flecks floated down when his hand went solid. I shook my head as it rained red. Paul, of course, remained unspoiled. The paint fell through him to puddle on the floor. The next few minutes seemed to stretch into hours.

"Is there anything there," Paul demanded.

"Yes." Andre pulled a huge clump away from the pattern. Floating down, he handed it to me. "Your turn."

My hands shook as I peeled the paint-stained baggie away from the paper it held. I unfolded it and read,

"You shall know them by their fruits." (Matthew 7:16)

"Know who?" Paul asked.

"That's the question, isn't it?" I replied. The doorbell rang. The three of us stared at each other.

"I suggest," Andre said smiling at me, "that you be the one to answer it." They followed me down the stairs. When I opened the door, Andre hissed in my ear, "See, you should always look first." It was Larry.

Believe me, I wished I had.

"Where's, Mom?" I demanded as I positioned myself in maximum "I don't want you here" posture.

"In jail."

"Huh?" I peered past him to his empty van, and then I really saw him. Larry's beard was scruffy and his eyes screamed bloodshot. "What did you do to her?" The squeal in my voice could've made bats restless.

His fists clenched as tight as my jaw. "I didn't do anything to her. It's a misunderstanding. I need to get some money."

"Money?" My mimicking was down pat.

He moved a step closer. "Hey, brat, I gotta get her out of there. Give me the money and I'll get off your doorstep." Before I could react, something solid moved between us. Larry's eyes widened. He took a reluctant step backward, than another. At the edge of the porch, the pressure gave way and Larry waggled backward and forward as he tried to regain his balance. He resembled a man fighting the wind. He lost.

I glared at him sprawled out flat on the ground. "Tell me what happened to my mother!"

He pushed to his knees and scurried back, trying to get distance between us. "How did you do that?" Larry demanded.

I crossed my arms. "My mother?"

"I told you, she's in jail." He scrambled to his feet. "I'm here to get some money, so I can get her out." He squinted as if trying to see what wasn't there. "How did you do that? And what's wrong with your hair?"

I pulled a red clump out of my bangs. "What happened to my check from the lawyer? You know, the one that's supposed to take care of me for the month?"

He frowned. "Check? I don't know anything about a check."

146

He bit his lip, an obvious attempt to make his last two brain cells work. "Your mother has money?"

And she didn't tell you about it!

Larry had regained some of his dignity or at least the arrogance that passed for it. "Are you going to help or not?"

"What makes you think I have any money?"

"Your mother told me you saved all your babysitting money." He said it like I'd been selling my soul. I bit my own lip. Could he be telling the truth? Or hatching a ruse to leave me dead broke? And, what if Mom sat in jail with an uncashed check she hadn't wanted her new hubby to know about?

"I'll get my keys."

He stopped kicking dirt against my porch. "What? Why? I can take the money…"

"I want to see her." I stepped back into the house to grab my keys and a coat. He followed me to the steps, stopping short of the front door. Good thing. I could feel my personal force field hovering nearby.

"You can ride with me," Larry said.

And bats could fly out of Hell. "No."

He shrugged. "Whatever paranoia turns you on."

"Wait for me in your van." He stomped away.

"I'm going," Andre said.

"Who's the sap?" Paul inquired as I pulled on my jacket.

"My stepfather. If they ever wrote a story about a wicked one, he'd play the lead."

"I'm going," Andre repeated.

"In the car?" I asked.

He shook his head. "But I'll be there."

"No. I can handle Mom and the sap."

"But…"

"No." How could I explain? I didn't want the rotten stench of my world with Mom oozing into my new life with Andre. He didn't argue, and I couldn't feel his presence. Well, maybe pouting would keep him out of trouble.

Paul lifted his glass in salute. "I'll be here when you get back."

I didn't realize until I got into the car that Paul had used the singular pronoun. "Andre! Where are you?" His essence, or whatever, focused beside the car. I rolled down the window. I might look like a lunatic talking to myself, but I really didn't care. Maybe it would make

Larry behave himself if he thought me crazy. "My problem."

"But we're a team."

"Not this time."

His lips brushed my forehead. "Okay, but he'll regret it if I have to come looking."

"Works for me."

Larry's voice floated across the gravel. "Are you going to keep babbling like an idiot, or are we going?"

"Going." My bug followed the van.

Mom's first time in jail. We'd always managed to avoid that indignity. Until Larry.

"I need to bail out my mom," I told the uniformed man behind the desk. Luckily, Chief Mason didn't witness this family reunion.

He yawned. "And that would be…?"

"Jilly Kelling."

The look on his face said, "What took you so long?" He asked, "How old are you?"

"Seventeen."

"You'll have to let him pay the fine."

"Told you," Larry said from behind me.

We'd had a heated exchange on the steps of the Ama police station, but I still had it in my head that he would take the money and run. Wishing I'd taken most of the money out of the envelope first, I shielded my movements with one arm and counted. I shoved the bills in Larry's hand.

"Holding out, weren't you kid," he muttered. I watched the cell door while he paid.

Mom came out trying to hand brush hair that looked like broken spikes. Her smudged mascara gave her the appearance of a rock star at the end of a bender. "Oh, Larry!" She ran to his arms.

I stood in the background while they signed some papers and Mom collected her personal belongings. She didn't acknowledge me until we stood on the station steps. Her hand went to her collar.

"What happened?" I demanded.

"It's all a misunderstanding, baby. I wrote a few itty-bitty checks on an account Larry had closed out." She giggled. "Only, I didn't realize it was closed, of course."

Of course.

"Anyway, the store owners said they wouldn't press charges if I paid the amount in full. Tessa, I didn't think you'd come. Not after your visit to the B & B. Larry said you were really mad."

Larry drew her close and gave her a squeeze. "Hey, no hard feelings. In fact, why are we standing here? Tessa can buy us dinner."

I ignored him. "You're lucky I wasn't in jail with you after that stupid note you and Larry sent to the police in Ama."

She sighed. "You're right. That was stupid. I admit that I wanted to ride in and rescue you, to take care of you."

"And make me do exactly what you wanted?"

"For your own good, baby."

I had nothing else to say, so I walked to my car, exhaustion flowing over me.

"Tessa?" Mom stood behind me. Larry had gone to the van. "Tessa, Larry tells me you have quite a bit of money." She pulled at her collar. "I had no idea you'd saved so much from babysitting. Anyway, I was wondering if you could loan …"

"Why haven't you cashed the check, Mr. St. George gave you?"

She glanced over her shoulder. "One should always save for a rainy day, baby."

"In case prince charming turns into a toad?" We glared at each other.

"It doesn't matter how much money you think you have," she said. "It won't last you through the rest of this month and another. Let me sell the house, Tessa."

"No, Mom."

"I overheard something. Some little redhead and her boy-friend came in hunting for her aunt. While they were waiting for auntie, they had a little conversation. There's something hidden in your house, Tessa. Something big."

I took a step backward. "You must have heard them wrong."

"No, no, I didn't." She eyed me. "What do you know, Tessa?"

"Only that I had to bail my mother out of jail." A deep breath then, "I found Wally."

"Wally? Who's Wally?"

"My old teddy bear. You remember, the one Uncle Jimmy sent me when I was born." I heard a sharp intake of breath. "Oh." Nothing else, just, "Oh." She would never understand what the bear had meant to me. Never understand how hard her betrayal hit. "It seemed kind of weird seeing him after all these years."

"I'm surprised your uncle still had him."

"Jimmy stored Wally in the attic."

"Did you, uh, did you happen to find anything else lying around that you remember being ours?"

I mentally forgot the pearl brooch. "An old pair of booties, a scarf full of holes, stuff like that."

"Oh."

"Mom, have you ever regretted cutting all ties with Uncle Jimmy?"

"Regretted it? Regretted it?" Her voice screeched upward a notch with each regret. "Oh baby, you were too young to remember all the nasty things he said to me. Me! Who did nothing but try to make his house a home. He probably regretted cutting ties with me. He lost a free housekeeper."

As I'd never seen my mother lift so much as a dust cloth, I didn't think my uncle had been too bereaved. "Just wondering," I muttered.Mom rubbed hands across her eyes, smearing her mascara to the point it made her cheeks look dirty. "Mom, are you all right?"

"No," she snapped, "I'm not all right. I just got out of jail and now all my daughter wants to talk about is a teddy bear." Her voice cracked. "Can't you get along with Larry, Tessa? Maybe we can find whatever is hidden in the house together?"

"I was sixteen."

She glanced over her shoulder then appeared to decide that getting support from Larry probably wasn't the brightest idea. "Tessa, baby, we've been over this. Larry came in a little tipsy. He thought it was me waiting on the couch for him." If she pulled any harder at her collar, she'd choke herself. "You made too much out of it, baby."

"He wasn't that tipsy." Wet tracks lined my cheeks. "You weren't there for me. You were supposed to protect me, but you didn't." Mom turned and walked over to the driver's window. I could see their heads come together. Larry gawked at me. Then his eyes dropped.

Something broke inside me and I stormed forward. He had no

time to react. I hit the side of the door as hard as I could. "You're not a man," I shouted. "Men don't take advantage of kids. I don't care how drunk you were or weren't."

Larry didn't move, only stared.

"You have no power over me," I said. "No more snarky remarks or leers. You leave me alone." I ran past Mom, ran out of my life with either of them. In my heart, I knew there would be no more dreams about Larry. He really had no power over me anymore.

The van backed out and left. Where were they going? Did I care? And had Mom joined the treasure hunt? Dang, Chloe had a big mouth. I sucked in my breath. Chloe and Buster knew something was hidden in the house. Did they know about the will? Were they treasure hunting?

Thirty minutes later, no one greeted me as I entered the house. Paul had probably gone and Andre possibly lurked in the library. I wanted to curl up in a ball in the middle of my bed.

"Psst." Paul stuck his head out of the mural room door. "Care to come in and play, my dear?" The head retreated. Horrified, I hurried. Paul said he'd forgiven Andre for the affair, but what if he'd lied, simply waiting until he found something Andre cared about? What if he planned on destroying the art Andre had so passionately created? I threw open the door to find a gleeful Paul awaiting me. "Leave it open," he demanded.

No idea how to stop a ghost, but I'd sure give it a try. I thought about yelling for Andre, but couldn't stand the thought of the look on his face when he realized the betrayal of yet another friend. "Paul," I hissed, "you can't do this!"

"Do what?" He frowned, confused. "I thought we wanted Andre to paint more of his lovely mural?"

Huh? We did? "Of course. What are we going to do?"

He floated over to the gazebo. "Destroy part of it."

He did harbor a grudge! "Paul, Andre shouldn't have had an affair with your wife. But that was, what, seventy years ago?" As I talked, I tried to get between him and the painted wall. "Will destroying his work really make you happy?"

He peered into his drink. "Have you been sipping this behind my back?"

I spread my arms out, trying to protect as much of the mural as possible. "You said you wanted to destroy it."

"Not irreparably, Tessa. Just enough so that it will drive Andre crazy."

"Oh! He won't be able to stand that it's not perfect, and he'll have to repair it." I faced the mural. "But we don't want to mess it up too bad, do we?"

"No, dear lady, we couldn't stand to do that." Paul waved his hand in the direction of a paintbrush. "Pick any color you wish."

"Me?"

"Why, yes. It's much easier for you." He strove to look innocent.

"I happen to know that you can pick up that paintbrush as easily as I can," I snapped.

"I see Andre has been a little too free with our secrets."

"I'm not going to be the only one to deface this," I told him.

"I'm with you in spirit." He grinned. "Pun intended."

"I'm not laughing."

"You should. It would do you good."

"Now look—"

"What are you two doing in here?" Both Paul and I faced the doorway. Andre stood there, surprise competing with anger. I waited for Paul to answer, but found him waiting on me. Andre stalked forward. "Well?"

Getting ready to deface your painting didn't seem like a good response. "We were admiring your work," Paul told him. Sort of true.

Andre stopped about a foot in front of me. "This is my room."

"Yes, but …"

"I demand the same respect that I give you."

"Sorry." I took the coward's way and fled. Behind me, Paul's voice rose in protest, countered by Andre's low, furious tones. I willed my body to stop shaking. The noise behind me stopped. Andre came out of the room, shutting the door behind him.

"Where's Paul?" I asked.

"Gone."

"Are we still partners?"

He smiled, although it didn't quite reach his eyes. "Always." He reached out and brushed a couple of leftover red flakes out of my hair. "How did things go with your mom?"

"Bounced checks. I paid the fines. We're not quite one big happy family, but at least they won't show up on the doorstep." At least I didn't think so.

"Sorry."

"Yeah."

"I'll see you later. I need to go and rest."

"Later," I echoed.

Before going to sleep, I went and stood at the top of the stairs. I probed the loose piece of carpet with my foot.

What had really happened to Uncle Jimmy? A part of me kinda wished Larry had been causing all the trouble. Better the scum you know …

The next morning, I wiped blueberry muffin crumbs off my sweater and pointed at the earring lying on the table. "What are we going to do about this?"

Andre reached out and fingered it. "I don't know."

Pushing my plate away, I folded my arms and grinned. "How about a little sleuthing?"

He leaned back and studied me. "You don't mean searching for clues, do you?"

"Nope." I took a deep breath and then plunged. "We need to find the owner of this earring."

"For all we know, it could have been your mother's from when the two of you lived here." Completely practical. How did his artistic side ever escape?

"No, for a couple of reasons. First, you are too much of a neat freak to have let that torn carpet stay unnoticed for decades. Second, this is way too tasteful for my mother. Did you ever see her wearing it?"

He frowned. "Not that I can recall." Leaning forward, he touched the lobe of my left ear. "Too tasteful for her, but not for her daughter?"

I fingered the diamond in my right ear. "These were my grand-mother's. I'm probably more like her than my mom."

"She knew how to let her natural beauty show through?"

How could I answer that without looking full of myself?

He saved me by picking up the earring. "You notice I'm ignoring the 'neat freak' part."

"Appreciate it." How could talking to him feel so natural, so normal? Would I lose my dream of a normal life because of a pair of gorgeous eyes belonging to a ghost who happened to be an excellent kisser? My mind immediately shied away from thinking about the kiss.

Andre held the jewelry flat in his palm. "Anna?"

Obviously, he had no such problems. One pity kiss and he was good to go. "I think so."

"You said she'd have been yelling bloody murder as soon as she discovered it missing?"

"If she lost it when she gave her little self-guided tour, then yes. But what if she lost it earlier?" I suggested.

I'd noted before how motionless he could go, as if only the still of the grave remained. "You mean, when she pushed Jimmy?"

I nodded. "Yes."

"What about the cheerleader?"

"Chloe and Buster know about the will."

He raised an eyebrow. "How do you know that?"

"Mom overheard them talking. They talked about something big hidden in my house."

"Okay, but maybe they don't know what it is. Maybe they've only heard rumors of a hidden treasure or something."

"Could be. Andre, I really, really want the creep to be Anna."

"Fair enough." He placed the earring back on the table. "Why?"

"Why do I want it to be her?"

"No, why would she push Jimmy? What did she have to gain?"

I didn't know and said so. "She seems very loyal when it comes to Charles and his family. Maybe, like we said before, he confided about being blackmailed and she decided to put a stop to it."

"Do you think the receptionist would be his chosen confidant?"

"Charles is the type that would feel the need to vent his frustration."

"And who better to vent it to than the sympathetic friend and employee."

"Exactly. That might even account for his uneasiness around her now. She might be a little too enthusiastic about helping him."

"It's a very good friend who will kill for you."

"But that friend might expect something in return," I finished. "Which begs the question—does Charles know she killed my uncle?"

156

"We don't know she killed him," he pointed out.

"True. But I think we have a place to start."

Andre frowned. "Do you plan to confront her like you did Charlie?"

"No." Confronting Charles hadn't scared me, but Anna as a villain terrified me. "Actually, I thought we'd pay a visit to her aunt. Anna lives with her."

"We?"

"Yes. I'll bring the earring and ask if it's Anna's. While I'm talking to the aunt, you can search Anna's room for the match, or anything else interesting you might find."

He gazed so hard at me that I had to resist the urge to grab the toaster and see if my pimple had made a return engagement. "You want to go to the home of someone you suspect of being a killer, taking the evidence with you, so she'll know you have it?"

That couldn't be what I'd said, because that sounded like a very stupid thing to do. "I want to talk to the aunt, not Anna. Anna will never see the earring. If Aunt Gleason identifies it as Anna's, we'll take it to the police. If not, there's no harm done."

"If it is Anna's, her auntie will want to keep it."

"Hmmm, could get sticky," I admitted. I snapped my fingers. "I know, I'll tell her I'm going by the law office and want to give it to Anna myself."

"And if she objects?"

I waved my hand. "You'll have to think of a diversion."

That didn't make him happy.

"If you don't come, and I get hurt, you'll be sorry." A bit of my own blackmail, but it ensured that he'd be with me.

Nerves made my stomach jumpy, but I kept my lips zipped since Andre was so set against the venture. Thank goodness, he decided to join me. Well, not exactly join me. He refused to get into the car.

I made a stop at the phone where I'd gotten Charles's home address. I found a listing for a M. L. Gleason and wrote down the number. I thought about giving Grandma Petey a call, but I was afraid of taxing Andre's already strained patience. "Do you know where Fir Street is?" I inquired of the air.

"No."

I checked the map at the back of the phone book. It appeared to be about three streets over from the downtown area. The box houses had been designed by a builder with no imagination and inhabited by people with a similar lack. The one exception proved to be Aunt Gleason's house.

Four twenty Fir Street should have been as cookie cutter as the houses surrounding it. But, the owner had taken care of that by painting the whole abode lime green. Yellow shutter accents completed a house no one would soon forget. Or duplicate. So, the sleek receptionist called this home? Bet the color scheme fit her aunt's idea of fine décor and not Anna's. I parked at the curb. Once on the sidewalk, I paused to calm my nerves.

"Are you sure you want to do this?" His voice at my elbow made me jump. So much for having a connection.

"Yes," I replied, barely moving my lips.

"Why are you talking like that?"

"In case Aunt Gleason is peeking out the window. We don't want her to think I'm talking to myself on the sidewalk." He didn't answer. "Do you think you'll have any trouble finding Anna's room?" I asked.

"I don't think I'll have any trouble telling her and Auntie's rooms apart. Did I tell you I've met Auntie?"

I almost moved my head, but remembered in time not to. "No! When?"

"She was a friend of Jimmy's."

This time I could tell he'd left. Did all ghosts have a flair for dramatic exits? After checking for a dog, I opened the gate in the chain-link fence and, still checking, strode up the walk. The doorbell was a yellow daisy with the ringer in the middle. I pushed it. The door opened so quickly I knew my progress had been observed.

From behind the safety of a latched screen door, the china-doll woman observed me, her eyes squinting almost shut behind coke-bottomed glasses. The white poodle that owned the yard barked behind her. "Hush, Tinkerbelle." Tinkerbelle ignored this admonition with a growl and a series of yaps. "Can I help you?" the woman asked.

I raised my voice so it could be heard over the poodle's. "Miss Gleason?"

"Yes?"

"You don't know me, but you may have known my uncle, James Duran?"

Her wrinkled face lit. "You're Jimmy's niece?" She fumbled at the catch. "I'd heard you and your mother were living in his house. I've been trying to get my niece to drive me out, but she's so busy." The opening of the screen door sent Tinkerbelle into a frenzy. "Bad dog." She smiled at me. "Don't mind her, she won't bite."

I had to take her word for it as I edged my way into the living room, careful to give Tinkerbelle all the space she wanted. With Tinkerbelle nipping at my heels, I entered a cozy living room filled with white wicker furniture. Whose decorating taste? Somehow Anna didn't hit me as the floral cushion type.

"Please sit down. Tinkerbelle, you are being a very bad dog. Do you want to go to your room?" The little poodle scooted over to a basket where she lay on her cushion and glared at me. Aunt Gleason sat on the edge of a rocker, her hands clasped in front of her, brown eyes shining. "You've met my niece, Anna, right?"

"Yes. She's very pretty." Well, I couldn't say nice. The word would have stuck in my throat.

"Oh, yes." She picked up a picture from the side table and handed it to me. "This is from her prom." Anna stared back at me with the same cool smile I'd encountered at the law office.

"It's a great picture." I handed the photo back.

Aunt Gleason fluttered her hand in a dismissive wave. "You're sweet, but you didn't come all the way over here to listen to a proud aunt."

"I wanted to return this to Anna." I produced the earring from my pocket. "I think she may have dropped it during a visit to my house."

She took the earring and held it so near her glasses that I was afraid she'd scratch the lenses. "I'm sorry, dear, but this isn't Anna's." She handed it back.

"Are you sure?"

She laughed. "You're thinking that with these eyes I shouldn't be sure of anything. But Anna always wears pearls." She pointed to the photo again. "They were a graduation present." Sure enough, in the picture Anna wore a pair of tasteful pearl earrings.

"I guess I made a mistake. I'm so sorry to have bothered you."

"Nonsense." She settled into her rocker. "It's very nice of you to attempt to reunite it with its owner. Not many people would put themselves out."

I felt just a teeny bit guilty at the praise. After all, I wanted to tie her niece to a murder, not reunite her with lost jewelry. "I hope you find the owner." She sighed. "I sure do miss Jimmy."

"You knew him?" I knew she did, but since my ghost told me, I couldn't very well say so.

She chuckled. "I knew you, dear."

I told myself to close my mouth. "Me?" It came out in a squeak. Why hadn't Andre told me that?

"You were a chubby young thing. I can still see a tiny bit of the little girl you were."

Okay, that did it. No more donuts. "Were you and my mother friends?"

"Not exactly. Your mother didn't like me coming to visit Jimmy.

Maybe she was afraid Jimmy would marry me. At the time, I think she planned on staying longer than a month."

"You and Uncle Jimmy were in love?" How did this image fit into the one I'd formed of a grouchy blackmailer?

Aunt Gleason studied her folded hands, a wistful smile playing across her face. "We dated. It looked like it might get serious. But then you and your mother moved in and things became…difficult."

Difficult - Mom's middle name.

"Uncle Jimmy let her run you off? How about after we left? Why didn't you get married then?"

"It was too late. Pride broke us apart. Stubbornness kept us from being more than friends."

"That's so sad!" Oh, boy, Anna and I could have been related by marriage. "Can I ask, well, Uncle Jimmy seems to have been rather cranky? A lot of people didn't like him. But you loved him?"

"Jimmy could definitely rub people the wrong way, especially people he perceived as weak. But he could also be a good friend. When I needed a new roof, Jimmy paid for it. I repaid him with a home-cooked dinner once a week. Is the afghan still in the living room?"

"The one made of granny squares?"

"She smiled with pride. "I crocheted that."

"I love it. It's great for snuggling under."

"I'm glad you're enjoying it." She shook her head. "I didn't always like the way Jimmy treated others." From nasty blackmailer to generous friend, my uncle hadn't been dull. She smiled. "Jimmy and I remained friends until the end of his life. He used to come over on Saturday nights and we'd watch TV together." But it could have been so much more. I didn't say it. She already knew it.

Before my mind could stop it, my mouth did say, "Did he ever talk to you about his ghost?" To my relief she laughed.

"Andre? Oh, my, yes. How did you hear about Jimmy's little joke?" She waved the question away. "No, I already know…it's a small town."

"Yes, it is."

She leaned forward, her face close to my chest. "I see you've been to in the attic. I remember that brooch. Your uncle bought it for your mother. It never seemed her taste though."

"You knew Jimmy put our stuff up there?"

"He told me once that all memories had been packed away. He seemed lonelier after the two of you left. Although, he'd never have admitted it."

Mindful of Andre waiting, I said goodbye, and promised to come back for a longer visit.

"I don't get out much." She tapped her glasses. "They took my license away a long time ago. I get to church on Sundays, but that's about it. So I always love visitors." She didn't invite me to bring Mom. Loneliness could be preferable over some disasters.

I repeated my promise and left. Going through the gate, I laughed out loud at the thought of Anna coming home one day and finding me there.

"Glad you're in a good mood." I stopped with my hand on the door handle and gawked into the car. Andre sat in the passenger's seat. "Can you please get in?" I clambored behind the wheel. "Don't you dare," he warned when I went for the ignition. "Here, do something productive with your hands." He shoved a photo album in them.

"Where did you get this?"

"Anna's room."

It was a scrapbook. "I'm not all that interested in her life story. By the way, she always wears pearls, and the earring isn't hers."

"Open the book." He didn't wait, but reached over and opened it for me. His closeness brought awareness of things that weren't there. Like smell. How had Andre smelled in life? Had he worn aftershave? Or maybe after a long walk, a little sweaty…I caught myself before I actually sniffed his neck. Andre frowned. "Are you okay?"

"Yep. What's this?"

"A memorial to the St. George family." Copies of birth announcements, death notices, even baby pictures filled the pages.

"She's obsessed."

"It does seem like it," he agreed. "But why?"

"Maybe it's the family she wishes she were born into." The observation hit a little too close to home. I chewed my lip. "Maybe she was."

"You mean…"

"What if Buster wasn't the only child fathered out of wedlock?"

"That's jumping to a conclusion."

As we talked, I flipped pages. "Andre! Look! This is Anna's birth certificate." We bent over the book. "The father is listed as B. St. George."

"Barney St. George?"

"I bet so. I'd also bet the rest of the family doesn't know about this."

162

"What's her motive for keeping quiet?" he asked. "Revenge?"
We stared at each other.

"The will," I said.

"It has already proven to be a great blackmail tool."

"Charles insisted he didn't break into my house the first time."

"Could it have been a woman?"

I thought. "Yes. Definitely yes."

"Interesting."

"Why do you think Barney St. George acknowledged Buster, but not Anna?"

"I don't know. Maybe when Anna was born, his wife would have cared. And by the time Buster came along, she didn't. Or Barney had stopped caring how his wife reacted."

"Ouch, doesn't sound like a marriage made in heaven."

"More like a mess of a marriage held together by money," Andre guessed.

"It must have been hard on Anna to see Buster acknowledged when she wasn't." I handed the book back to him. "You'd better put it back." He took the book and faded. "Hey!"

Andre reappeared. "What?"

"How do you do that?" I asked.

"I thought we'd already gone over that."

"I mean, how do you make the book disappear too?"

"I just can."

"Well as long as you have a good explanation."

He grinned and vanished.

At this point no good could come from airing the family's dirty laundry. But I tucked the knowledge away for future use. Getting bored, I checked my watch and realized I'd been ditched. I spy a big fat chicken.

Pulling away from the curb, I realized I'd learned something else. My mother had moved us in, broke up whatever brewed between my uncle and Aunt Gleason, and then moved out again. Uncle Jimmy had lost everybody in his life. No wonder he'd been so bitter.

Since Andre had left without so much as a goodbye, I wasn't in any particular hurry to get home or share the rest of my plans with him. Sleuthing called. One stop had to do with the mystery. The other had nothing to do with Charles and Co. Something I didn't want my persnickety ghost to know anything about.

The St. George Community Library had been a bank in a former life. In this life, the old vault stored back issues of magazines. Offices off the main lobby had been repurposed as reading rooms. As much as I loved libraries, any library, this one didn't appear modern enough for what I wanted.

Then I spied them. Two computer monitors to the left of the main desk. A boy of about twelve or thirteen occupied one. A matronly woman typed away at the other.

The woman behind the desk gave me a friendly smile. "Hello. I don't believe I've seen you here before."

"No, it's my first time." I walked over to the desk. "I need to use a computer."

"There's a fifteen-minute time limit when others are waiting. Except for children doing school work. So it won't be long." The elderly lady stopped typing long enough to give me a dirty look. She'd probably been hoping for a long session. "While you're waiting," continued the helpful librarian, "would you like to fill out an application for a card?"

Although Uncle Jimmy's library probably had almost as many books in it, I took the form. Growing up, the library had been my refuge. Every town had one and it beat an apartment that never felt like home.

As I finished filling out the form, the lady behind the desk said, "Mrs. Whitley, I'm afraid your time is up."

"Let me log off," snapped the woman. She gathered her things and, with another withering glare in my direction, stomped off.

"Go ahead," the librarian told me. "You can get your card after you're done."

"Thanks."

Before getting to my real reason for coming, I typed in the URL for my friend's website. A yellow skeleton with a purple and pink checked heart background appeared on the screen. Princess Punk is what we'd called it. I'd designed the site and felt flattered that Wendy still used it. I also noticed the picture of us had been deleted. The new pictures were of her friends in Arkansas, including the yummy guy she'd written me about. I left the site without leaving Wendy a message. What would I say? Living in Ama now with a gorgeous guy. Too bad he's dead.

I loved creating websites. Unlike life, they could be anything. I'd never created one for myself, though. Instead I'd made them for temporary friends at different schools. It helped me fit in.

"Find something you really like to do," a school counselor once told me. Maybe she hadn't been an idiot after all. I remembered the Vo-Tech brochure. Didn't Vo-Tech have computer classes? But no use planning the future until I solved the problems of the present.

Back at the search engine I typed in "The Daily Oklahoman." Among the hundreds of other URLs that came up was a link for the "Oklahoma Electronic Archives." The smaller print said that I could see full-page replicas of the Oklahoman dating back to 1901. Exactly what I needed. Luck stayed with me. They were having a free preview.

I clicked the search engine and was asked to select a date. I knew it had been in the summer of 1923, but didn't have an exact date. So I put in the month of July and the year. Once they appeared, I typed "murders" in the search. You'd think a double poisoning would stand out, but I couldn't find it. Of course, it could also have been in June or August. I glanced at my watch. About seven minutes had passed. Although no one waited to use the computer, someone could walk in at any moment and my time would end. A thought struck my brain. Maybe I was a little off.

Had either Andre or Paul said Maria had been convicted of murder? Back at the search bar I typed in "Poisonings." Found it: Tragic Accident: Woman Accidentally Poisons Husband and Visiting Artist.On Thursday, July 19th, Maria Atkins called the local switchboard and told the operator, Anita Kellogg, that her husband appeared to have died and that another man was very ill. Miss Kellogg quickly informed the hospital and the authorities. By the time they arrived, both Mr. Paul Atkins and Andre Noel, a visiting artist, were dead. Mrs. Atkins, also ill, was taken to the hospital where she remained in guarded condition until this morning. It has been determined the culprit of the tragedy was a bad batch of mushrooms.

Under the article was a grainy picture of a dining room. The caption underneath said, 'Mr. Noel's work in progress'. I leaned forward until my nose almost bumped the screen. The original mural! As with its successor, it remained unfinished.

I leaned back. Nowadays, the police would have been suspicious of poisoned mushrooms, but not in the 1920s. Maria had gotten away with it. How had she felt about that?

"Isn't her time almost up?" a voice behind me demanded.

Mrs. Whitley stood at the front desk, unruffled. "She has a few more minutes," countered the librarian.

"I'm done." I escaped out of the archives, grabbed my purse and started toward the door.

"Wait." The librarian waved my card at me. "You'll want this."

"Yes I will. Thank you." I took the card and rushed out of the library. What had I accomplished? Nothing, except make the past more real to me.

Now to the other reason I hadn't gone home. I stuck my hand in my pocket and felt the hardness of the earring. It wasn't Anna's. Chloe's? My legs walked themselves to Ma and Pop's store. My first friendship in Ama was about to be very short-lived.

Chloe waved as I entered the store. Vera stood behind the second cash register. She winked and popped a bubble.

"I didn't know you worked here," I said.

"Gotta help with the rent," she replied.

Poor baby. Talk to me when you've helped push your car down a driveway at three in the morning so the landlord won't know your family was bailing on the rent. "Been there." She laughed.

"Here to buy more groceries?" Chloe put in.

"Actually I wondered if we could talk."

"Take a break," Vera said. "I'll yell if we get a crush."

"There are chairs in the back," Chloe said. She led between the aisles and through the swinging door that read "Keep Out, Employees

Only." We sat at a small lopsided table next to the vending machine between crates of canned peaches. "How's your ghost?" Chloe asked.

"He's fine." I couldn't wrap my tongue around the words, "did you break into my house", so I laid the earring on the table.

Her eyes widened. "Oh, Tessa, I'm so sorry." She said something else, but it was muffled because she'd buried her head in her hands.

"Yours?" She didn't look up, but nodded. "Did you lose it the night I moved in? The night you broke into my house?" My voice cracked at the end. Guess I wouldn't make it as a hard boiled interrogator.

Her head jerked. "What? No! I lost it right after your uncle died. You can't really think I broke in?"

I swallowed. What I thought and what I wanted to think warred in my brain. "Tell me what happened."

"You'll think I'm a dork."

"Better than a burglar."

"Yeah, guess so." She sniffed and wiped her eyes with the back of her hand. Her green mascara smeared, making her look both piti-ful and ready to join the circus. "A couple of days after your uncle died, Buster picked me up from cheerleading practice. I made a joke about wanting to see the haunted house and, on a dare, he took me. We didn't mean any harm. Really. The laundry room window was un-locked and we got in. All we did was wander around trying to scare each other. Really, that's all. When we reached the top of the stairs, Buster pretended to grab me. We play fought and that's when I lost my earring. I didn't discover it until too late to go back and get it. How did you know it was mine?"

"You knew about the mural room. When you came to the house, you mentioned the room with the painting in it."

"How did you know your Uncle Jimmy didn't show it to me?"

"My ghost told me."

She laughed, a bit shaky, but real. "Will you forgive me, Tessa? It was dumb, but we didn't mean anything by it. My aunt would kill me if she knew."

"I promise she won't learn about it from me."

Chloe touched the earring. "I guess I should thank you for returning it." She eyed me. "Am I still your first friend in Ama?"

"As long as you want to be."

She grabbed my arm. "Remember, if you ever need anything, just ask. I mean it. Anything!"

"I will." Okay, still over the top weird. I believed her. Still, I didn't ask her about the will.

"We need to get together and hang out," Chloe said.

"Sure."

"I mean it. You, me, Alec." She grinned.

Please don't blush! "Sounds nice."

"Hey, you don't have a boyfriend back home, do you?"

"Not really. Well, there is someone I've known for a long time. But we're not really together." After all, I'd known Andre since five years old. "It's complicated."

Chloe grinned. "I'll let Alec know he's got some competition."

Hadn't I told him I didn't have a boyfriend? "Uh, Chloe, why don't we keep that between the two of us?"

Her eyes widened, but she grinned. "You bet, Tessa. After all, we girls have to stick together." She went to wash her face and I left.

"Hey," Vera called as I came down the aisle, "come here."

Curious, I walked over to her register. "Chloe will be back out in a minute."

"Yeah, we've got a real rush going." She popped a bubble. "Chloe told me you're feeling like an outsider, which only makes sense because you are."

"Thanks for the pep talk."

"All I'm saying is that it's not always bad being an outsider. But you've got to do it by your own rules."

I studied her tattoos, particularly an angel with blood red wings. Interesting with her pearl earrings, plastic and fake, nothing like Anna's dainty ones. I liked Vera's better. "Thanks."

"Anytime."

Leaving, I felt I'd made my second friend in Ama. I'd also realized everyone had their own version of normal. And they didn't all include white picket fences. Something to think about. What better place for quiet contemplation than the cemetery?

Fifteen minutes later found me in my spot beside the fence. Maybe I should kick myself for not asking Chloe about the will, but I really didn't want to lose my first friend in Ama. And I really had started thinking of the cheerleader as a friend. A slight breeze rustled the plastic flowers on a nearby grave. The distraction sent my thoughts in another direction.

If I died, would I join Andre? I believed in heaven and hell and wasn't sure where ghosts fit into that. Did it make me a sinner for wanting to stay on earth with tall, dark and handsome? Did I need to die with business left undone? Maybe Andre was the business?

I'm a nut, I'm a nut, and I'm crazy…

I rummaged through my purse and found a pen and the back of an old receipt, the receipt for the gas at the beginning of the trip, so long ago in terms of my mental health.

What did I consider a normal life?

1. Not moving in the middle of the night to avoid paying rent
2. Having friends
3. A family

I'd found my place in Ama, Oklahoma and I intended to stay. I'd gained friends, well one friend, and maybe two if I counted Vera. Alec? Not sure how Alec counted. But in my mind, even with family skeletons and drama, he represented a normal life. The only family I claimed at the moment was Grandma Petey.

But, what about Andre? He didn't count. It tore my heart out to admit it. I had no future with Andre, normal or otherwise. The big girl part of me said, "Grow up." The little girl part wanted to cry.

"Why didn't you tell me you planned to talk to Chloe," Andre demanded.

"You left me," I reminded him. "At least now we know the earring wasn't a clue."

"Did you find out anything else?" He still sounded irritated.

"No." Anything I'd learned at the library didn't count.

He ran his fingers through his dark, wavy hair. Good thing I'd made the decision to just be friends or the gesture would have done all kinds of warm things to me. "This is getting really dangerous."

"Getting?" I tried for levity. "That train pulled out of the station a long time ago."

He glared. "Not funny." He left the living room to stir the soup.

As a ghost he couldn't report the whole mess to Chief Mason himself. Relieved, I pulled the afghan up to my chin. Knowing Aunt Gleason had crocheted it, made the throw even more snuggly. The mail lay on the side table along with a copy of the Ama Review. I picked it up and read the headline: Man Killed in Late Night Hit and Run.An unknown vehicle had hit a man walking along Waterloo Road about midnight. A farmer and his family heading into town had found the victim early in the morning. A picture showed him standing next to a pickup bed filled with offspring. A caption underneath read "Scared the kids to death." The article read, "We found him lying there

170

in the ditch. My wife saw him and screamed, Stop, Freddie! I thought it might be an injured dog. She's always taking care of strays."

But it hadn't been a dog. It had been a man. Leafing through the rest of the paper, I wondered, a little uncharitably, if the dead man had been sober. Then I saw it. "POLICE CHIEF'S REPORT: A green Chevy was towed from a no parking zone around 3:00 a.m. in the morning."

The hit and run had occurred on Waterloo Road. My road! "Andre," I yelled. "You have to get me into the morgue."

Andre paced from one side of the room to the other, pausing occasionally to run his fingers through his hair. A scowl covered his face. Paul, who'd joined us mid-argument, leaned against the fireplace, an amused expression on his features. Me? I strove to give the impression of innocence.

Paul rattled his glass and moved to stand in front of our agitated friend. "She's right, you know." Andre stopped and glared. What would have happened if he'd kept going? Would they have passed benignly through each other? Or would electrical charges have started a chain reaction that could have burned the house down?

"Don't glare at Paul like that. It's me you're mad at," I said. So Andre stopped glaring at Paul and glared at me. "Is it so crazy?" I asked.

"Yes," Paul said.

"I wasn't asking you," I snapped.

He made a wobbly bow. "A gentleman always answers a lady."

Andre snorted. His brown eyes, gone from milk chocolate to semi-sweet, remained on me. "It is crazy," he said softly.

The softness told me I'd started winning. "I have to know if it's Mr. Dockins."

"The detective that found you?" Paul asked.

"Yes."

"You could ask the Police Chief," Andre said.

"And say what? That I read the man's car had been abandoned and assumed he'd been murdered?"

"No, you could say you know he drives a green Chevy and were concerned when you saw one had been abandoned."

I took a deep breath. "I think Mr. Dockins was talking to Anna on the phone at the convenience store. And we know from the conversation I overheard that he was blackmailing both her and Charles."

Andre's eyes narrowed. "So?"

"Maybe one of them got tired of being blackmailed."

"So Anna ran him down?" Andre asked.

"I don't know." Could Snotty Gleason be a killer? "It could have been Charles." But of the two, I knew who I put my money on for cold blooded homicide.

"You should talk to the police."

I folded my arms. "Not yet."

He folded his.

"Now, now, kiddos, how about a compromise?" Paul said. "Let's go talk to the Police Chief, or at least Tessa can." He raised a hand to ward off my protest. "It is the more practical thing to do. But..." he waved a chubby finger in Andre's direction, "...if for some reason we can't report it, it won't hurt to have a peek around the morgue. After all, I can understand why she doesn't want to wait until the next edition to find out if the dearly departed is her Mr. Dockins." Well, he wasn't exactly my Mr. Dockins, but I wouldn't nit-pick.

My housemate looked like he wanted to chuck both of us out. Then he shrugged those gorgeous shoulders. "At least if you get arrested for breaking and entering, I'll know you're safe in jail." I threw a pillow which flew right through him and hit the fireplace. But I felt better.

Andre set out on his own for the Police Chief's office, but to my delight, Paul rode with me. "I don't understand his fear of cars," I said, navigating the driveway.

"I think he must have been dropped out of one when he was a baby," Paul replied. He took a long sip and then gazed out the window. "I, however, used to love driving my Packard. One of the original Sunday drivers, I'd take her into the country and open her up."

"Wow. What happened to her?"

"My wife drove her into a pond."

"Ouch."

"My feelings exactly. Has Andre started painting again?"

"As far as I know, he hasn't even gone back into the mural room."

"Pity."

"I agree."

"So what are we going to do if this is your Mr. Dockins?"

"I don't know. But I can't believe his death isn't connected to all the other weird happenings."

"Maybe it was an accident?"

I kept one hand on the wheel and ticked off points with the other. "He ran from me. He died on the road to my house. And, he started this whole mess, at least for me."

"If it's him."

"If it's him."

Paul craned his neck. "Where do you suppose they found the gentleman?"

In spite of a shudder, my eyes scanned the passing scenery. We could see better in the daylight. What did I expect? Splashes of blood on flattened leaves? Or maybe skid marks where the car had bounced him off its hood? Like all respectable small towns, Ama locked its doors around 5:00 p.m. Even the Ma and Pop's had closed.

I pulled into a space in front of the Police Chief's office and got out of the car. Paul rose out of his seat and sailed through the roof. It didn't appear as strange to me as it once would have. Andre met us on the porch. He pointed to a sign on the door. *"Police Chief at Bingo. In an emergency you can reach Deputy Geller at 555-6707. Or, if you really need to speak with Chief Mason, you can find her at St. Matthew's."*

I hadn't pegged the Chief as a bingo player. But I'd accompanied my mother to bingo often enough to know you don't interrupt a player without a good reason. I wasn't about to disrupt her to appear nosey, or worse, guilty. "Okay, now we get to do it my way."

"Why not call the deputy?" Andre asked.

"That wasn't the deal. Now, we need to find the morgue."

Andre stuffed his hands in his pockets. "There isn't one. After a doctor examines the body, The Eternal Rest Funeral Home takes it." He pointed across the street.

"Is it where they took Uncle Jimmy?" I asked.

"Yes."

"Do you want to wait?"

"No."

I recommend taking a ghost to your next break-in. Andre walked through the door, unlocked it, and opened it for me. I didn't have to touch a thing. Inside, we stood at the end of a long hall. I shivered. Being in a place where the only other people there have

173

already met their maker is not my idea of fun. "I can't see a thing," I whispered.

Andre took my hand. "One thing ghosts are good for is seeing in the dark."

Oh please don't let me run into someone's coffin! We inched forward. An unpleasant odor wafted in the air. "What's that smell?"

"Formaldehyde." Ugh. I tried breathing through my mouth, but the air had a funny taste. Andre reached forward and pushed aside a curtain. "This appears to be a viewing area." He stuck his head through the door. Pulling back, he said, "There are some tables in there."

Creepy crawlies. "Any occupied?"

"Don't seem to be."

"Okay, let's go in."

"There's a door on the other side." Still holding my hand, he led us.

I was wondering where Paul had gone when an icy finger ran down the back of my neck. "Boo!"

Andre's hand clamped over my mouth before the blood-curdling scream could escape. "Not funny," I gasped. "Not funny at all."

"It was from my vantage point," chuckled the unrepentant ghost.

Andre put an arm around me. "Are you okay?"

"Yes." I glared at Paul.

Andre moved his arm and started us forward again. At the door, my heart started its drum solo again. A note had been taped to the frosted glass. It read:

OFFICIAL POLICE BUSINESS

DO NOT ENTER

Andre turned the knob.

I saw Phillip Dockins for the third and last time.

I'm not one to throw up but, that night, the funeral home's bushes got something besides water. When I'd finished, the guys, who had discretely moved away, moved back to my side. "I want to go home," I said.

"I'll drive," Paul said.

I let him.

Once home, I headed for the stairs. "My head hurts, my knee hurts, and my stomach feels like someone punched it. I know it's relevant that someone killed him. It's even more relevant that he was killed on the road to my house. But all I want to do now is take a hot shower and go to sleep. We can talk in the morning." No one argued.

The next day found me worn out and confused. It didn't help that Andre had left to rest in that place he couldn't describe. Or maybe it did. My "let's be friends" pledge was a lot easier to keep when he wasn't around. I paced the downstairs twice and still couldn't sit. The rain had started again, thundering and lightening as if a war raged in the sky. Every creak made me jump. Okay, that scrape sounded suspiciously like a door being pushed open by a mass murderer! Knock it off, Tessa. You'll go nuts thinking every noise is the boogie man. Another scrape and I ran for the kitchen. "Andre!"

No answer. Thunder cracked overhead. Outside, the wind whipped the trees and the clouds gave the day the eerie feeling of dusk.Okay, much more of this and I'd give myself a heart attack. So, I decided to search the only place Andre and I hadn't torn apart yet—the basement.

A moment later, I stood in the small alcove between the kitchen and the unused dining room, staring down into the dark. What did I imagine waited for me? For starters, spiders with huge webs, woven in places designed to smack the face of the unwary. Be smart, girl! I hurried back and grabbed the flashlight from the utility drawer in the kitchen. The basement door creaked, a sound loud enough to wake the dead. However, all the dead around my house were nowhere to be found.

A set of wooden stairs greeted me. I felt for a light switch, found one and flipped it on. A bulb sputtered but came on. I'd need my flashlight for peeking into corners.

Rats! Basements always had rats, right? "Don't be such a baby," I scolded myself. The wooden railing looked splintery, so I hugged the stone wall. My heart be-bopped as I inched down, every horror movie I'd ever seen replaying in my mind. What if the door slammed shut? Or the light went out?

Rounding the last step, I got my first peek at the basement. Masses of jumble filled the place. Uncle Jimmy could have hidden an elephant down here and no one would have been the wiser. Apparently when he'd decided to discard something, he'd simply opened the basement door and tossed it down the stairs. Heaps of old clothes, empty cans and magazines scattered the floor. Along one wall, an old porch swing sagged. I inched around a dresser missing a drawer, ever on the lookout for spiders and rats.

How to find anything? Even a junk store wouldn't have wanted all this trash. Okay, be methodical. Start in one corner and work my way around. Overhead, thunder boomed. I swallowed my fear.

The deeper into the basement, stronger a wet, moldy smell grew. No wonder! A small window stuck half open. I buttoned my sweater and toed a pile of soaked clothes. Gross. This place was going to have to be fumigated. I reached up and tugged at the window. No use. I wiped the rainwater off my face and decided to forget it.

I had to find that stupid will or people would never stop breaking in. I kicked at the wet clothes with the toe of my tennis shoe. No paper in the pile. Next came some broken shelves, pushed against the far wall. The cardboard boxes shoved haphazardly on them might hold spiders, or forgotten knickknacks, or the will. Could it be that easy?

The damp cardboard ripped as I tugged. Great. The bottom would probably fall out of the box if I pulled it off the shelf. Reluctant to actually set my flashlight down, I propped it between my legs and used both hands, one underneath, to yank the box.

The sharp sound of glass falling against concrete stopped me. Stillness stretched across the basement. "Andre?" I whispered. A shuffling, then stillness.

I swallowed. "Who's there?" It wasn't so much a demand as a squeak.

Something arced through the air. A shoe? Someone was throwing shoes at me? The footwear caught the light and the bulb shattered. The room went from dusk to dead of night. I stumbled over the moldy clothes and into the corner. The silk string of a spider web brushed my cheek and I bit my lip to keep from crying out. Idiot! The big baddy is in front of you, not above you.

I pointed my flashlight across the room. Something bulky detached itself from the gloom. "Who are you?" I shouted. Hopefully the intruder would think the challenge came from bravery and not pure panic. The bulk kept his back to me as he shuffled toward the stairs. As he neared the bottom, he reached down and picked something up. Without turning he threw. A bottle smashed over my head.

I ducked into a fetal position, still clutching my flashlight. I wasn't going to be like one of those idiots in the movies who lost her flashlight only to be killed while frantically searching for it. No, I'd shine it right into my killer's eyes. I…the sound of the slamming door stopped my thoughts cold. I was alone.

Slowly I stood. On tiptoe I pushed my face close to the still half-open window and listened. Rain poured down my face and drenched me as I struggled to hear any sign that the bulk had left. Nothing. If he'd come in a car, it could be parked anywhere. The window faced the back of the house, so he could even be parked in my own front yard and I wouldn't know it. The sound of a scraping door replayed through my brain. Being right didn't feel so good at the moment.

I pushed away from the wall. Had the thief found what he'd wanted? "You've got to go upstairs," I whispered. Water dripped from my clothes and hair and I couldn't even make my arms work to wipe my face. Instead I held tight and shivered. "Move!" I told myself. But instead I backed into the corner and slid down until my butt hit the floor. I didn't want to play "find-the-clues" anymore. I didn't want to be a detective. Tears joined the rainwater. Andre would have to come find me.

He did.

I must have drifted off because one moment I huddled alone, and the next he bent over me. Without a word, he scooped me up. I leaned on his shoulder as we floated through the basement and up the stairs. At the door he didn't stop. I gasped as every molecule went weightless. Colors swirled and I felt a tug. Then we stood in the alcove. "You took me through the door," I gasped.

"Yes." He didn't ask me a single question until after he'd brought me a cup of hot tea. I didn't really like hot tea, but the cup felt warm

178

and firm in my hands. Andre put me on the couch, wet clothes and all. He wrapped me in the afghan, my hair held back by a towel. I knew I'd have to change my clothes at some point. But even in the familiar, safe living room I couldn't fight off the numbness of fear. I didn't even jump when the fireplace lit itself.

Andre sat beside me, his chocolate eyes worried. I tried a smile, but couldn't hold it. "What happened?" he asked.

"I went clue hunting."

"Without me?"

"Yeah, but I wasn't alone. I had company."

"What? Who?"

I explained. His confused frown changed to outrage.

"What are you thinking?" I asked.

"That this time you tell the police everything."

"No, not yet." I rushed on to quell his protest. "Andre, if I tell, I risk everything. No one but you will take my side. Mom can swoop in and grab me. She'd bully me into leaving. I really don't trust Charles St. George to protect my interests. His solution will be to rent my home right out from under me and you know Mom will take the check. Please." So close to having a real plan for my life—get my GED and look into doing something I liked, maybe even web design. No drifting anymore. I couldn't blow it all so close to my goal.

Andre shimmered solid. He reached out and pulled the towel from my hair. His lips brushed the top of my head and the world went spinning. "'I'm so sorry," he whispered. Good intentions flew out with the wind. Just kiss me and everything will be all right.

I leaned against his chest and pretended the cold in his arms came from being outside, not from being dead. "You don't have anything to be sorry for," I whispered back.

His arms tightened. "Yes I do." He released me. I would have hung on, but he went insubstantial, so in the end I found myself hugging myself. "I wasn't there for Jimmy and I haven't been there for you."

"You idiot," I said. "Oh, don't look insulted even though it's the truth. I'm surprised you don't have chains dragging off you like that ghost in 'A Christmas Carol.'"

"Tessa—"

"—Andre, you collect guilt like my mom collects rent notices. I'm not your personal responsibility. I don't expect you to hang around

179

me twenty-four hours a day like an otherworldly babysitter."

"Drink your tea," he said.

The hot tea helped the shakes. In spite of my declaration of independence, I asked Andre to walk me to my room. I needed a long soak in a hot bath. But, at the top of the stairs, my brain started working again. "Andre, what if he searched the house? I mean, I don't know how long he was here before I encountered him."

Were the clues still in the library? They were. But we'd left them lying in a stack, the first clue on top. They'd been scattered around the table. "Forget the bath," I ordered Andre. "Stay right outside my door while I change." I almost asked him to check under the bed, but pride kept me quiet. Before leaving the library, I grabbed the stack of clues. If people were going to insist on rummaging through my house, they needed to be in a safer place.

Once in my room, I yanked off my tee and stripped out of my soaked jeans in record time. I pulled on dry clothes, shoved the clues in my nightstand drawer then joined Andre in the hall.

Downstairs, he insisted on covering me with a blanket from the closet. He spread the afghan near the fireplace to dry. "I'm going to make you some more tea."

I felt a slight shift and Paul appeared beside me on the sofa. "Did you know your fish pond has been smashed?"

"What?" I threw off the blanket and rushed to the door. On the porch, I viewed the rubble. "I don't believe it." I stayed on the porch while Andre and Paul investigated. Squinting, I could see rain drops slashing through the both of them. "How come we didn't hear anything?" I asked when they rejoined me.

"The storm," Andre replied. "I think someone took a sledge hammer to the pond."

"Why?" I wailed. I leaned on the porch rail. "So much for watching the fish swim while eating strawberries. Wait!" A dim bulb in my brain suddenly glowed. *You shall know them by their fruits.* "Mom told me about the strawberries."

"You think she and Larry read the clues?" Andre asked. "And then busted up the pond trying to find the will?"

"It's a theory. Nothing's ever said the will is hidden inside the house. From overhearing Chloe and Buster, Mom knows something's here, something supposedly worth a great deal."

"Do you think she'd be smart enough to figure out strawberries by the fish pond from the clues?"

"Who knows? Maybe together she and Larry managed to have a complete thought. How long has it been since Jimmy kept fish in the pond?"

Andre shrugged. "Years. But I don't think he stopped because he buried something in it. He simply didn't want to mess with them anymore."

"But he still grew the strawberries?"

"They were wild strawberries. It's more that he never bothered to dig them out."

"The real question is," Paul said, "did your Mom and this Larry fellow find the will?"

"That is the question," Andre replied.

Very early the next morning, Andre tapped on my bedroom door. "Meet me in the kitchen," he called.

I pulled on some clothes and hurried downstairs. "If the house is on fire," I said around a yawn, "you should have just let me burn."

He didn't smile. "I didn't want you to get the heebie-jeebies if you couldn't find me later."

I stopped yawning and woke up fully. "Where are you going?"

"I want to have a search through Larry's van."

Okay, interesting. "Why?"

"Because I can't picture that flat tire carrying a sledge hammer into the Bed and Breakfast they're staying at."

"Couldn't he have gotten it from our garage?"

"I checked. There's an inch of dust on all the tools. Your mom and Larry had to have brought it with them."

"What are you going to do if you find a sledgehammer?" I don't know if a ghost can actually gnash his teeth, but Andre gave a pretty good impression.

"Let's just say when they check him into the loony bin yelling 'I've seen a ghost,' he won't be lying." He disappeared.

"Don't you dare take off without me," I yelled. No answer. "Andre?" Ding-dang it. I ran for my shoes and my car keys. He'd decided to go proactive and leave me out. NO WAY.

I fired up my bug and headed out the drive. He'd probably get to the B & B before me, but hopefully no bloodshed would have occurred. If we did find a sledgehammer in Larry's van, I wanted to be the one to swing it at his head.

Fifteen minutes later, I slowed to a stop in front of the B & B. Larry's van stood alone in the small parking lot. Except for the irate ghost next to it.

"Don't you be mad at me," I said jumping out of my car. "I'm mad at you."

He grinned. "Then we'll have to declare a truce."

"Sounds good to me. Have you found anything?"

"See for yourself." He reached his hand through the back door and pulled out a sledgehammer. Mud and pieces of stone from my fish pond covered it. "I think this is proof, don't you?" Andre said.

"Yes I do."

He hefted the sledgehammer in one hand. "What do you want to do with this?"

"If we take it, will it still be proof?"

"If it has his fingerprints on it."

"What about yours?" I asked.

He grinned. "Ghosts don't leave fingerprints."

I popped the trunk on my bug. Andre placed the sledgehammer inside. Then he disappeared.

"Hello, Tessa. What are you doing here? Ready to apologize for the way you treated your mother and me?"

I faced my stepfather. "I'm here on a treasure hunt."

"And have you found any?"

"Well, so far I've found a sledgehammer." His mouth opened, but no sound came out. "You and Mom read the clues after locking me in the basement."

"Your mom and I were on our own treasure hunt. We just needed you out of the way for a moment." He yanked open the back of his van. "Tessa, where's the sledgehammer?"

"Mom thought of the strawberries after reading the clues, didn't she?"

"Yes. Now about that hammer." He took a step closer.

A small current ripped through the air. In a moment my invisible force field would be between us.

No, Andre, this is my fight! I reached out and grabbed Larry by the shoulders. "Sorry to ruin your honeymoon." His eyes widened as my knee made contact. I put all the rage I'd built up in the last year into the move. Larry gasped, grabbed low and hit the ground. "Stay away from me," I told him. "Stay away."

The doorbell rang the next morning while I still decided whether to be awake or not. When it rang again, I muttered, "Andre, why don't you get that?" However, while he might do windows, he didn't do doors. I threw on my robe and hurried down the stairs. Chief Mason towered in my doorway.

Had Larry called the police on me? "May I help you?" I croaked.

"I certainly hope so." She appeared to be waiting for something. Oh. Like the proverbial vampire, she wanted an invitation to enter.

"Come in." I followed her into my living room and waited for her to make herself at home on my couch.

"May I speak to your mother?"

"She's still—"

"—on her honeymoon?" I swallowed and nodded. "Then please, Miss Kelling, have a seat." I did, sitting as far away as possible. "As I'm sure you know, your mother enjoyed our hospitality for a night."

"Yes."

"And that she's been staying at the local B & B?"

"Yes, on her honeymoon."

She sighed. "It's your family, your business, Miss Kelling. But, you're underage, so I do have to ask. Do you want your mother here while I talk to you?"

Good grief, Larry did call the police! "No, I'm good."

She reached over and flicked the edge of the newspaper lying open on the coffee table. "I see you've read about our little hit and run?"

"Yes."

"We've identified the body as that of a Mr. Phillip Dockins. Mr. Dockins was a private detective. I believe you knew him."

"I met him once. He's the one who told me about my uncle's death."

"That's the only time you ever talked to him?"

I struggled to keep myself from squirming. "Yes."

"Then why would he run away from you?"

"Huh?"

"At the convenience store by the highway. The clerk says that Mr. Dockins used the phone, but ran away when you approached him. She says you were yelling something at him, but she didn't hear what. She didn't know your name, but I recognized your description and that of your car."

"I was yelling hello. I recognized him and wanted to thank him again for finding me. But we didn't talk."

"Why did he run?"

"I have no idea. Maybe it had something to do with his phone call, not with me."

"Lousy timing on your part?"

"I don't know what else it could be."

She wrote in her notebook. "The man got run over on a road that leads to your house. He left a perfectly fine running vehicle in town. And you have no idea why?"

"Chief Mason, the one time I talked to Mr. Dockins, he gave my mother and me the news of my uncle's death and the information on how to get in touch with my uncle's lawyer, Charles St. George. That's the only contact I've had with him." I decided to take a chance. "You don't think he was hit by accident?"

She gave me a sharp look. "Why do you say that?"

"Because he had a perfectly fine running car, and he was on foot in the middle of the country."

Chief Mason might have wanted information from me, but had no intention of giving any out herself. She stood. "May I see your car, Miss Kelling?"

I also stood. "My car?"

"Yes, please."

"It's parked at the side of the house. I'll…"

"I can find it."

"Yes, ma'am." I saw her out and then hurried to the kitchen where one of the windows overlooked the side yard.

"She thinks maybe you're the one who hit him."

I didn't even turn at the sound of his voice. "I know." We watched the chief walk around my car, paying particular attention to the front, right bumper. "She can see that it hasn't been in an accident," I said. Chief Mason closed her notebook and started for her truck.

"Andre, I've never been suspected of killing someone before."

"New experiences are growing experiences." I didn't know whether to hit him or cry. My dreams of a normal life seemed to be fading along with Chief Mason's trust in me. Not that she'd had that much to begin with. "You should have told her everything."

The sun chose that moment to shine bright and with the light come renewed determination to solve the mystery on my own. "Let's hunt for clues."

This had to be the last one. Maybe because of the old adage that trouble came in threes. We searched the kitchen even though Andre insisted the will couldn't be hidden there. He was right. Nothing stuck behind the alphabetized spice rack. Nothing taped to the back of the fridge.

Not wanting to miss anything, we even trudged back to the attic, this time taking a flashlight for the descent. During the search, I tripped over a grimy painting of a bowl of fruit.

"'You shall know them by their fruits,'" I quoted. Andre watched as I cut the back off the painting. Nothing. I felt along the frame to make sure something hadn't been sealed under the varnish. Nothing. Remembering the rose in the stained glass, I even scraped at the fruit in the bowl and found nothing.

"I do believe," Andre said, "that there is nothing here to find." I tromped downstairs covered in spider webs and a black mood. "Go work on your room," Andre ordered. "Pretend none of this is happening for at least one hour." I escaped upstairs, glad to put the whole mess behind me.

Entering my room, the first thing I spotted was Wally sitting on my bed, washed and mended. "Thank you," I shouted.

"You're welcome," Andre shouted back.

I placed Wally back on the bed and studied the yellow paint sitting in the corner. It would have to sit a little while longer because I wasn't in the mood to mess with it. Instead, I picked up Haunted Mesa and curled on the bed beside Wally.

Later, I wandered downstairs. Outside the bay window, a truck crept up the drive. For an isolated spot, my house sure got a lot of traffic. Had the Avon lady found me? Buster's truck stopped a few feet from my front door.

"Hi!" Chloe bounced out of the truck and trotted over to greet me, engulfing in a warm hug. Buster climbed out behind her.

I smiled. "Hello."

He smiled back and it went clear to his blue eyes. "Hi ya." Definitely a family resemblance to another pair of blue eyes. Oh Lord, don't let the burglar be Buster!

"Sorry to drop in again without calling," Chloe said as she released me, "but you still haven't gotten a phone."

"Soon as Mom gets back from her honeymoon," I replied.

Buster eyed my house. "Needs a lot of work, huh?"

I studied my cherished home through his eyes. The moulding needed painting and the porch rails had split in places. I closed my eyes and when I reopened them, I saw my dream. The perfect, soon to be vine-covered, cottage. "Want to come inside?" I asked.

"Actually," Chloe replied with a grin, "we're kidnapping you."

"What?"

By then, each had an arm and propelled me toward the truck. I hadn't even had a chance to say good-bye to Andre. My eyes searched the bay window. From behind it, he blew me a kiss.

Chloe pulled. "Don't worry, your house will be here when you get back." Buster opened the back door to the SUV. "Climb in," Chloe ordered.

"Where are we going?" I asked, sliding across the seat.

"You'll see." She had her phone out, madly texting.

"Who are you texting?"

"You'll see." Buster opened the driver's door and Chloe climbed in, crawling across to the passenger's seat. He hopped in behind her and started the SUV.

"Chloe, I don't even have my purse."

"So? You're not driving and I'm not taking you shopping."

Buster grinned at me as we pulled out of the drive. Chloe finished another round of texting and then turned in her seat with a big smile. "Don't worry, this kidnapping isn't long term. Just long enough to have fun."

Fun? Like anyone else with friends.

"So, how's your ghost?" Chloe asked, still hanging over the backseat. Andre's kiss on the cheek must have convinced her that he was a good guy.

"He's fine. He fixed my teddy bear."

She stared at me openmouthed and then giggled. "How handy."

"He certainly is."

Buster snorted, but we both ignored him.

"Have you heard the latest?" Chloe asked. "You haven't already, have you?"

"I don't think so. Mom and I aren't on any of the grapevines yet."

"Well, I know my aunt talked to you about Mr. Dockins." Actually auntie had grilled me. "Well, they've found out that he had a lot of gambling debts. I mean a lot!"

"Your aunt must be chatty around the dinner table."

She didn't even blush. "I sometimes hear things. My aunt has a tendency to talk loud when she's on the phone. Anyway, they've pretty much decided that someone he owed money to bumped him off." She leaned in, her voice lowering to a whisper. "They said he was running when he got hit."

"And "they" don't believe he was out for a late night jog."

She laughed and slapped my leg. "Right. They think someone drove him to that spot, made him get out and then chased him down." She grabbed her arms and shivered. "What an awful way to go. My aunt says they probably chose your road because it's so isolated and so few cars come down it."

"Wonderful."

Her eyes widened as she clasped her hands over her mouth. "Oh, I'm so sorry. I'm sure you're safe."

"As long as I don't owe any huge gambling debts?"

She giggled. "Right."

Buster cleared his throat. "Uh, Tessa, Chloe said she told you about us checking your house out after Jimmy died."

"Yeah."

"No hard feelings? I mean, she was such a 'fraidy cat that I couldn't even get her past the bottom of the stairs. Can you believe it?"

"No hard feelings." Couldn't even get her past the bottom of the stairs? Chloe had lied again. She hadn't seen the mural room with Buster. I took that information and locked it away in my brain. Today would be about fun. And no clues, ghosts or slightly absentee mothers were going to spoil it.

We entered town. Before long, I realized we were headed toward Alec's house. My heart sped up a couple of notches. Alec stood in the doorway, a loopy grin covering his face. "Hey," he said as I climbed out of the SUV.

"Hey," I said back.

Chloe pounded up the steps. "What did you rent?" she asked.

"Zombie 16."

She sighed. "I said get something romantic."

"As in chick flick? No thanks!" We filed inside. As I walked past, Alec smiled again. "Hope you like popcorn, 'cause I made plenty."

"Good grief," Chloe exclaimed when she spied the huge bowl sitting on the coffee table. "How much do you think we eat?"

"Didn't want to run out," Alec mumbled.

"Put the movie in," Chloe ordered Buster. "You two can sit on the couch," she said.

Awkward.

Buster settled into the oversized easy chair pulling Chloe down with him. She snuggled in with a sigh. Double awkward. "Do you two plan to sit?" Buster asked. "Or are you going to stand for the entire movie?"

Nervous, I plopped right in the middle of the couch. When Alec sat, his left leg brushed mine. I scooted.

Buster laughed. "Did you bite her?" Chloe playfully slapped him.

Alec grabbed some popcorn. The movie started. Alec and I sat on the opposite sides of the couch. He made it a little less awkward by putting the bowl of popcorn between us. About halfway through, Chloe and Buster apparently got bored. I glanced and there were no eyes on the screen. Great.

Something whizzed past. Buster yelped as a piece of popcorn bopped him in the head. Alec grinned and tossed a handful in his mouth. Buster reached across me and grabbed a handful of popcorn, but Chloe grabbed his hand before he could unload. "Stop acting like three-year-olds," she ordered.

"He started it," Buster whined.

Alec snorted. "Just trying to make some entertainment for Tessa and me. It's either watch you or the movie and to be honest, both are boring."

Chloe bounced off Buster's lap. "It's not like we don't know the ending," she said. "The guy they abandoned to die in the lake, is the guy drowning everyone. The brunette is the one who is going to survive 'cause she's not the slut."

"What do you suggest doing instead?" Buster said.

Alec stretched and stood. "Tessa, want to go for a walk?"

Buster groaned. "You've got to be kidding."

"You're not invited." Alec looked cute standing there with his hands shoved in his pockets. "Tessa?"

"Sure." I didn't even bother to check and see if Chloe minded that we ditched her. After all, this had been the whole point of the "kidnapping."

Outside Alec shrugged. "Sorry about that."

I laughed. "Don't worry about me. I'm having fun. You know, I forget that you and Buster are cousins. You act more like brothers."

"Oh great. Me and Casanova. Yeah, thanks."

I laughed again. It felt good and normal. Getting together with friends to watch movies, talk and have fun. The life I wanted. Then I realized how much I missed my ghost.

"You okay?"

I'd not only paused in the middle of my thoughts, but also in the middle of the road. "Yeah, just thinking."

He took my hand. His fingers felt warm, alive. "Want to share?"

"You're lucky to have so much family. It's always just been me and Mom."

He got a funny look in his eyes. "Believe me, the more family, the crazier."

"I don't think anyone can outdo Mom for crazy," I said.

"You'd be surprised. Anyway, I guess you really understand what I was trying to tell you about Anna before."

What? Bubble burst as reality settled in.

"She's never really had any family either."

Actually, she's got yours only nobody knows it.

"It's not right," he said.

"Huh, what's not right?" I peeked back at the house. Watching Chloe and Buster grope or listening to Alec defend Snotty Gleason. Talk about a bad coin flip!

"That Anna is the outcast?"

I started paying attention. "What are you, her knight in shining armor?"

He grinned, but it didn't shine in his eyes. "Sorry. I'm being a jerk." Did Alec know Anna was family, his family? Or did he have a cougar crush? The street ended at a small stream.

"Beautiful!" I exclaimed. "And right in the middle of town. Wow, I wonder if I have a stream on my property." Good grief, I was babbling worse than a brook.

Alec faced me. He slipped one hand under my chin, bent to kiss me, and bumped my nose. Hard. He laughed. "Great! I'm so smooth."

"It's okay." So, standing by a stream, feeling like the only two people in the world, I kissed him.

The sound of a horn pulled us apart. Elma waved from the driveway. Her sour gaze told me she wasn't exactly ecstatic to see me with her baby boy.

"Sorry, I've got to go see what she wants," Alec said.

"No problem."

Elma didn't look any happier up close. "Hello, Tessa. Alec, did you forget you're supposed to pick up your dad from the hospital? His car is in the shop."

Alec slapped his forehead. "Sorry, Mom, I'm on my way. Uh, Tessa..."

"I assume Tessa came with Buster and Chloe? They can take her home." She smiled at me. "I'm sure Tessa understands."

"Sure." I did understand. I was so far on the wrong side of the tracks that the train didn't run to my neighborhood anymore. Definitely not the kind of girl she wanted her baby boy hanging around.

"Let me take the basement," Andre said.

"No." I pushed myself off the couch. He tilted his head to one side. Was there anything that ghost did that didn't come off as sexy?

"Are you sure? You've been quiet since coming back from Willard's."

"Tired I guess." I headed for the dining room. Okay, Tessa, stop feeling guilty. You can't cheat on a ghost. "Chloe lied again," I told him. "Buster said they teased around downstairs, but she refused to go upstairs with him. So she didn't see the mural then."

"So we can't cross her off our list?"

It killed me to say it. "No, we can't."

In the basement, Andre replaced the bulb and wrestled the window shut. I peeked. Yep, definitely some ectoplasmic muscles showing under his sleeves. The thought of the pressure of his lips came swooshing back and suddenly the basement felt way crowded. "How do you think we should start?"

I blinked. "Beg your pardon."

He frowned. "I said, how do you think we should start?"

With me not touching anything wet, moldy or spider infested. "I guess we should start in one corner and work our way around. Then we can tackle the middle."

"Sounds good. I'm not too keen on staying down here any longer than I have to."

"At least you can't smell the place." Stuffed nasal cavities would have been a blessing.

"I'm jake with that," he said.

"Remember," I warned, "we're not cleaning. We're searching." He grinned. After a few minutes, I said, "I spy something disgusting."

"I'm afraid that gives me too many items from which to choose," Andre replied. "You've got to be a little more specific." I held out a jar of jam, a dirty red bow tied around the top. The contents had crystallized and molded. "He probably got it as a Christmas present and didn't like the flavor," Andre said.

"So instead of throwing it away, he tossed it down here?"

Andre shrugged. "My turn?"

"Sure."

"I spy something old."

"You've got to be kidding! That describes everything in this dungeon."

He motioned toward a cardboard box he'd been carefully rummaging through. I peered into the box and then stepped back with a groan. The last thing I'd ever wanted to see was Jimmy's old underwear, but there it was. "Okay, my Uncle gets his official hoarding badge." Two hours later, searched not only around the walls, but finished with the middle. "I think we can say we've definitely examined this place top to bottom," I said as I searched for spiders in my hair. "There's no will here."

"Agreed," Andre said. He looked me over. "I spy something that needs a bath." I sniffed my clothes. Gross! At least I hoped it was my clothes that reeked. He, of course, had not one hair out of place.

He waited until we'd reached the top of the stairs before disappearing to rest. Exhaustion weighed me down, or maybe it was the grime. But, I decided to go outside before going upstairs to soak. My lungs would thank me for the fresh air. Not to mention, my feelings about Andre and Alec had my head hurting.

Once outside, restlessness took over. I wandered out to the road and then down to the cemetery. I had no desire to roam through the headstones, especially with the sun touching the tops of the trees. Twilight in the graveyard didn't appeal to me. Unlike modern cemeteries, this one had gravestones as individual as the people who rested beneath them. Angels, Bible pages, even a gargoyle, represented those who had gone to meet God. Feeling slightly brave, I crossed the gravel road to read a stone carved in the shape of a heart.

194

She Sleeps Alone

Could be real sweet or a real burn, depending on how you took it.

A tingle crossed the back of my neck. The tingle didn't feel unearthly, so I peered around in the gathering gloom. A woman stood about ten feet away. She reached down and placed a pot of mums on a grave. Feeling intrusive, I backed away, right into the shallow ditch. My butt hit the ground before I could even yell.

The woman turned. Anna!

I swallowed and scurried to my feet. "Sorry."

"Come here," she ordered.

Resisting the urge to stick my tongue out, I grudgingly joined her.

She wrinkled her nose as I drew near. "Ewww, what happened to you? Did you take a bath in a dump?"

"Cleaning house," I replied.

A nasty glare crossed her face. "You were hunting for the will." Her voice cracked in a way that made me step back again.

"That's none of your business." Confirmation! She knew about the will. Did that let Chloe off the hook?

"It's my business when you start involving my aunt. How dare you visit her!" Eyes slightly too wide for the situation, Anna gestured to the grave at her feet. "This is my mother's. Do you plan to visit every woman in my family, dead or alive? Or are you stalking me?"

"Jimmy's buried here too." *Hope she doesn't ask me to point out his grave.*

Anna's fists curled. "Answer me! Why did you visit my aunt?"

Okay, the police could use her as bad cop any time. "I'd found an earring and thought it might be yours." The answer seemed to calm her.

She reached up and fingered an earlobe. "I always wear pearls."

"That's what your aunt said."

"Why don't you stop pestering everybody? Sell your house and go back to wherever. No one wants you here." *Stay away from us new girl.*

"I know about you," I said.

She frowned. "What?"

That's it, Tessa, rile the crazy woman. "I know you're the sister."

"You're nuts."

"Maybe, but Barney St. George was your father. And that gives you about the same motive as everyone else for killing my uncle."

"Your uncle died by accident."

I shook my head. "I don't think so."

A bit of fear, then anger burned in her eyes. "Dear Dad acknowledged Buster, but not me. And I came first! My father demanded Mom move to Oklahoma City where I was born. I couldn't visit my aunt without first getting his permission. Before my mother died, she made me promise not to ever tell the truth. Can you believe she loved that creep? I didn't ask his permission to bury her here, though. I didn't ask his permission to move back either."

"Did you break into my house the night I came to Ama? Were you trying to find the will?"

"You bet I did. After I moved back, I confronted dear old dad. He told me to be patient that he had plans. He had to have meant the will. He must have acknowledged me, left me something. If not...", her face twisted, "then I'll get what's mine another way. You were supposed to spend the night at the bed and breakfast."

I ignored the accusation in her voice. "Mr. Dockins was blackmailing you, wasn't he?"

"Yes. Charles and I made the mistake of trying to hire him to break into your house. He blackmailed us instead. Dockins said he'd tell you everything if I didn't pay him. You don't know how shocked I was to see you walk into the Cafe that morning."

"His way of telling you to shut up?"

"Yes." My nerve failed when it came to asking her if she knew what had really happened to the detective. Alone in the cemetery, with Anna, didn't seem the best place to get the information. She moved a couple of steps closer. "Have you found the will? Does it name me as Barney's daughter?"

"No, I mean, we haven't found it." The bravado I'd felt a few moments earlier completely melted away. "Sorry."

"I don't believe you!"

"What?" I backed away as she reached into her purse. A gun!

Dodging tombstones, I prayed I didn't break or tear anything. I really didn't want my tombstone to read "Found with Her Pants Split." I landed in the dirt. No dignity, but pants intact. One of my worst fears, the graveyard at night. But no ghosts danced into my line of vision. No unearthly howls grated across the night. Andre would probably be offended, but hey, it was only me and my imagination in the graveyard.

"Tessa!"

Oh yes, and a psycho. I sprinted toward the nearest trees, wishing they were a couple more inches round, or my butt was a couple less. I willed my breathing to slow down so I didn't gasp like a fish deprived of water.

"Tessa?" Anna's voice carried across the headstones. "You little idiot, I just wanted to scare you." Yeah right. The bad guy, or in this case gal, never let the witness go. Not in any movie I'd ever seen.

She picked her way back toward the trees. I got down on my hands and knees and scooted behind the nearest gravestone. Uncle Jimmy! I'd found his grave. An owl hooted. Anna ducked and peered around. So I wasn't the only one spooked by our surroundings. How could I use that to my advantage? I grabbed a handful of pebbles. It always worked on TV. I threw one. It landed to her right. She instantly whirled that way. I took the opportunity to scurry a little further away. My shoulder whacked a stone, but I kept going.

A pebble landed a few feet away from me. "I watch TV, too," Anna called out. I could hear her making her way across the grass.

I found myself beside a stone angel almost as tall as I was. Her stone skirt billowed out and around the headstone in front of her. I scooted under it. Crunch. Anna's footsteps sounded close. I pulled my knees to my chin and closed my eyes like a two year old who reasoned if I couldn't see the boogie woman, she couldn't see me. Something soft draped my cheek. My eyes opened to find a gauzy material enveloping me. I fought down panic. A voice in my head whispered, "Shhhh." I obeyed. Steps ran past me. I huddled, praying I wasn't trading for a worst disaster.

"Tessa?" Anna yelled. "Oh good grief, you are so not worth this. Listen, try telling this to Chief Mason and I'll deny it. She'll chalk it up to you being as loony as your uncle." Her steps crunched away.

Silence.

The wispy fabric drew back and only stone surrounded me. I took that to mean my enemy had gone away. Scrambling, I ran back to my side of the road. I turned. The angel stood upright and unyielding. "Thank you," I whispered.

I ran home where Andre met me on the porch. "Tomorrow," I promised. "Tomorrow I go to the police."

"What happened?" he demanded. I filled him in on my adventure with Anna, except for the angel. Not ready to talk about that experience, even with my resident paranormal expert. "You should have gone to the police a lot sooner," he accused.

I didn't know what to say. You're right? All the frustrations and guilt that had been pulling my emotions between Andre and Alec caught up to me. I burst into tears.

Andre's arms went around me. "It's going to be okay, Tessa, I promise. We'll figure out who's causing all this trouble. Then you can get your life back. You can be best friends with the cheerleader. You can go on dates at the local malt shop. That is, if they still have malt shops." His hand rubbed my back. "You can have the wonderful life you deserve. I promise." He bent forward, touching his forehead to mine. "After we solve this mess, I'm moving on. I'm not good for you." He disappeared.

My chest burned with the breath I held. I let it out with a long, scream. "No!"

Even knowing he'd probably gone where I couldn't follow, I still ran. A fingernail tore on the kitchen door. "Andre?" But no ghostly hands checked the meatloaf. The mural room! I shot out of the kitchen and hit the stairs at a run. "Andre!" On the third step I re-skinned my knee, but barely paused. If Alec had appeared at that moment with a wedding ring and asked me to marry him, I'd have shoved him aside. How could Andre think of leaving me? In the upper hall, I careened from wall to wall, finally barging into the mural room.

He appeared in front of the painting. "I thought I'd better come back before you really hurt yourself," he said.

"Go solid," I demanded. He did and I pounded his chest with both fists. "Don't you dare talk about leaving! I've spent my entire life wondering if I was crazy for believing in you." His arms held me. I shook with fear, frustration and plain anger. He kneaded my hair in a wild gesture that said this was hard for him too. Good.

"You need to go to school, have friends, date." he said.

I pulled away. His hands went insubstantial right before they yanked out a hunk of my hair. "Your guilt doesn't get to make my decisions," I yelled. "I decide what's normal for me!"

"I get to make decisions too," he said softly.

"Promise you won't leave?"

He doctored my knee and my finger, but he wouldn't promise.

Sometime around midnight, I dreamed. Strawberry vines covered my room, with big, red berries threatening to drop into my mouth and choke me. Vines crept along the sides of the bed, tightening around my arms. One thick vine wrapped around my neck and squeezed. I woke clawing and screaming.

The will! I knew where it was hidden!

I shot out of bed in search of Andre. Both the library and the mural room were empty. Back in the hall, my eyes fell on the mutilated rose in the stained glass. A blood red rose. Blood on the blades of grass. Jimmy was dead. Mr. Dockins was dead. A shiver started at my toes and ended at the top of my head. Was I next?

Then anger boiled through me. I'd fight for my home. Mom couldn't snatch it away from me. No intruder would scare me from it. And even if Andre abandoned me, I'd still keep my house. "Andre!" I shouted.

At the top of the stairs, I paused and sniffed the air. I knew that scent. A hand shoved me from behind. I tumbled headfirst down the dark stairwell. Grabbing and clawing, I almost stopped my fall at the landing, but the hand pushed me again. My arm cracked hard on the wood. I hit my head and knew nothing else.

I woke in Andre's arms. "This time you go to the hospital," he said.

"Did you see …?" I tried to ask.

"No one's here," he said. He picked me up and carried me toward the front door. Someday, I'd have to get the boy to pick me up when I wasn't hurt.

My arm and my head competed for attention. "Wait. How are you planning to get me there if we can't call an ambulance?"

"I'm going to fly you."

"No," I wiggled in his arms. I stopped when he adjusted his hold to keep from dropping me. "You've got to drive me."

"I can't drive."

"You'll have to. I'm afraid to fly." Injured, I won.

Andre deposited me into the passenger seat of the bug, not an easy thing to do considering its size. The door shut and a moment later the driver's side opened. It stayed open. Perhaps he contemplated learning to drive after seventy years? Maybe he'd simply shrugged his invisible shoulders and left? The driver's seat shot back. I would have giggled if a sharp pain hadn't shot through my arm about then. I guess even ghostly long legs had to have room.

"What next?" he asked.

I tried to remember the rules to starting a car. Luckily my bug was an automatic. "Turn the headlights on." He found them with only a little fumbling. "Now, put the key into the ignition. No, that's the house key. It's the other one." I sensed his frustration. "Okay, that's great. Now, put your foot on the brake, no that's the gas." A wave of nausea hit me when I tried to point. I gasped.

"Are you alright?"

"Yeah." I swallowed hard. "Okay, left is brake and right is gas." By some miracle the car got started. I explained the gearshift and watched as it moved by itself to DRIVE. "Wait!"

"What?"

"Before we start," I whispered, "I need to see you. I know it's a lot to ask with all the concentrating you're doing, but please?" He materialized beside me, the strain written on his face. He sat in that still way of his, waiting. "I don't suppose you could drive the whole way like that?" He shook his head. I sighed. "Okay, just thought I'd ask."

"It would be so much easier if you'd let me fly you."

Up off the ground without even a plane under me, my already queasy stomach flipped at the thought. "No thank you."

He sighed. "As you wish." He disappeared again. The car crept forward and I could see the pedals moving, but the steering wheel wasn't turning.

"Andre, you'll have to turn the wheel or we'll drive into that clump of trees." The wheel jerked too far. We left the driveway and bounced along toward the rubble that had been my pond. Before I could mention this, the wheel jerked back. We sort of headed for the drive, reached the gravel, jerked to the left, and came to a jolting stop.

Except for the motor, there was silence. Somehow I didn't think it would help Andre's confidence to hear me shouting, "Lord, please don't let me die!" After a moment, the car inched forward again. Bit, by agonizing bit, we made our way down the driveway.

I bit my lip and tasted blood as we bumped along. I could see the main road ahead. "Remember," I cautioned, "if another car comes along, you need to become visible until they're out of sight." I decided to ignore his nasty reply.

He managed to turn out onto the road without putting us into the ditch. Unfortunately, we were headed in the wrong direction. "Ama is to the east," I snapped. "You've been there."

"Not driving, I haven't," he growled back.

The next few moments of getting Andre through the mechanics of turning the car around were some of the most hair-raising I've ever had, but we finally headed in the right direction. Again, we moved forward inch by inch.

"Uh, could you go a bit faster?" I ventured.

His reply was really hostile, but the car picked up speed. We weaved at each curve in the road, which, no matter how mild, caused him to slow down to a turtle's pace. But I didn't complain. In fact, after a couple of miles, I even relaxed.

Then a dog came out of nowhere. He blinked in our headlights then raced back to his side of the road. Andre jerked the bug the other way and found a barbed wire fence coming up fast. I screamed. The jostling of my arm, and the panic of near death, caused a good, loud scream.

The car stopped. My head snapped forward and then back. The driver's door opened and closed. My door opened and Andre appeared. "I'm sorry, Tessa." He disappeared and my seatbelt unhooked itself. He lifted me into invisible arms.

"Andre, don't do this," I begged. Cradled close to a firm, but invisible chest, I left the ground. Tears stung my eyes. I couldn't do this. I couldn't fly. I threw up.

I hoped I hit him.

Chief Mason frowned from the chair beside my hospital bed. "How did you say you got to the hospital, Miss Kelling?"

"I drove part of the way, until I crashed my car, and then I walked." She stared at me. I tried on my best innocent expression. I won.

"We're hunting for Charles St. George and Anna Gleason. Of course, there's no proof either of them pushed you."

"They both admitted to breaking into my house."

"You mean to look for a will, that no one, including them, has seen?"

"Yes. But whether they've seen it or not, Charles and Anna believe it exists."

"True enough." She stood. "At this point, we don't know if your uncle was pushed, but I admit, your story has me wondering. However, we're concentrating on who pushed you now. I wish you'd told me about the second break in."

"I should have." I don't think that really satisfied her.

She shook her head. "So, Anna is old Barney's daughter? I don't suppose you know what kind of gun she had."

"No."

"Get some rest."

"I have no choice." And I didn't. A bad sprain and a slight concussion had made the attending physician decide to keep me overnight.

Chief Mason turned to someone standing behind her. "Nice you could come and admit your daughter into the hospital, Mrs. Kelling."

Mom started to protest, but something in the police chief's eyes must have told her to shut up. I needed to learn that trick.

"How did you manage to come in time?" I asked after the Chief left.

Mom's hand went to her collar and then back to her side. "The police chief banged the door down. She was very rude. I have the feeling the owner of the B & B is going to ask us to leave."

"How's Larry doing? Still using ice packs?"

"You really hurt him, Tessa!"

"You guys broke into my house."

"It doesn't work with you and me, does it, baby?" Were those tears in her eyes?

"No, Mom, it never seems too."

"You need to rest. I'll be back to see you later." Boy, talk about your threats.

I leaned forward and grabbed her arm. "Mom, I meant every word I said the night I bailed you out of jail. Keep Larry away from me. If you won't come without Larry, then I want you to give Chloe permission to take me home tomorrow."

She yanked her arm away. "Chloe? Who's Chloe?"

"The police chief's niece."

Her hands bunched the covers as they tightened. "Who's going to take care of you after you get home?"

"Grandma will come if I need her."

"Have it your way, then." She released the covers, straightened her collar and walked away. Neither of us said good-bye.

Grateful to see the door shut behind her, I tried to get comfortable. It wasn't easy. I hated sleeping on my back. Besides, I should be remembering something. Something just before I fell.

Andre materialized next to me.

"I'm going to be okay," I told him.

"I know. I listened in."

"There's something I should be remembering."

"Maybe you got a glimpse of who pushed you?"

"No." I remembered not to shake my head.

"Well, don't worry, it'll come. Are you okay otherwise?"

A knock at the door and then Chloe stuck her head around

the corner. "Hi. Are you ready for some company?" Andre had already faded.

I smiled and told her to come in. Buster trailed behind her. Alec wasn't with them. The wave of relief surprised me. His threat to leave made me realize, ghost or not, Andre fit my normal. It was simple as that.

Chloe hurried over to the bed, her tearful eyes and mournful expression making her look like she was attending my wake and not my sickbed. "Oh, Tessa, I can't believe someone pushed you down the stairs. Buster and I were at home with Aunt Josie when she got the call. We drove here with her, but she made us wait in the lounge until she'd finished talking to you."

"Thanks for coming."

She laughed. "Hey, I take being your first friend in Ama very seriously."

Buster moved closer. "I can't believe Charles is the one who did this to you."

"I don't think he was," I told him with all sincerity. No, it could have been your half-sister.

He shuffled his feet. "Mom said to tell you she sends her best." Very proper, no mention that someone in her family might have tried to kill me. Elma probably blamed me, after all, if I hadn't come to town …

"Thanks," I said. And Alec? In the end, my ghost, not my dream guy, came through for me.

Chloe squeezed her guy's arm. "We know you found Charles' glasses, and that he broke into your house."

"Really?"

Chloe blushed. "I listened at the door while my aunt talked on the phone to one of her deputies."

"So you know about…" I stopped and glanced at Buster.

"Yeah, we know what Anna claims." The bitterness in his voice made me leave the subject alone.

Chloe hugged herself and peered around the room. "Is your ghost here?" Buster rolled his eyes.

I laughed. "Chloe, I have a favor to ask you. Can you take me home tomorrow?"

She frowned. "Sure. But what about…"

"Mom said it's okay. She'll clear everything with the hospital."

"Then yeah, I'd love to be your chauffeur." She gave me a gentle hug. "I'll bring an overnight bag."

I had an ulterior motive for asking her, besides getting rid of Mom. "We never made it upstairs." That's what Buster had said.

They left and Andre reappeared. "You need to go to sleep now."

"You'll stay?"

"As long as you want me to."

"I think maybe your little kiss has given Chloe a crush on you. Should I be jealous?" My heart skipped a beat.

He didn't answer. Instead he bent and kissed me gently on the lips. Then, another kiss, and me too loopy to do a darn thing about it. Andre straightened and started toward the nearest chair.

"No." Without moving any of my injured parts too much, I managed to scoot over. "That's too far away. Sit with me."

Wearing a bemused expression, he sat on the bed, his shoulder touching mine on the pillow. He stretched his long legs and said, "If a nurse comes in, I'll fade away."

"Sounds good. Now, tell me a story."

"What do you want to hear?"

I took a chance. After all, I was all banged up so he couldn't get too mad at me. "What made you decide to become a painter?" I could tell the question took him by surprise.

At first I thought he wouldn't answer, but then he took my hand and gently rubbed it. "My mother's hands." I didn't say a word. In fact, I hardly breathed. "She was blind from birth. But she never let that keep her from enjoying life. In fact, my father said he first fell in love with her smile." He paused.

My curiosity wasn't a good enough reason to make him relive painful memories. "It's okay. You don't have to tell me."

Even in the half-light of the room, I could see his smile. "If you really want to hear a boring story, I think I'd like to tell it to you."

"I'd really like to hear it."

As he talked, he traced my fingers one by one. "My father worked long hours as a stone mason, so I grew up helping my mother. I helped her cook and clean, even garden. She loved putting her hands in the soil. She could identify a lot of flowers by their texture. A stone wall enclosed our backyard. You'd recognize it if you saw it since you've seen my poor rendition in my room. In the middle of the garden grew an apple tree. My father placed a picnic table near it, and when I was little, my mother would sit reading Braille books while I played. When she grew tired of reading, we'd play a game. She'd say, 'bring me something new.' I'd search the patio for something interesting to bring her. Sometimes it would be a leaf, an apple, a rock, or even a bug. She would take it in her hands, and we'd take turns describing it. She would say the shape. I would say the color. She'd describe the texture, and then I'd make up what I thought it could be used for. My poor dad had more rock paperweights."

He chuckled softly. "Even without sight, my mother saw beauty in everything. She especially loved paint, loved to swirl her hands in it. We spent a lot of hours at the picnic table painting. She'd ask me, 'What color is the sun?' I'd help her find the yellow. 'What shape is it?' I'd tell her. And together, we'd swirl the yellow in a circle. Every time I paint, I remember her hand in mine." He stopped talking.

"How did your parents die, Andre?"

"In a car accident."

"I'm sorry."

"It happened a long time ago."

The medication was messing with my brain. I tried to make myself understood. "I mean I'm sorry about Jimmy."

"He was my best friend. I don't understand how he could have hurt so many people."

"I know."

"You need to rest."

I leaned my head on his shoulder and fell asleep, leaving the problem of what to do if a nurse entered the room to Andre.

I can say this for pain medication—it makes a lot of things better. I shifted in my bed, although I'd given up on being comfortable. Chloe immediately leaned forward and straightened my pillow. "Sorry to put you out," I told her for at least the fifth time.

"Are you kidding? I'm loving it." She clasped her hand over her mouth. "Oh, I didn't mean you getting hurt." She sat by my bed in a rocking chair Andre had carried from the front room before we'd arrived.

"I know. But it has been exciting hasn't? Besides, I'm not feeling much pain at the moment." I'm not ashamed to admit it. We giggled.

Chloe and I were alone in the house. The long arm of the law hadn't managed to snag Charles or Anna yet. The police were being unknowingly aided by a very angry ghost. Paul had gone with Andre to help. Knowing Paul, the help would be iffy at best.

Chloe frowned. "Buster'll be over after work. Until then, it's just you and me."

"What?"

"Uh, where did your mother go?"

"Back to Oklahoma City." I said it because I hoped it. There had been no sign of her or Larry when I got home.

"Oh."

"It's a long story. I'll tell it to you someday." My arm ached, which told me my pain medicine was wearing off. Good, I needed a clear head for this next part. "Chloe?" Something in my voice warned her. She stopped smiling. "Buster said you were so scared he couldn't even get you to go up the stairs. You didn't see the mural room with him. When did you see it? Please tell me the truth." I half expected the tears again. But she held herself in a tight grip.

Her eyes dropped, but her voice stayed steady. "I came once by myself to talk to your Uncle Jimmy. He let me in. But when he found out I wanted to talk about the will, about what his joke was doing to Buster and his family, he ordered me out. He stormed upstairs, and I stood in the foyer not knowing what to do."

"Not knowing whether to follow your butt or your head," I said softly.

She looked confused and then grinned. "Yeah, something like that. Anyway, I decided to follow him, to try and make him listen. I found the mural room while searching for Jimmy." She stopped.

"How did you know about the will?" I asked.

"I overheard Anna and Charles talking. I'd stopped in at his office to use the bathroom. No one was out front, so I went in. When I came out I heard them talking in his office. They never knew I was there."

Someday, girl, you need to think about a job as a CIA agent. "Go on."

"Tessa, your uncle was tearing Buster's family apart. I only wanted to make him understand that."

"I know."

Her hands kneaded the bedspread as she talked. "Anyway, Jimmy found me standing in the hallway. He started screaming at me about trespassing and how he'd tell my aunt what a little sneak thief her niece was. I shouted back that I'd tell her what a blackmailer he was. At the top of the stairs…"

"Go on."

Now the tears came. "I didn't push him, Tessa. You've got to believe me. He came charging after me, said I'd better keep my mouth shut. We struggled and he fell. I didn't push him! I pulled away and he lost his balance."

"I believe you." I did. "But why didn't you call anybody, or try to help Jimmy?"

"I did! I called Willard as soon as I got out of the house. Elma said he was already on his way."

Andre. Andre had found Jimmy and fetched Willard. If only the ghost had known Chloe had called for help. Then he'd never have had to leave Jimmy, not even for an instant. And that also meant Willard knew how Jimmy had died. And he'd never told Andre.

I took a deep breath. "You've got to tell your aunt."

"Yeah." She wiped her nose with her sleeve. "I thought if I could make everything perfect for you here, be your best friend, then I could make up for the trouble I caused."

"We'll get this sorted out, I promise."

She shrugged. "Are you hungry? I'm hungry. I'm going to go fix us some lunch."

"There's chicken salad in the fridge." She practically flew out of the room. I didn't blame her.

Rest was all anybody wanted me to do. I had to admit, though, the pain pills helped in that endeavor. I clumsily got two more out of the bottle. My eyes closed. The feeling that I should be remembering something came back. But sleep overtook before I could capture the memory. I dreamed I heard shouting, and then someone playing drums out in the hallway. Then Anna stood over me. I fought, but I couldn't wake up.

When I did wake up, I had to pee. Getting up from the bed with my legs practically crossed took some doing. Half groggy, I opened the door to the bathroom across the hall and stopped. Someone already occupied it, although I didn't think they would mind my intrusion. My hands clamped to my mouth to stop the scream trying to issue from my throat.

Charles St. George lay dead in my bathtub, his necktie knotted tightly around his neck. Scuff marks on the side of the tub told me it hadn't been drums in my dreams. Leaning against the door jamb, I tried to breathe and the musk smell made me choke. And that made me remember. Remember the smell of musk just before I was pushed.

I stumbled back to my room. Anna and her gun waited there for me. She motioned with it and I eased onto the bed. "You pushed me," I whispered.

"Yes, I did," she said. "Not," she added with a dreamy smile, "that you had the decency to die like your uncle did. How did you figure it out?

"I remembered your perfume. You didn't wear it when you broke in."

"When I broke in, I didn't want to be caught." She shrugged. "You were supposed to die when I pushed you." She frowned. "Why are you wiggling like that?"

"I have to go to the bathroom."

Anna sighed and motioned with the gun. "Go on, we can't have you jumping up and down like a two year old." She marched me into the hall.

"Can I use the one downstairs?"

"No." She giggled again. "Say hi to Charles."

So, I ended up back in the room with the corpse. And from Anna's reaction, I knew who'd killed him. Averting my eyes, I did my business.

The lady holding the gun wasn't sane anymore.

Anna banged on the door. "Hurry, Tessa. We've got things to do."

Leaving the bathroom, I noticed the door to Jimmy's room stood cracked. Had Chloe hid in there? She should have been able to strangle the chicken, as well as spoon out chicken salad in the time she had been gone. I mentally crossed my fingers. Maybe she'd seen Anna come in with the gun and ducked out of sight?

"Sit," Anna ordered. I sat. Anna stayed near the doorway.

"You wanted the money bad enough to kill Charles?" I asked.

She snorted. "It's not about the money, you idiot. I told you, it's about dear old daddy acknowledging me!" She thumped her chest. "I'm Barney St. George's darling daughter and that will tells *everybody*."

"Why did Charles have to die?"

She sneered. "He's a wimp. After all the plotting, Charles developed a conscience. Would you believe he'd decided to go to the police after he confessed all to you?"

"Who killed Mr. Dockins?"

She smirked. "No one blackmails me and gets away with it. If that idiot had broken in when we asked him too, *before you arrived*, we'd have the will."

"But he blackmailed you instead. Then he found me, so it would be hard for you to break in. Not that it stopped either of you."

"Exactly. Dockins took money from Willard for finding you and then expected Charles and me to pay him to keep his mouth shut. But that's all old news." She held out the two clues, along with Uncle Jimmy's instructions. "I found these in the nightstand while you were sleeping. You really shouldn't leave important papers lying about. By the way, who's Andre?"

"I hope you get to meet him," I shot back. My head spun in slow circles, and I clung to the end of the bed. I realized all the drawers in my dresser had been pulled out, and my closet door stood wide open. How long had I lain asleep while Anna poked about?

"Tessa? You look a little loopy. Now, stay with me. We're going on a treasure hunt."

"May I put my robe on?" I asked.

She shrugged and didn't offer to help. I had to remove the unfamiliar sling, and gritted my teeth to keep from yelling as I slid my hurt arm through the sleeve. Her phone rang. She answered. "It's about time. We're upstairs." She ended her call and turned her attention back to me. I heard footsteps running on the stairs, and then Alec stood in the doorway.

"What are you doing here?" I asked.

"Helping Anna. I'm the only one she trusted with her secret." His eyes pleaded. "Please, Tessa, no one has to get hurt. All we want to do is find the will. Anna deserves..." He caught sight of the gun. "Anna? What are you doing?"

"It's the only way I can get her to cooperate, Alec." She put an arm around him and squeezed. "We need her to help us find the will, to make things right."

"But..."

"Don't wimp out on me now, Alec." She pushed him aside and tossed the clues on the bed. "Which is the newest?"

I ignored her. "What was your part in this, Alec?"

He hung his head. "To get close to you, so I'd know if you found the will."

My dreams of a normal life, in a Norman Rockwell house, with the cute guy shattered. It had been too easy for him. "Why? What did she promise you?"

His head shot up. "Grandpa had no right treating Anna the way he did. She's family! She needs me. I'm the only one who can help her!" A clueless knight in shining armor. Just not my knight.

"You're a jerk." A jerk I'd kissed. A jerk I'd kind of liked.

"Cute," Anna cut in. "But if I wanted teen drama I'd watch more TV. Tessa, which one is the last clue."

I thought of lying, but didn't know where it would get me. "That one," I said, pointing.

She picked it up again and read. "You shall know them by

211

their fruits."

"It's from the Bible," I offered, "in case you've never read it."

"I don't care where it's from, what does it mean?"

"I don't know. We haven't solved it yet."

Her eyes narrowed. "We?"

"My ghost and I."

Her voice got as tight as her grip on the gun. "Tell me what the note means."

"Obviously it has something to do with fruit." Fruit. I'd had a dream...

"Try harder," she snapped.

"The next clue could be taped to the bottom of a bowl of waxed fruit or taped to the bottom of the fruit bin." Bright red strawberries, with vines that were strangling me...

"A bowl of waxed fruit?" she asked.

"There's one on the kitchen table." I didn't mention that Andre and I had already searched it while following the second clue.

"Come on."

I didn't move. "Charles is dead."

"Tessa, I'll shoot you," she growled.

"You're lying, right Tessa?" Alec said.

"I'm not lying. He's right across the hall in the bathroom. Go see for yourself." He did. I heard him yell.

Anna hurried out of the room. "He was threatening to tell," she shouted. They seemed, for a moment, to have forgotten little ol' me. I ran to my door and locked it. The knob rattled. "There's no place to run," Anna shouted. "Open it or I'll shoot the lock off."

"You killed Charles," Alec shouted.

"Quiet," she said.

I backed until my bottom hit the windowsill. I fumbled for the catch, breaking two more fingernails down to the quick getting the window open one handed. The screen popped out at the same time an explosion splintered the door behind me.

I crawled out onto the roof.

"Get back here," Anna shouted. *Please don't let me stumble!* I shuffled as near the edge as possible. The shingles bit into my feet and the wind whipped my hair into my eyes. Slow now, girl, you don't want to walk off. Anna's head poked out the window. "I'll shoot you." I glanced back over my shoulder. The barrel of the gun pointed at me.

And then I felt it.

"Andre," I shouted. "Catch me." I stepped off the roof. The wind caught my nightgown and pulled it up to my armpits. Thank goodness I hadn't been too out of it earlier to put on underwear. Then Andre's arms went around me and drew me to him. Our descent slowed. He set me on my feet.

"How did you do that?" Anna shouted from above.

Someone else appeared in front of the window. "Boo!" Paul shouted.

Anna gasped. She froze, then turned and ran. A moment later, we heard a scream.

Andre appeared beside me. "As I always seem to be asking, are you okay?"

My arm felt like needles stuck out of it, and my head pounded in a particularly hard rhythm. But I lived. "Since you always seem to be around when I'm falling out of something, yes I am." I bit my bottom lip. "Andre, Chloe went to the kitchen to fix lunch and I haven't seen her since." He disappeared.

As I ordered my head to stop spinning, Alec staggered out the back door. He stood for a moment then slumped into a sitting position, his head in his hands. Chloe ran out of the kitchen followed by Buster. "Sorry, Tessa," Chloe started. "I got to talking to Buster." She stopped short when they spotted Alec. "Alec?"

Buster sat down beside him.

"Charles is dead," Alec whispered.

"What? How?" Buster demanded.

"Anna strangled him."

Buster groaned.

"What? Why?" Chloe asked.

Andre appeared behind them. "Anna's still around here somewhere," I told him. "And she's got a gun."

"No she doesn't," Paul said, appearing next to Andre. He held the gun with two fingers. "Naughty little thing, that one."

"Did you know we have a dead man in the bathtub?" Andre asked me.

That's when the sheriff arrived.

The ghosts disappeared, but not before I found myself holding the gun. I glanced at Chloe.

"I called my aunt," she said. "I wanted to set things straight. At least, my part in it all."

Sheriff Mason led Anna by the arm. They were followed by a deputy. "Caught her trying to leave," she said. "Seems I'm late to the party." She held out her hand. "I'll take that." I didn't argue, but handed her the gun. "Is it yours?"

"It's Anna's."

"You killed Charles," Buster yelled. He came off the porch headed for Anna who shrank back.

Chief Mason stepped between them. "Simmer down, Buster. What are you talking about?"

"She strangled my brother."

"He's upstairs in my bathroom," I said.

"Go check it out," Chief Mason ordered her deputy. "Chloe, come get him."

Chloe hurried over and pulled on Buster's arm. "Come on." She got him back on the steps next to his cousin.

Chief Mason turned to me. "Talk."

I spilled everything except about how Jimmy died. That was Chloe's story. I explained about my house being broke into twice, the will, Anna being Barney's daughter, all of it. Oh, and about the ghosts, my lips stayed sealed. I didn't want to be locked in the loony bin with the rest of them. "Anna has the honor of smashing the window in my door, and Charles has the honor of smashing my pumpkin. Anna also pushed me down the stairs and killed Mr. Dockins and Charles." Should I say something about Alec? He sat pale and stunned, unable to react to anything. It would probably come out later, but at that moment, even though I hated him for using me, I didn't want to give Buster anymore grief.

The police chief eyed the secretary. "Ms. Gleason, I'm not sure what to say but…why?"

In a halting voice, Anna explained about the will and her hope of being in it.

"You thought Barney St. George would leave you the money? Chief Mason asked.

"I didn't want the money," Anna shouted. "I wanted him to say the St. George's were my family. You idiot, you ruined it all." Claws out, she flung herself at me. Chief Mason moved fast. Anna screamed as her arms were wrenched behind her, and she was cuffed. The deputy came out of the house. He shook his head. Chief Mason spoke into her cell.

"There was a ghost," Anna shouted. "Two of them. One of them pinched me."

"Trying for an insanity plea?" asked Sheriff Mason. "Take her away."

I watched the deputy lead the secretary away. In the distance, I heard the wail of an ambulance.

I spy something evil.

I owed Chloe. She could have fallen apart when Andre and Paul appeared and disappeared. But she didn't. Instead she helped me tell a plausible story to Chief Mason about how we'd managed to turn the tables on Anna.

"Miss Kelling," the sheriff said, "I don't suppose you have a clue where your mother is?"

I shook my head. This time, I truly didn't.

All this pain because a man wanted to play games. The next morning, I sat on the back steps, shaking, but calm. Sheriff Mason and I had come to an agreement. I could stay at the house, and we'd pretend it was under my grandmother's watch. I think she'd decided that was preferable to Mom's tender loving care. Sweater weather had returned and the sun felt cleansing on my face.

Chloe had left with Buster. I believed Chloe's version. My uncle would have been furious that someone threatened to spoil his fun.

Alec? He'd slunk off as soon as possible. Would he come clean to his family? I really didn't care as long as he stayed far, far away from me.

Andre had gone to rest.

That left me all alone, sitting on a porch in a mental place I really didn't want to be.

What if Andre didn't come back?

Those thoughts were too painful, so I thought about the will. Yes, I knew its location. Obvious once you thought about it, or rather dreamed about it. "You will know them by their fruits." What fruit had Andre never been allowed to touch, not even to weed? What fruit had my uncle grown, although allergic to it?

I grabbed the spade and walked out to the strawberry patch. I dug in the area farthermost from the rest of the garden. Digging in the hard, red dirt with only one hand made things difficult. But not as difficult as carrying my heavy heart.

What if Andre didn't come back?

I'd finally figured out he was part of my normal. So what if I didn't have a mommy who had baked cookies or a daddy who had read me bedtime stories?

I had a grandma and a ghost. What girl needed more? But with or without the ghost, I'd stood on my own two feet and intended to stay there—bum leg, sore head, bruised arm and all. I'd survive. My plan had changed from simply existing to living.

"Well, Uncle Jimmy," I told the sky. "I fulfilled your requirements for taking care of Andre. If he moves out, it's not my fault, it's yours."

What if Andre didn't come back?

Frustration made me come down hard with the spade. I succeeded in splattering clods of dirt everywhere, me included.

"Let me help you." Andre stood by my tree, a shovel in his hand. I backed out of the way. As he put his back into it, he asked, "How did you decide to dig here?"

"Wild strawberries grew by the fish pond. Why deliberately grow more of something he couldn't eat?

"Makes sense."

I'd already dug three holes, making the area look like we were tossing grenades for fun and fitness. Andre dug another one, and then started on another. Then, the shovel grated on something metallic. I inched closer. Andre soon unearthed a gray metal box. He stood back. "Your turn."

Mindless of the dirt I sat down cross-legged.

Andre crouched beside me. "Is it locked?"

I scraped dirt away from the catch and tried it. "No." Inside, a sealed baggie lay in the bottom, several folded pieces of typing paper inside it.

Andre grinned. "I do believe you found it." I unzipped the baggie. Andre leaned over. If he'd been able to breathe, I'd have felt his breath on my neck. I pulled the paper out of the bag and unfolded the pages. "Who was right?" Andre asked.

"Charles."

"Too bad he's dead."

"Then I guess it's Buster?"

Andre chuckled. "I guess it's not our problem to figure out."

"Listen to what Charles Sr. wrote: 'My son, Charles, is a wimp, but he'll invest and take care of the rest of the family. That includes his mother and brother, Buster, my brother Willard and his family.' There isn't even any mention of Anna. Even here, he doesn't acknowledge her."

"I'm sorry about Alec."

I blushed. "Yeah, not quite one of the good guys, was he?"

"I'm still not quite sure why he helped her."

"White knight fixation. He wanted to save her, to be the hero who brought Anna into the family where she belonged. She played him."

Andre flicked a corner of the will. "You need to give this to Chief Mason."

All my fears burst to the top. "Who's going to make sure I eat all my vegetables if you leave?" I blurted out.

In that instant way he had of moving, he knelt in front of me. "I'm not leaving. I'm still not sure if it's what's right, but I'm not going anywhere."

"Promise?"

"Cross my heart."

"Seal it with a kiss?"

"What?" I reached out and grabbed his shirt with both hands. Those luscious lips responded to my demanding ones. Without breaking contact, I maneuvered until I sat in his lap. Andre pulled away and buried his head against my neck. "This is a bad idea, Tessa."

"I don't care." And, I didn't.

EPILOGUE

I walk out of the Vo-Tech building, pulling my scarf tight around me. Fortified by a bowl of Andre's delicious vegetable soup, I've come to register for classes.

It isn't high school, but a lot of the high school students take classes at the Vo-Tech. Both Buster and Chloe are taking computer classes. First my GED and then a class on web design.

That's the gift I'm giving myself, time to find out what I really want in life. I've finally thrown out my little girl ideas of normal. Normal now equals what makes me happy. And Andre makes me happy. There've been no more kisses so far. He seems determined to settle into the role of my big brother. But I've never wanted a big brother.

As I wait for the car to warm up, I munch on a candy bar. At first I'd thought of asserting myself by putting a bowl full of candy right in the middle of the kitchen table. But I know they'd disappear faster than my arrogant housemate when he loses an argument. Instead, there's a bag of chocolate tucked away in my nightstand drawer; the one I finally got back open after painting it shut. It turned out to be the right size for holding midnight munchies.

Grandma Petey is coming for Christmas. I haven't decided yet how to tell her about Andre, but I will. At least after I make sure her heart is good and strong.

Paul visits frequently. He's helping Andre teach me how to play poker. We play for pennies, and last time I won!

Chloe's still my friend. The judge ruled Jimmy's death an accident and released Chloe into her father and aunt's custody. Chloe brought Buster by after things settled down a bit. The poor boy's in shock at his family's self-inflicted tragedies. He's apologized over and over for the harm they did.

As for Alec, the one time I ran into him, he hung his head and ducked into the nearest store. He did tell his family about his part in Anna's scheme. Willard apologized, but Elma doesn't speak to me. I think she blames me for the crack in the St. George perfect-family facade. As far as I know, Willard hasn't told Andre that he already knew how Jimmy died. Maybe someday I'll ask, but for now, I need a drama-free zone.

Although Chloe loves Buster, she's got a slight crush on Andre. She follows him around the kitchen and he says she's becoming a great cook. One thing is for sure—she'll never use instant anything again.

My bathroom is coming along. Andre drew a beautiful beach scene on one wall, although he still has to paint it. He hasn't started working on his mural again, but I have hope.

I've gone back to the cemetery several times. Not, to visit my uncle, I'm ashamed to admit, but to visit my angel. So far, she hasn't moved, or spoken, again. But I'm patient.

I make a stop at the local video store and pick up a copy of one of my favorite old movies, The Ghost and Mrs. Muir. My housemate has never seen it and I look forward to introducing him to it. Pulling into the gravel driveway I stop the car and gaze at my house. It feels good to come home. I might even invite my mother to stay sometime in the future. The very distant future.

"Hello!" I call to Andre who appears on the porch. He's wearing his gray slacks, but instead of the blue sweater, he wears a pale green button down shirt. Okay, not only is he prettier than me, he obviously has access to better clothes.

"We've got a visitor."

Curious, I hurry inside then stop. Charles sits on the bottom stair step. I blink and turn to Andre. "What's he doing here?" He shrugs his elegant shoulders.

The ghost that had been Charles in life looks up and sees me. "I'm sorry."

Guilt. Is that all ghosts think about?

About the Author

Susan York Meyers
Author

Susan York Meyers is the author of two chapter books, Callie and the Stepmother and The Princess and the Pee, as well as two picture books, The Mystery of the Red Mitten and Grrr...Night!, which won the Creative Women of Oklahoma Award. Stone Girl, is an early young adult novel.

Susan worked in elementary school libraries for over twelve years and is familiar with both books and the children who check them out. In addition to her writing for children, Susan has a published book of poetry for shoe lovers, entitled Shoe Haiku. She also wrote Two Little Old Ladies: It's All in the Attitude, a humorous inspirational book. Meyers is an inspirational speaker and also speaks to writing groups.

Meyers lives with her hubby and Kira, the dog that thinks she's people. You can find out more about Susan and her books at susanameyers.com. Be sure to sign up for her newsletter which comes out four times a year.

For additional copies or for author visit information, contact:

Doodle and Peck Publishing
413 Cedarburg Ct.
Yukon, OK 73099
(405) 354-7422
www.doodleandpeck.com

CPSIA information can be obtained
at www.ICGtesting.com
Printed in the USA
LVHW081721170919

631358LV00011B/213/P